DEAD
END

a zombie novel by

Anthony Giangregorio

Also by Anthony Giangregorio
from Permuted Press

The Rage Plague

Dead Cage

DEAD END

a zombie novel by

Anthony Giangregorio

Permuted Press
The formula has been changed...
Shifted... Altered... *Twisted.*
www.permutedpress.com

*Thanks to my wife, Jody and my son, Joseph
for their contribution to this work.*

A PERMUTED PRESS book
published by arrangement with the authors

ISBN-10: 1-934861-18-9
ISBN-13:978-1-934861-18-9

Cover art by Chris Kaletka
Edited by Thomas Brannan
Layout by Ryan C. Thomas

CHAPTER 1

The ductwork creaked on its supports, making Adam wince

After a tense heartbeat passed, he decided the duct would hold his dwindling weight and he continued forward.

His destination was the CVS pharmacy at the end of the mall. The Mystic Mall, to be precise. Dust and stray spider webs gathered on his face, making him want to sneeze. But he held it in, his jerking body causing the duct to creak again.

After waiting for another few heartbeats, he moved on. The ductwork had never been built for a man to crawl around in, but that was exactly what he was doing, and had been for a little over a month now.

He would use the ductwork to crawl into stores, grabbing what he could and then shimmying back up again like a gerbil in a cage. He'd managed to make himself a nice little home in a furniture store on the second floor. The only problem was, he was alone. As far as Adam knew, he was the only living human for a hundred miles. Or more.

He returned to his store and lounged a bit. As he sat, his mind wandered back to how it had all began, the story that had brought him here to this mall, scavenging like some sort of caveman.

Two months ago he'd been a cashier at his local video store. The money wasn't great, but he was able to watch all the movies he wanted for free. His favorite had been horror movies, especially the end of the world stuff. Zombie movies were at the forefront of his choices. In almost every zombie movie he'd seen, the world would end when the dead overran the living. Now, as he blew dust from his lip, he thought back to all those movies, still not believing he was living one of them. He thought back to how it had started.

Two months ago to the day, the world had ended. Not with a bang, but with a moan.

Two states over, an eighteen-wheeler had overturned and spilled its contents across the highway, the hazardous liquid contaminating a nearby cemetery. The haz-mat cleanup crew arrived soon after and, in their white body suits and breathing gear, cleaned up the mess.

The local news briefly covered the accident, everyone thanking God no one had been seriously hurt. Even the driver of the rig had sustained only minor abrasions.

After that, it was quickly forgotten.

Forty-eight hours after the chemicals bled into the soil of the graveyard, the first corpse thrust its desiccated hands through the top-soil and climbed out into the light.

The disease spread like wildfire. One bite from the infected and victims would turn undead themselves in a matter of minutes or days, depending on their physiology.

A pair of truckers got infected early on and had continued across the United States, not knowing that they carried with them the death of the nation. When they finally succumbed to the disease, they spread the infection to more people than could be counted. The government finally realized that this plague could not be controlled.

Through investigation and detective work, Federal agents found the source of the outbreak—the spill at the cemetery—but by then it was far too late to contain. It had become an epidemic.

Adam's mother had been attacked when she went to the grocery store for canned goods and bottled water. The news people were still trying to get a handle on what was happening and his mother had decided that stocking up on supplies would be a good idea. She'd been bitten on her arm as she exited the store. She escaped her attackers, but the damage was done: she was infected.

Adam still remembered his mother's screams as she thrashed in her bed, as the infection slowly took over her body. His dad sat with her for as long as possible, until he was absolutely sure there was no hope. Then, with dread in his eyes, he had walked Adam to the kitchen and asked him to wait there.

Dad patted him on the shoulder briefly and, with a sadness in his eyes Adam couldn't understand, he turned and walked back upstairs, the third step from the bottom creaking under his weight as he plod-ded up, his feet becoming heavier as he got closer to the landing.

Adam could hear him rummaging in the hall closet and got a sink-ing feeling in his stomach. Dad was looking for his revolver. That was the only time he ever went into the hall closet.

Adam could hear the creaking floorboards on the second floor as his father moved across the hallway. He heard the bedroom door open and his mother's wails of pain drifted down the stairs until the door closed once more.

Then her screams stopped as she succumbed to unconsciousness. Hours went by, his father standing a silent vigil over her bedside.

Adam remained at the bottom of the stairs, waiting.

Then she died. She returned ten minutes later, no longer his mother.

The house was silent, only the sirens from outside drifting into the house to break the quiet. Adam stood at the bottom of the stairs for what seemed like days. His legs ached from standing too long and he finally decided he should just sit.

The sound of a single gunshot drifted down the stairs, making him jump. The shot seemed to echo forever as Adam thought about what it meant. He was about to go upstairs, when the echo of another gunshot bounced off the walls.

With eyes wide and filled with panic, he ran up the stairs two at a time, his heart pounding in his chest. Pushing through the bedroom door, he stopped in horror at the visceral scene in front of him.

His mother's brains covered the headboard, the blood and grey matter already starting to slip down the painted wall to disappear behind the bed.

On the carpeted floor next to her was his father. At his first glance, Adam knew he was dead, as well. The smell of gunpowder and copper filled the room and he slowly moved closer to what were once his parents. Next to his father's left hand was a small piece of notebook paper. Small red dots of blood splatter covered the white page. Adam leaned down and picked it up, a large lump of grief growing in his throat.

The words *I'm Sorry*, were written hastily in his father's hand. Adam let the paper fall to the floor. It drifted down to land in the spreading puddle of his father's blood, the thin carpet not absorbent enough to hold the viscous fluid.

He stood there quietly, listening to the sirens wail outside the window. The sound of crunching metal and shattered glass exploded in an aural cocktail and floated into the room from an accident on the street in front of his house.

He barely noticed, caught up in his own grief for his family. He was angry at his father for what he'd just done. The selfish bastard had taken the easy way out.

Now he was alone in a dying world.

Time went by slowly after that. Adam didn't notice. He stood in his parent's bedroom for another hour before coming out of his stupor. Then he began the arduous task of burying them. One after the other, he wrapped the bodies in blankets and dragged them down the stairs. With muscles screaming from the weight of the bodies, the weight of the two people he loved most in this world, he pulled and pushed his parents to the backyard.

He snatched up his shovel and started digging. The whole time he was outside, he could hear the city falling apart. Sirens wailed, gunshots sounded, and smoke from numerous fires floated on the horizon, the wind scattering and spreading the roiling clouds of darkness.

Once the two shallow graves were finished, he gently rolled his parents into the holes, then quickly covered them up.

When he finished, he wiped the sweat from his brow and made the sign of the cross. While he wasn't overly religious, it felt like the right thing to do.

He said a few prayers and cried a little more.

With a weary sigh, he wiped his eyes and walked back into the house. He was alone now. He had no brothers or sisters, and most of his extended family lived out of state.

With another heavy sigh, he opened the back door and stepped into the house, making sure to secure the door with the deadbolt.

The house was deathly silent with the absence of his family. Not knowing what to do, he sat down on the living room couch and zoned out. He was in shock. Murder/suicide. Not the kind of thing one plans for when they get up in the morning.

He sat quietly on the couch for hours, until his growling stomach would not be denied. Despite the fact he was starving, he still didn't want to actually eat much, so he made and ate a quick cold cut sandwich and then washed it down with some tap water.

Absently, he turned on the television. The anchorman for CNN was droning on about the epidemic and how FEMA was being called in to help. Rescue station locations scrolled across the bottom of the screen as well as all the school and business closings. He watched it all in a daze, still finding it hard to believe what was truly happening.

So far, no one had used the word *zombies*. The news had only referred to them as "the infected." But Adam knew better. All the signs were there, if only they would accept it. He knew they wouldn't. Just like every other emergency, such as with Louisiana and Hurricane Katrina, the government was always slow to react. This time would be no different.

He turned the television off, deciding he'd heard enough. So far the power was still on and he could only pray it would stay that way. He picked up the phone on the kitchen wall, pleased to hear a dial tone. If only there was someone to call.

Adam had always been somewhat of a loner. His movies and books had been enough to keep him company. Still, it would have been nice to have at least one person to call, to talk with, to share his grief and fears.

He turned to the stairs that led to the second floor, still expecting his parents to come down from their room and yell at him for having had the television on too loud or something.

He let out a long sigh, the sadness welling up inside him. He felt tears and decided he needed to occupy himself before he started crying again.

A scream floated into the room, coming from the front of the house in the direction of the street. Adam ran to the window. A man and a woman were running down the sidewalk, their car left behind where it had struck a telephone pole, the front end wrapped around it like a young lover. The accident he'd heard earlier remained where the vehicles had collided, immobile. Steam drifted from under the hood of one of them, a Honda.

The man and woman darted by the front of the house and continued running, their faces were painted masks of fear. Adam craned his head against the window to see what they were running from and let out a shocked gasp.

Five zombies shambled down the street, each in a state of disrepair. The first one in line looked to be a middle-aged man. His stomach was torn open and his intestines dragged along behind him like a child's jump rope. The zombie behind him kept stepping on the ends of the guts, causing the man to jerk as he was stopped for a moment, then he would continue on when the pressure was released; bile squirted with each compression of his entrails and splattered on the pavement.

The second zombie in line, the one that kept stepping on intestines, was a woman, or used to be. Now she was nothing more then a mess of ripped flesh and exposed tendons and muscles. While she walked, her exposed muscles flexed and contracted like elastics, her moist organs glistening in the sun. Every now and then a piece would fall out of her and land in the street with a meaty *thwap*.

The zombies behind her didn't mind, though. Every time a piece fell to the road, one of the others would bend over and pick it up and start to chew merrily. The other three zombies in line were in a similar state of damage, except their torsos seemed to be intact.

The last one in line was a boy in his late teens, only a few years younger than Adam. The boy was wearing one high top sneaker, on his right foot, the other missing. He walked at a slant due to the height of the one piece of footwear.

The boy stopped when he was directly in front of Adam's house. He seemed to sniff the air as he looked around the street. Then his head turned to look directly in Adam's direction.

Adam jumped back from the window, hoping he hadn't been seen. After only seconds had ticked by, he peeked out the side of the curtain and let out a sigh of relief when he saw the boy was gone. His heartbeat started to slow down and he was about to continue on with his day, when the front window shattered, sending splinters of razor sharp glass into the room.

Adam fell to the floor and rolled to his side, acting on instinct. The sun's rays spilled into the room as he crawled on the carpet like an inchworm, his arm over his eyes to save them from flying glass. When he pulled his face clear, he was looking out the window at the zombie boy.

Evidently, he had seen Adam and had scurried across the lawn to get at him. The zombie boy was trying to climb through the window, his torn clothes catching on the exposed shards of glass still left inside the window frame. Adam rolled to his feet and looked over the zombie boy's shoulder to see the other four ghouls now walking on his front lawn toward his house.

The zombie boy managed to climb into the room, leaving large chunks of flesh behind on the windowsill. The dead boy didn't mind. The blood-slicked glass reflected the sunlight, painting the room around Adam the color of blood.

Adam backed up against the far wall of the room, shock and panic freezing him to the spot. His heart felt like it was on the verge of exploding, while like a slowed frame in a movie, the zombie boy moved closer to him, the other walking dead not far behind.

CHAPTER 2

Adam was frozen in fear as the zombies moved closer. He scanned the room for a weapon, but nothing was within reach.

He placed his hands in front of himself and prepared to be eaten.

Suddenly, a voice rang out from the front yard through the broken front window. "Get down!" The disembodied voice was strong and confident.

Adam dropped without thinking.

Shots rang out and one of the zombies was thrown forward as the barrage of bullets hit it in the back and propelled it into the wall next to Adam. The corpse bounced off the wall and slumped to the floor like a puppet with its strings cut.

The other zombies continued toward Adam. The zombie boy was now within reach and Adam snapped out of his fright, actually managing a half-assed punch into the zombie boy's jaw.

Its head rocked to the side and the boy let out a belch that stank of death and decay. The head turned back to stare at Adam and the white orbs flashed malevolence. The dead boy seemed to smile a slight grin and without hesitation, dove at Adam's exposed face and neck.

Another shot filled the room and the boy's head exploded into a dozen pieces. Grey matter and bits of skull splattered against the wall, sounding like the patter of rain. Three more shots sounded in quick succession and the rest of the walking corpses collapsed to the floor with different parts of their anatomies missing. What they all had in common though, was one precise shot each to the head.

Adam blinked the sweat from his eyes and looked out the front window of his house. The smell of gunsmoke and death filled the room as he stood on wobbly legs. His neighbor stood at the window with a smile stretched from ear to ear.

Adam squinted through the sunlight barring his vision and moved closer to the window.

"Paul?" he asked incredulously.

Paul nodded. "Hell, yeah, it's me. Looks like I showed up in the nick of time. Where's your dad?" He asked this while looking over his shoulder for more signs of trouble.

Adam looked down at his feet and stepped over one of the prone corpses.

"Dead, like Mom," Adam answered quietly.

Paul frowned. "Sorry to hear that, I really am. Your Pa was a good man."

Silence lay between the two men until a crash floated across the street, coming from the direction of the town square.

That had Paul moving again. "Look, Adam, me and the Missus are holed up in the cellar of our house. We've got enough food, water and ammo for at least a month. You're welcome to join us. What do you say?"

Adam didn't have to give it much thought. He had nowhere else to go and it would take a lot of time to barricade the large picture window, time he didn't have, and he'd always liked Paul and his wife, Josey.

"I say, sure, why not."

Paul nodded curtly and climbed into the room, using the barrel of his .22 rifle to knock aside the loose glass in the frame. He got caught for a moment and then shimmied inside with Adam's help.

"You know, Paul, you could have used the door. It's still right over there," Adam said, gesturing to the front door.

Paul grinned back and flashed his white teeth. "Yeah, I know, but it's cooler to climb in the window."

Adam shrugged and stepped aside to make room for his neighbor.

Paul looked around the room and at his handiwork. He kicked the closest zombie in the ribs to make sure it was dead. The air in its stomach expelled and the zombie let out a fart that filled the room.

Adam raised his arm to his face and let out a disgusted grunt. "Oh, sweet Jesus, that smells."

Paul agreed. "No shit. The moment you become one of them you start to decay from the inside out. I still don't get what keeps them moving. I saw one that had a giant hole where its stomach was. I could see clean through it, and the goddamn thing was still trying to eat. The meat just fell into the hole and then fell out and hit the sidewalk. And get this. The damn thing would bend over and pick up the chunks of meat and eat them again." He shook his head as if he was seeing something strange. "Craziest thing I ever saw. Well, come on, boy, let's get what we can get from here and bring it over to my house."

Adam nodded and the two men started to strip the cupboards of Adam's kitchen bare. Adam remembered his Dad's revolver and retrieved it along with a box of shells.

When they'd gathered everything worth taking, they carried it across the backyard to Paul's bulkhead, which led to his basement. The two horizontal red metal doors were locked, and after Paul knocked on them three times in rapid succession, the doors were pushed open from the inside.

Adam and Paul looked down into the narrow stairwell at Paul's wife.

"Thanks, Josey. I brought Adam back with me. His parents are . . . he's alone. We raided his cabinets, though, so he's bringing his own food," Paul said as he stepped over the stone threshold and started down into the steep stairwell.

Josey stepped back so the two men could enter the cellar. Once all the supplies were loaded, the bulkhead doors were quickly closed again. Just before Paul slammed them shut, he caught a glimpse of more zombies stumbling into the yard from the street, attracted to the noise they were making.

Slamming closed the bulkhead doors, the shambling ghouls were lost from sight.

He backed down the stairwell and closed the heavy wooden door that brought him into the actual cellar. He ducked under a couple of supports that ran the width of the house and walked into a wide open area directly under the living room. If Paul had been taller than his five foot eight, his head would have scraped the low ceiling, but instead, he just made it. Adam was about the same height and was managing fine.

Adam helped carry the rest of the supplies into the middle of the cellar and took a seat in one of the lawn chairs set up against the far wall. Paul was talking in a hushed voice with Josey and he saw her look over at him.

She left Paul and walked to him, leaning near his face, her right hand on his upper arm in a friendly manner.

"Adam, honey, I'm so sorry about your parents," she said.

"Thanks Josey, that means a lot," Adam said.

She patted his arm one more time and turned away, then immediately got to work taking the food supplies out of their boxes and placing them on the metal shelves that lined one wall of the cellar.

Adam watched her for a few moments, marveling at the efficiency the woman displayed. Josey was in her late thirties or early forties. She had dark brown hair and a slim figure. She wasn't drop dead beautiful, but she was still pleasant to look at.

Paul came in and sat down next to Adam, placing his rifle on the floor next to him. He was a regular-looking guy. He looked like he would be more comfortable in a three piece suit on Wall St. than toting around a rifle, shooting zombies. His hair was thinning on top and he had cut it short to distract from his bald spot. His appearance was rounded out with thin lips and a pair of wire-rimmed glasses that rode on his face like they belonged there.

When he removed them to rub his eyes, the deep indentation on his nose signified how often he wore them. Though Paul would hate to admit it, he was blind as a bat without them. He kept extra pairs in the bureau, always had.

There was a small black and white television sitting on a work-bench. At the moment there was a sitcom on about three friends living with a gay man. Then the screen switched over to the Presidential seal and a moment later the President of the United States came on. On the bottom of the screen, words scrolled by in a thin line, proclaiming that this was an emergency address to the nation.

The three of them gathered around the screen. Adam stood next to Josey and despite the fact she needed a shower, he still felt himself becoming slightly aroused as her left breast brushed against him.

"What do you think he's going to say?" Paul asked the room, really just thinking out loud.

Josey shushed him quickly. "Quiet, Paul, I want to hear this," she snapped.

"Sorry, dear," he muttered concentrating on the screen.

The President sat behind a large oak desk. His hair and make-up was perfect and he started to read from the notes lying in front of him. His voice was strong and sure.

"My fellow Americans. This unknown infection invading our borders is, unlike the threat of Sars and the Bird flu, a reality and is sweeping the nation in full force. At the most recent estimate, more than a quarter of our nation's populace has been infected by this unknown virus, which somehow mutates the body and then kills it.

"Now, the word zombie has been thrown around in a few of the meetings I've attended and I have to say *that* is the most ridiculous thing I've ever heard. The victims are still human; the laws of nature still apply. Whatever is happening to our friends and loved ones will be corrected. You have my word.

"If anyone you know is exhibiting symptoms of the disease, much like those of the common flu, please notify your local police. Once the infection has fully taken over, these people will no longer be your friends and loved ones. They must be taken away and interred at local rescue stations until a cure can be found. Martial Law is now in effect. Citizens are to turn over their weapons. Anyone that does not comply and is found on the streets with a weapon will be shot on sight. Looting will not be tolerated and will be met with force. All airports will be shut down until further notice. No air travel will be allowed until further notice.

"If we are to survive this, we must all work together. Have faith, my friends, and God will see us through this dark time. Keep posted to your televisions and the internet for any breaking news on how to help yourself and your neighbors.

"God bless you all, and God bless the United States of America."

The screen went dark and the Presidential seal once more filled the screen. A second later a news anchor came on and started to paraphrase what the President just said.

Josey walked over to the television and turned the volume down. She frowned as she looked at the two men in front of her.

"I don't know about you two, but I don't like that at all," she said.

Adam sat straighter in his chair. "What do you mean? He said things were gonna be all right, we just have to be patient."

"It's not what he said, Adam, it's what he didn't say," Paul added. "He didn't say anything about a cure. All he said was that people were being brought to what sounds like concentration camps. Rescue stations, my ass."

"I know, Paul. I'm just glad you stockpiled all this stuff down here," Josey said, waving around the room at the shelves of bottled water and dried food.

Adam's eyes perked up while he scanned the room more closely. In one of the dark corners, where the shadows played across the dusty shelves, he could make out what looked like MRE's from the military and five gallon plastic drums of water.

"You mean this stuff was here before everything started happening?" Adam asked.

Josey nodded. "Yup. You see, my husband is a survivalist. He always thought sooner or later something would happen and he would need his stockpiles."

Paul nodded and walked over to the shelves. He turned to look at Adam and his wife.

"You bet your ass I did, but I always figured it would be a rogue meteor or a nuclear war, not zombies. I mean, walking dead people?

It's friggin' ridiculous."

"It may be ridiculous, honey, but it's happening." She looked to Adam. "That's why we're down here. Figure we'll stay here for as long as we can; let the world work itself out." Josey sat down in one of the lawn chairs.

Adam nodded, absorbing everything he'd heard. At the moment he didn't know what to do and figured he was as safe here as anywhere else. He stood up and walked over to Paul.

"I still haven't thanked you for saving my ass. If you hadn't shown up when you did, I don't even want to think about what could have happened."

Paul slapped him on the back and grinned. "No problem, son, happy to help. Maybe you can return the favor before all this shit blows over." He lowered his voice so only Adam could hear. "Besides, being trapped down here with only the wife to talk to would have driven me fuckin' crazy," he muttered.

"I heard that," Josey said from across the room.
Paul cursed under his breath. "Sorry, dear, you know I was just joking." He smiled sweetly in her direction, turning on the charm.

She smiled back and playfully gave him the finger, then turned and continued what she was doing. She'd laid out Paul's rifle and was cleaning it. One of the new skills she'd been taught by her husband in the first few days they had been in the cellar.

Paul watched her and smiled, then gave Adam another slap on the back. "Come on, Adam, I'll show you how to clean a rifle."

Adam stood in the corner of the room and watched the couple working. His mind was filled with images of his parent's bodies and the zombie boy who had tried to kill him. The images of heads being blown apart as Paul came through the window and saved him. Shaking his head as if that would work, he forced those images down, banishing them, not liking where they might take him.

He was pretty sure they'd be back when he went to sleep tonight.

Putting on his best smile, he walked over to his two new friends. Whatever was going to happen next, at least for now, he was safe.

Outside in the streets surrounding Paul's house, sirens continued to wail and gunshots kept sounding, the sounds permeating the stone walls of the cellar. Little by little, the world was falling apart while Adam learned how to strip and clean a rifle.

CHAPTER 3

The next week went by in a bored blur for Adam. There wasn't much to do in the small cellar and cabin fever started to set in after the fourth day.

The television was their only window to the outside world and through it the three survivors watched as civilization crumbled.

At first the news was more positive as the military and State police strived to contain the infection. But after only a few days, it was clear to the three survivors that things had shifted for the worst.

On the fifth day, the electricity fluctuated off and on and had then, thankfully, remained on. All three breathed a silent sigh of relief. Paul had stocked candles and flashlights, as well as batteries, but was hesitant to use them, and he continuously kicked himself for not having a generator.

If the power actually turned off, it would signify how bad things had become. The news anchor for CNN was droning on about the casualties across America. But it was when he told his viewers that reports had come in from overseas that the infection had spread to other countries that the survivors' morale grew dim.

Slapping her hands on her thighs, Josey raised herself up from her chair and turned off the television.

"Hey, I was watching that, what did you do that for?" Paul asked, sounding like a five-year-old.

Josey folded her arms across her chest. "Because I've heard enough, that's why. How much doom and gloom can we take before we decide to eat a bullet?"

Sitting next to Paul, Adam nodded in agreement. "She's got a point, Paul. It seems that whatever's happening is just getting worse. It's not like the TV is gonna change that."

Paul sulked in his chair. Then he sat taller and nodded. "Yeah, I suppose you're right, but what if something happens and we don't know about it until it's too late?"

"Hmm, that's a good point, honey. Tell you what, let's leave it off for an hour and then we'll turn it back on, okay?"

"Yeah, that's fine with me," Paul answered back, feeling better.

"Good. So who's up for a game of cards?" Josey asked, walking over to the shelf and retrieving the deck of cards.

Adam stood up and walked over to the small card table in the corner of the cellar. It served the three of them well as a dinner table, the double-duty table getting more than its fair share of use.

"I'll play. You coming, Paul?" Adam asked hopefully. The night before, Paul had whipped him good in gin and he wanted to get even.

Paul nodded and raised himself from his chair with a slight sigh. "Yeah, fine, let's play cards."

***

The second week passed uneventfully, mostly. There were only two things that happened.

The television was still on, but it only showed snow. The last news report had been less than a day past. The anchorman had said the military had ordered all nonessential personnel out of the city. That it was a mandatory order. Anyone not obeying would be arrested and detained . . . or worse.

The anchorman said they would bring a remote broadcaster to continue reporting, but nothing had come through the set but snow.

The first thing to happen to break the drudgery of the day was when a National Guard truck arrived on the street. The men looked imposing in their Interceptor body armor and ballistic helmets. Every so often, one of the men would fire his rifle into the distance, but whether they were shooting at live or dead targets was unknown.

Through a booming loudspeaker, a man with a hard voice said this neighborhood needed to be evacuated, that to remain in your homes, no matter how well defended, was unlawful. All citizens needed to report to the nearest rescue station and from there would be given further instructions.

Josey stood on her tiptoes at the cellar window, looking out at the green-and-brown colored truck.

"Should we go with them? You heard what they said." Josey's voice kept lilting up and down while she raised herself up and down

14

on her tiptoes, trying to get a better look at the soldiers on the street.

Paul made a disgusted sound out of the side of his mouth. "No way, I don't trust those idiots as far as I could throw them. We stay here. This is one time when it's not safer to be in numbers. More people means an easier target for the zombies. Friggin' weekend warriors."

Fifteen minutes later they heard pounding on the front door above them, then a crash and the sound of booted feet searching the house.

"Dammit, my wedding China is still up there," Josey lamented, the sound of crashing continuing.

"Forget it, honey, you can't eat China," Paul told her.

This went on for a little more then five minutes, then the boots receded and the house became quiet once again.

"This house," Adam whispered, "is clear."

The Guardsmen checked the other houses on the street, a few of Paul's neighbors being carried out in restraints. Once they were placed in the back of the truck, it rumbled off to the next street. Minutes later the loudspeaker could be heard again as the soldier repeated his instructions.

In the basement, spirits were low. The government was now physically removing people from their homes. How bad could it be out there if it had come to that?

The other thing to happen that week occurred a few days later. Adam had just finished using the chemical toilet that Paul was smart enough to have installed, when a loud crash filtered into the cellar.

All three of them rushed to the front window of the cellar and looked out onto the street. A mini-van had plowed into the house across the street and had ended up sticking half-in/ half-out of the structure.

Before any of the occupants could escape, the few zombies on the street attacked the van, pulling the people out of their seats through the shattered windows of the van.

One of the occupants held what appeared to be a blowtorch and the man used it to try and fend off his attackers. Unfortunately, he couldn't see what was happening behind him, and while he stuck the torch into a zombie's face, another attacked him from the rear.

The man screamed in fear as he was pulled into the wreckage of the house; the zombies seeming to become one entity as they surrounded him. Two zombies tore into his flesh, tearing the man limb from limb. On the other side of the van, a woman was screaming as her throat was ripped out, the blood spray arcing across the front of the vehicle like a fountain. The spray quickly slowed to a trickle, her life's blood only seeping out of the jagged wound as her heart ran out of blood to pump, and then she, too, was devoured.

While Adam watched in horror at the visceral scene, he prayed she was dead before the feeding began.

Suddenly, crying floated across the street to penetrate the basement and all three of them looked at one another in recognition. The crying was high and scared and it took only a moment for Josey to realize what the scream belonged to.

"Oh my God, there's a child in the car! Paul, we've got to do something, we can't let those things get a child, not in front of us."

Paul looked across the street. He counted at least seven of the undead moving about the wreckage. Although the ravenous ghouls didn't seem to move that fast, he would still be outnumbered. He looked to Adam. "What do you think? I'm not going out there alone; I'll need your help."

Adam looked at Paul, then out the window to the crashed van. The zombies were banging on the side windows and it would only be seconds before one of them realized it could crawl through the busted driver's window and into the front seat to get at the child.

Another piercing scream cut through his thoughts and he nodded. "Yeah, I'll help. I can't just let a kid get slaughtered."

Paul nodded. "All right then, let's move. I'll take my rifle and you take one of the pistols."

"Will you two hurry? Those things are almost in the car!" Josey wailed while she watched the van, her hands curled into fists of worry for the hidden child.

Adam ran to the work bench where he'd previously cleaned the rifle Paul was now picking up. Instead of the hammers and screwdrivers typically found on the wall above a workbench, Paul had collected an assortment of firearms. Over the years he'd managed to find a Police Glock, a Browning Hi-Power, a SIG-Sauer 232 with five boxes of 9mm ammo, a .44 Magnum and an assortment of shotguns and rifles. Adam's .38 revolver was now hanging on the wall as well, now part of the armory.

Adam reached up and palmed the Browning; Paul had told him previously that the weapon would be better for his inexperienced hands. After checking to make sure it was loaded, he joined Paul at the cellar doors. Josey was already there; ready to throw the doors open and close them quickly behind the two men after they'd exited.

Paul looked to Adam, small beads of sweat appearing on his forehead.

"Okay, once we're in the yard, we stay to the shadows and sneak up on them from behind. The second you have a shot, just point and shoot, but be ready for the weapon to kick a little. When it does, you need to compensate for muzzle climb and lower the gun again. Just make sure the safety's off or this is gonna be a short trip. You got all that?" Paul asked quickly, the gleam in his eye showing his nervousness.

Adam nodded and swallowed the saliva that had built up in his mouth. "Just point and shoot, got it."

Paul let out a deep breath and moved up the five stone stairs that led to the metal bulkhead. "All right then, let's move. We're running out of time to save that kid. If it's not already too late."

Josey cocked her head toward the front window. "No, I can still hear him, but hurry," she called to him.

Paul nodded and pushed open the metal doors, stepping into the cool evening air. It was early May and the New England weather had been excellent this year. After being inside the cellar for almost two weeks, it felt good to breathe fresh air again, even if it was only for a little while.

The two men moved silently across the yard and rounded the house until they were on the front lawn, the metal sound of the bulkhead slamming behind them signaling that Josey had secured the doors again.

Moving closer to the street, the sounds of the child's screams became louder, as well as the groans and moans of the zombies. A chill went up Adam's back when the muffled moaning floated to him.

Paul noticed this and placed his hand on his shoulder. "You all right?"

Adam nodded. "Yeah, I'm peachy. We're about to have a gunfight with corpses."

Paul frowned. "Yeah, I know what you mean; it didn't seem so real when we were just seeing it on the TV. You gonna be able to do what has to be done?"

Adam nodded. "Yeah, I'm with you. Let's go."

The two men moved down the street and stopped on the sidewalk, studying the scene before them. Since they had left the cellar, at least five more zombies had arrived. Now there was around twelve of the undead moving about the van. Some were still feeding on the man and woman, while others were still trying to gain access into the van. While Adam watched, he saw one of them accidentally open the driver's door, then lean inside. The screaming from the van went up in pitch as the child saw the monster now reaching for him.

"Shit, time's up, it's now or never," Paul snapped. "You take the left side and I'll take the right. Remember, you're the one with the gun, just stay calm and you'll be fine."

Then Paul was off. He ran at full speed across the street with his rifle at chest level. When he was no more then six feet from the van, he slowed to a stop and raised the weapon to his cheek. Sighting down the barrel, he lined up and shot the first zombie he saw.

The crack of the rifle filled the street and echoed off the abandoned houses. The zombie was thrown forward and into the ripped opening of the house from the force of the bullet punching through its chest. Paul could see arms and legs flailing as the ghoul struggled to get up amidst the shattered timbers of the house's front wall.

Ignoring it for the moment, he lined up his gun sight on the next walking corpse. Before he pulled the trigger, he recognized the dead woman as his neighbor from three houses over. Mrs. Johnson was her name.

Whenever he'd been on a late night walk after dinner, he'd usually see her on her porch. He would wave to her and continue on down the street. But this wasn't the neighbor he'd waved to for countless years; it was some abomination created by Hell itself. Setting his jaw tight, he sent a round through her skull. The bullet struck her head in the right ear while she tried to lean into the van. Her head jerked to the side, as if she'd found something curious, and she dropped to the rubble strewn ground, remaining still. The left side of her head was a gaping mass of exposed flesh, the bullet blowing the side of her head open on its exit path.

Paul had no time to examine his marksmanship as two more zombies turned and started toward him. As quick as he could, he turned to the new ghouls and shot the first one in the chest. The impact spun the zombie around and for a few precious seconds it started to walk away, then it realized its direction was skewed and turned back towards Paul.

Paul lined up the second zombie and shot it in the face from no more then three feet away. Its head was thrown back like a giant hammer had struck it and the zombie fell to the street with the back of its skull missing. Then Paul swiveled on his boots and shot the other zombie again, this time hitting it in the forehead. The creature fell to the street and twitched for a moment as its brain leaked out of the exit wound in its head, then it too, remained still.

Paul glanced in Adam's direction and saw he was doing a good job of keeping the ghouls at bay.

With his rifle in hand, Paul moved closer to the van. Adam had wasted the first three bullets shooting the two dead men and one woman in the chest and stomach. Then he started taking headshots and things moved swiftly. The closer he came to the walking corpses, the better his marksmanship. One after the other was knocked down like ducks in a shooting gallery until there was only one left; the one in the van's front seat.

Paul was first to the driver's door. Pulling the door open as wide as he could, he reached in and grabbed the collar of the ghoul's light windbreaker. The child was still screaming bloody murder as Paul pulled the man from the van and pushed him to the ground. He realized it was Mr. Botson from two streets over. Paul had wanted to buy a really sweet lawnmower the man had for sale last year and the asshole had tried to raise the price, knowing Paul wanted it badly.

Mr. Botson snarled and hissed at Paul the entire time he tried to regain his footing. Paul didn't hesitate. He spun the rifle around and used the gun like a baseball bat, the end of the gun barrel, burning his hands from the heat given off from the discharge of so many bullets, and let swing.

The rifle stock struck Mr. Botson square in the temple, sending his head back to smack into the earth. No sooner did his head rebound then he was ready for more. Paul swung again, this time feeling the skull give. The impact vibrated up the stock of the weapon and into his shoulder. Stepping away, he could see Mr. Botson's head was cracked like a melon, brains seeping out of the gaping head wound. Lifting his rifle's butt to his eyes, he frowned to see he'd cracked the gunstock with the man's head.

"Knew he had a hard head." He looked down at the dead man. "Next time, give me the damn mower for what you promised."

The corpse didn't answer.

Shrugging, Paul reached out to the van's side door and, after finding it locked, reached inside to the door locks. With a quiet click the doors unlocked, allowing Paul and Adam access.

Adam pulled open the sliding door on the other side of the vehicle, while Paul did the same on his side. The child's screams were louder now that the doors were open. Paul reached in to grab the child, but the tot shrieked louder. Paul was about to just reach in and grab the kid when Adam stopped him with a raised hand.

"Wait a sec', Paul, let me try. You keep watch, okay?"

Paul nodded and moved away from the van. Anything was better than listening to the screaming kid. "Fine, go for it. I was never really that good with children anyway."

Adam chuckled at that and reached into the van, his mouth curved into a lopsided grin.

"Hey, buddy, what's your name? Mine's Adam." He spoke calmly while he undid the child's seatbelt. While he did this, he gave the kid a quick once over with his eyes. The small boy looked to be about eight or nine. With the exception of a small cut on his forehead from stray glass, he appeared to be unharmed.

All the while he was unbuckling the seatbelt, Adam was talking in soothing tones to the child. As the seconds ticked by, the child seemed to calm down slightly and soon the screaming stopped, although the whimpers and whines continued.

Adam held out his hands to the boy and cupped each one, motioning for the child to climb out of his booster seat and into his arms.

With tears falling down his plump cheeks, the boy did as he was asked.

"Where's my Mom and Dad?" The boy asked through breaks in his whimpers, his small shoulders trembling with terror.

Adam looked over his shoulder at the boy's mother. There wasn't much left. In a matter of minutes the zombies had torn her body apart. Now she resembled something found on the floor of a butcher shop.

Adam tuned his body so the child couldn't see. "Uhm, your parents had to leave, they asked me and Paul to take care of you for a while." Adam nodded to Paul. Paul waved a hand at the boy and then turned his attention back to the street.

"Adam, we've got company," Paul said, stepping away from the van. Another six or seven zombies were moving closer to their position, drawn to all the shooting. If the would-be rescuers didn't move fast, they would have to deal with yet another group of the undead, and their ammo was low after dispatching the first group of walking corpses. Plus, they now had the child to protect.

Adam nodded to Paul and then looked at the boy, flashing his best smile. "So, what's your name?" He asked while stepping away from the vehicle.

"Timmy McCormick," the boy said. His tears seemed to have dried up. Adam was now moving across the street with Paul by his side. Adam had placed the Browning behind his back and was now using both hands to carry Timmy. Timmy saw the new zombies moving down the street towards them and let out a frightened scream.

"Ahh, more monsters, don't let them get me!" Then his pleadings became muffled as he buried his face in Adam's chest.

Adam patted Timmy on the back. "Don't worry, buddy, you're safe now."

The first of the ghouls had reached Paul and he was about to raise his rifle and take the zombie out when Adam called to him.

"No wait, if you shoot, you'll just attract more of them, right? Let's just avoid them and get back to the cellar."

Paul turned to the zombies and then to Adam, conflicted. He wanted to shoot the bastards, not run away, but Adam's reasoning was sound. If they were going to survive in the cellar, they needed to stay hidden and unnoticed.

"Fine, you get back and I'll take care of these guys," Paul said.

Adam just grunted from the weight of Timmy and took off towards Paul's backyard. Adam wasn't exactly a big man himself and Timmy had to weigh at least fifty pounds. Fifty pounds of dead weight!

With Adam darting across the street, the boy bouncing in his arms, Paul moved toward the new group of walking dead. Using the rifle like a club, he swung at the first one in line. The end of the rifle struck the dead woman against her shoulder, causing her to stumble to the side. There was a piece of rubble lying in the street and Paul leaned over to retrieve it. It had the shape of a square and Paul idly noticed it was one half of a cement block. Just one of many pieces that had been thrown around the area when the van had plowed into the decorative fence lining the damaged house's property.

Paul hefted it for a moment, gauging its weight, then threw it overhand at another ghoul, a teenage boy of around thirteen. The cement block struck the boy in the face, pulverizing his nose and pushing his eyes deeper into their sockets, popping them like eggs. The block peeled off his face like a piece of flypaper, leaving behind something that looked like it had been hit with the flat end of a frying pan.

The shattered, empty sockets dripped a clear viscous fluid down the boy's demolished face. Now blind, he wandered off in another direction, inarticulate groans eschewing from his shattered mouth, spitting teeth as he moved away.

Paul bent over and picked up another piece of rubble and threw it as hard as he could at the next one in line. This time he only caught a glancing blow at what had once been a housewife, her hair still in rollers. She stepped back from the impact, regained her balance, and continued onward like nothing had happened.

Paul had had enough. No matter what he did, they just kept coming. If he couldn't shoot them, then what was the point of staying out here? Backing away, he ran to his neighbor's house and jumped the chain-link fence, running around to the backyard. There was a small fence separating his property from his neighbor's and he hurdled it easily. Landing in his yard, he saw Josey waiting by the bulkhead doors, waving him forward. Adam was nowhere in sight and Paul assumed he must have already made it inside the cellar. With a quick look around his yard to make sure the coast was clear, he sprinted across the light green grass and jumped into the stairwell. Josey closed the metal doors with a muffled slam and latched them.

Paul moved down the steep stairs and into the cellar, breathing heavily from his exertion, adrenalin still pumping.

Stepping into the cellar, he saw Adam by the table, the boy curled up tight in his lap.

Adam looked up and grinned at Paul. "What took you so long?"

Paul was about to answer and then decided *why bother?* Instead, he plopped down in a chair and reached for a bottle of water. Beer would have been better, but they had run out over a week ago.

They had saved the child and for now were safe again. Although he didn't regret going out there, he wasn't relishing having to do it again.

He walked over to the television and turned the knob. A blast of static filled the room and the familiar emergency broadcast signal came on, which at least was better than snow. Paul was walking back to his seat when the television and cellar lights blinked out, plunging the room into darkness. The small cellar windows let in a few suffused rays of light that filtered into the room, so for the moment, they weren't in absolute darkness.

The electricity had finally gone off. That did not bode well. Paul looked at Adam, then Josey, in the dull gloom of the cellar and his shoulders sagged a little.

"Shit," he whispered.

CHAPTER 4

Reverend Bernard Williams of the First Church of Christ was crazy.

Schizophrenic was the clinical term. He was diagnosed late in life, after preaching the word of God for more than ten years, and he had taken medication to keep his sickness in check. He was a fully-functioning member of society.

Then the dead started coming back to life.

At the beginning, he'd been fine. He helped his parishioners deal with the loss of loved ones and the slow crumbling of the American way of life. It helped to keep him focused. But then it had all gone horribly wrong. One of his parishioners had gotten infected and returned to the church, hoping for help. The young woman had died in terrible pain, and no one was prepared when she sat back up and tore her mother's throat out. Pandemonium ensued as people tried to escape the carnivorous woman. The first to try to leave the church were crushed against the doors of the back room by the crowd of people behind them trying to escape; they clogged the frame, making the doors impossible to open. It was an old church, and only the front entrance had been brought up to code for public buildings.

The dead woman was soon joined by her revived mother, and the two women dove into the crowd of frantic parishioners.

Rev. Bernie, as his people called him, stood at the top of his podium and watched his people being slaughtered one by one only to be revived by something inexplicable. Soon only the undead filled the church.

Then one of the undead parishioners turned on Rev. Bernie, seeking to add him to the ranks of the walking dead.

With panic in his heart, he ran out of the main theater and barricaded himself in his chambers, the large, heavy oak door more than enough to stop the zombies. He stayed there for more than a week, surviving on junk food that had been confiscated from his younger parishioners at Sunday school and the still-running water in his private bathroom.

At the time he'd had almost a week's worth of medication and he had taken it diligently every day. Then . . . he just ran out.

Now Rev. Bernie sat in his office and stared at the walls. There was a four-foot statue of Jesus sitting on a mahogany pedestal in the corner of the room . . . talking to him.

"The time is now, my son," the statue said, in a peaceful soothing tone. "The Rapture has come and you have been left behind. What are you going to do about it?" The question seemed to imply there was something to be done.

Rev. Bernie knelt in front of the statue. The light from the window directly behind it gave the four-foot sculpture an eerie glow.

"I don't know, my Lord; all my parishioners have been killed, turned into monsters."

The statue of Jesus Christ shook its head. "Not at all, my son. They have merely been transformed into the Devil's henchmen, Warriors that will defy the will of God, my Father. But you can stop them."

Rev. Bernie listened intently, waiting to be told what to do. "But how, my Lord? How can I stop them? I am not only one man?"

Jesus smiled. "True, you are one man, but you have me behind you. With the Son of God by your side, how can you fail?"

Rev. Bernie nodded as a plan formulated in his mind. First he would need more parishioners. Surely, there were others who needed to be comforted by the word of God?

Standing up, he walked to the door and slowly opened it an inch, prepared to slam it shut if the zombies were still outside the door.

He may be crazy, but he wasn't stupid . . . or suicidal.

With a creaking of old hinges the door opened a finger's width. The church was quiet. Sucking in a deep breath, he pushed the door open a little more.

Empty. The hall was empty.

With the courage he felt knowing Jesus was behind him, he crept back into the theatre. The front doors to the church were wide open, the ghouls long gone. As he walked down the aisles and looked down the pews, he saw bodies that had been ripped to shreds. A cold chill went up his back as he recognized the arm and the purse still attached to it as it lay on one of the seats. The arm had belonged to Mrs. Magilacutty; a sweet old woman in her late eighties. She had confided to him one morning that she was scared to death of dying from old age. Looking at the remnants of her ripped arm, he wondered if she'd be pleased to know that worry had been unfounded.

Reaching the doors of the church, he pulled them shut. His eyes caught a glimpse of the street before slamming and locking the doors. Cars were stopped at crazy angles everywhere he looked, some having been in accidents. Bodies were spread across the sidewalk and street, some whole, some in pieces. He distinctly caught the odor of smoke from some nearby building, and the worst thing of all was the fifteen zombies that had turned when the noise of the slowly closing doors reverberated across the street. The stench of death floated in front of them and assailed Rev. Bernie.

The first one in line made it up the stairs and hit the closing doors just as Rev. Bernie slammed the lock. Muffled pounding permeated the heavy oak doors as the first zombie attempted to gain access. Seconds later, the sounds of flesh on wood grew louder as more of the undead joined the first.

Rev. Bernie smiled at that. The Devil's minions would not sully the Lord's house again, he would see to *that*. He stopped and looked around the theatre, deciding the first thing to do would be to clean up the large room.

With a bounce in his step, he went off to the custodial closet to retrieve a mop and other cleaning supplies. He had a lot of work ahead of him, but with the Lord's help, he knew he would make it.

It took five long hours for Rev. Bernie to clean the blood and gore from the floor and pews of his church. The time was lost in a blur, his mind wandering as he worked. When he had finally swabbed the last spot of blood and picked up the last chunk of flesh, he carried the mop and rags to the custodial closet and left them there in a heap.

Walking back into the theatre, he paused at one of the stained glass windows that surrounded the left and right sides of the church. He stared at the picture, lost in thought. Jesus was struggling with his cross, the heavy timbers crushing him under their weight. On both sides of the tortured man, people stood, hurling negative epithets and curses at him.

Rev. Bernie jumped in his skin when Jesus turned to him and

spoke. "You have done well, my son, but your work is far from over. You must first destroy the soldiers of Satan. Then, you must fortify this church, so wanderers will have a sanctuary to come to when they seek shelter."

Rev. Bernie looked up at the picture, marveling at Jesus. "But how, my Lord? How can I do these things? As I said before, I am not only one man?"

Jesus smiled gently. "You already have the tools at your disposal; you just need to use them." Then the picture transformed, returning once again to a stained glass window.

"No, wait, I don't understand," Rev. Bernie pleaded, but it was too late, Jesus was gone. The picture was inanimate.

Rev. Bernie sat down in one of the pews and thought about what the apparition had said. He already had the tools he needed? But where? He was brought out of his reverie by the sounds of the zombies at the main door.

Standing up, he went to the back storeroom where supplies and spare oil for the lanterns were kept. Through the back window he could see the rear of the church. The small yard was fenced in on both sides and the leftover pieces of chain-link fence were leaning against the rear of the rectory, the house that was also owned by the church.

Studying the supplies in the closet, an idea crossed his mind. Now that the medication in his system had worn off, he felt more aware of his surroundings. The haze he had lived under for so many years was gone, he felt more awake and more intelligent then he had in years.

He retrieved the oil and the few spare buckets and then got to work on his plan to rid himself of the demons that now resided at the front of his church. Without realizing it, he started to hum one of his favorite hymns, the moans and the groans from outside fading away until they weren't there at all.

It took more then two hours to piece together what he needed to secure his church. He set up scaffolding (leftover from renovations) by the front doors. He then carried buckets of the flammable oil up to the front. With the scaffolding set up, he now had access to the window above the doors.

He climbed to the top, perfectly level with the three-by-three foot window. Using some tools from the box he'd found in the cellar, he managed to pry off the frame for the window.

Rev. Bernie stuck his head out and was pleased to see that the crowd of undead monsters was directly below him. More then twenty of the disgusting things milled about on the stone steps, some half-heartedly banging on the doors.

He pulled his head back and made sure he had everything he needed. Oil, *check*, spare piece of wood with a rag tied around it and soaked in oil, *check*. And of course, a lighter, that had been acquired from the lost and found. *Check*.

He picked up one of the three buckets of oil and put it through the window. When he was confident there were a number of zombies below, he poured the flammable liquid out at them.

Most of the oil hit its mark, although the wind caught a portion of it and spread it across the stone steps. The Reverend smiled when the bucket was empty. He poured the contents of the other two buckets out the window in quick succession. The zombies barely noticed and continued banging on the doors.

Rev. Bernie was ready for phase two of his plan. He flicked the lighter on and held it under his homemade torch. The flame caught immediately, the orange and red flame blossoming like a giant match, reflecting in the Reverend's eyes and making him look like a demon himself, all out of place in this house of God.

Holding the torch out the window, he lined up a few zombies and with a mischievous evil smile touching his lips, let go of the stick. The torch floated down to the steps, the wind fanning the flames, threatening to extinguish the torch before it reached its target. But the torch stayed lit and struck the head of an oil-soaked woman in a pale blue dress.

The walking corpse burst into flames. The dead woman's arms flailed, she not comprehending what was happening. She let out an ephemeral screech as the fire entered her lungs, scorching it from the inside out. The blazing human caricature plowed into its brethren, the fire jumping from form to form until all the zombies were a blazing mass of burning flesh. Hair was the first to go, then the eyes literally boiled inside their sockets. Rev. Bernie didn't know if the demons below felt pain, but he knew he was sending them straight back to the Hell where they belonged.

The redolence of charred meat floated up to him, making him want to gag. Pulling a handkerchief from his pocket, he covered his nose to keep out the distasteful odor.

Below him on the landing, the last remnants of the zombies fell to the stone steps. Burnt husks of what were once human beings adorned the front of the church.

A small fire was still burning on the front doors, but Rev. Bernie was confident the hard wood would resist the flames. Most of the flames on the zombies were slowly dying out, the fuel consumed.

Rev. Bernie looked out on the street. All was quiet; at least for the moment. He had no doubt there would be more of the demons if he didn't work fast.

The first half of his plan had worked well, even better then he'd hoped. As he climbed down to the floor, he could only pray the second phase would go as well. He really didn't doubt it, though. After all, he had God on his side.

CHAPTER 5

Adam was dreaming.

He was fishing with his father on a small lake in the middle of Malden, Mass. The clear blue sky was marred only by a few white clouds and the air smelled fresh as only a spring day could. The birds were singing in the trees, and over on the shoreline, a family of squirrels was playing; chasing each other in and out of the blossoming flowers scattered across the green grass.

Dad had a beer in one hand and a fishing reel in the other. They'd come to this spot before. Although the fish were sparse, that really wasn't why they were here. They were here on this lake to spend some quality time together alone.

Just father and son.

A hundred feet away, a small motorboat chugged by, the owner moving slowly across the water, causing slight ripples that touched the boat and made it rock gently. At least one person on the lake was being respectful of others, Adam thought, looking across the once smooth surface, where a couple of teenagers were riding jet-skis. If there were any fish nearby, they would definitely be gone now, thanks to all the commotion the small engines were making in the water.

A gentle wave caressed the bottom of his boat, causing it to rock only slightly harder.

He relaxed and enjoyed the gentle rocking.

Dad had just let out another cast, the line soaring out into the middle of the lake. Then he started to reel it back in. After a few minutes with the line still more than half out, he felt a gentle tug on the rod.

"Hey, son, looks like I got one," he said.

"That's great, Dad, reel it in," Adam coaxed.

He started to do just that, a little more quickly now, the thin string cutting through the water like a razor. As the line drew closer, so too, did the man's struggling increase.

"Jesus, son, I don't know what I caught, but its heavy."

"Need any help?" Adam asked from the other end of the boat.

His father shook his head. "Nah, I'm okay. I should have it in the boat in a minute. You can help then."

"Cool," Adam answered back, looking forward to seeing what his father had hooked.

Dad gave one more heave and something smacked the side of the boat. From Adam's vantage point, he couldn't see what it was, but he could smell it.

If he was watching a cartoon he could imagine the waves of stink lines that would emanate off the object his dad had caught; the smell of death and decay nearly overwhelming him.

Adam looked through his arm which he'd brought up to cover his nose and mouth and saw Dad bending over the side of the boat to retrieve the object.

"What's the matter, boy? It doesn't smell that bad. In fact, I think it smells kind of nice."

"Are you crazy?" Adam gasped through his arm, his voice muffled from the material. "That thing smells like death itself! Throw it back in the water."

His dad smiled a little at that and grunted with the exertion of pulling the object into the boat. It hit the deck with a squishy, meaty sound, brown water immediately dripping off it to pool in the bottom of the boat.

His father looked up, stretching muscles from the exertion of hauling it out of the water.

"I can't throw it back, son. It's your mother and I love her." Then he bent over and helped the corpse to sit up.

Adam's eyes went wide with shock as he looked at what was left of his mother. Her skin was a mottled blue color from being in the water. Her once beautiful blue eyes were gone, replaced by gaping eye sockets. Her lips had swollen to nearly twice their size, now resembling two fat, wriggling night crawlers.

But despite all of this, it was the hole in her forehead that freaked him out the most; the hole where his father had shot and killed her before she could return as one of the undead.

His father kneeled down and placed his arm around her, the water-logged clothes of his mother transferring moisture to his sleeve. He didn't seem to mind.

His father's teeth flashed in the sun, white as the clouds.

"Come here, son and give your mother a kiss. She's missed you."

Adam started to shake his head in disbelief. How could this be happening? From somewhere deep below in his mind, he knew this was all a dream, but he couldn't break free of it.

His father bent over his mother's face and kissed her, his tongue sliding into the orifice that was once her mouth, her blackened swollen tongue entangling with his. The slurping sound of the kiss drifted across the lake. Adam felt his stomach churning and he looked away, retching.

When he looked back, his father had finished kissing her, but now he looked different. His skin was a pallid blue like hers, and as Adam watched, blood started to pour from the side of his head. His father stood up, turning away for a second. In that second, Adam saw the gaping wound where his father's ear once was. The wound was identical to the one after he'd shot himself in the head.

Adam started to back up, but quickly realized he was already at the end of the boat with nowhere to go.

His father helped his mother stand up and the two of them stood in front of him, his mother dripping brown, scummy water into the boat. Adam's eyes caught the water near her feet and saw small things wiggling around in it, hundreds of maggots twisting and squirming.

His father and mother took a step closer to him, his mother raising her hands like she wanted a hug.

"Join us, son, it's not so bad. There's no more pain here. All your suffering will be over," his father told him.

"We could be a family again," his mother said through swollen lips, her voice like sandpaper and steel nails rubbing together.

Adam looked around for a way to escape. He was about to jump into the water and try to swim for it when he stopped. The water was now filled with hundreds of arms, the hands grasping up for him.

As he watched, the surface of the lake became covered with the bodies of the undead, each one bloated from being underwater. Arms with skin peeling from them reached for him, grasping the air. Gurgling moans surrounded the boat as the zombies attempted to talk with waterlogged lungs.

On the boat, his parents moved closer. Adam looked along the deck of the boat for a weapon, but there was nothing nearby.

"No!" He screamed. "Leave me alone, you're dead!"

His father chuckled. "So what? That doesn't seem to be a problem anymore." He stepped closer.

Adam raised his arms in front of him, forming fists with his hands. "Stay back or so help me . . ."

His father chuckled. "You can't stop us. Eventually, you will either feed us or join us; the choice is up to you."

As his parents moved closer, Adam tried to step back a little more, despite the fact he was out of room. He tumbled over the side and fell into the water. It was cold and he struggled back to the surface, the sun shining down on the churning lake.

His head broke through and he sucked fresh air, relieved to be alive. But the corpses in the water surrounded him, and before he could do more than scream, they fell onto him, pulling him down into the icy depths of the lake.

The light receded and he wondered, how could the lake be so deep? The air in his lungs was spent and his chest wanted nothing more than to exhale and breathe, but he knew to do that would be death.

Deeper and deeper the corpses pulled him, until he realized even if he escaped, there was no way he could make it back to the surface before he drowned.

A voice next to his head made him turn. His father was there, drifting down with him. His voice seemed far away, the water muffling it, but Adam still heard him as he spoke.

"Just give in, Adam. It's over, you've lost."

Adam pushed himself away, even though he'd already realized the same thing. His lungs were screaming for oxygen and spots were appearing in front of his eyes.

He was at his breaking point and knew it. He expelled the spent air in his lungs and involuntarily sucked in cold water into his body. He jerked as the fluid filled him, his lungs fighting it, expecting air but getting water instead.

He jerked again, but only for a moment, his body shaking in its death throes. Then he remained still. With eyes that saw nothing, he started to sink into the depths of the lake, the other zombies by his side.

Adam snapped awake, looking around frantically; wondering what had woken him. He quickly realized he was lying on the floor of the cellar, the gloom of the room reminding him of his dream. He looked down and saw he was drenched in sweat, his bedclothes damp from perspiration.

Throwing the covers off himself, he stood up; the dream dissolving from his mind like a wisp of smoke in the wind. It was nearly midnight, the battery operated clock on the wall proclaiming the time with glow-in-the-dark hands. The others were sleeping, as well. Paul was on one cot and Josey and Timmy were curled up together on another one.

Josey had adopted the boy from the second she'd taken him from Adam's arms nearly a week before. In the first few days, the boy had constantly asked where his parents were, the scene of their massacre blocked from his memory. Josey had lied to him and said they had to go away for a while and they had asked her to watch him. Timmy had simply nodded and walked away.

Now he barely asked at all. It was almost as if he knew what had happened and had just decided to let it go. Paul had some spare wood on one of the shelves and he'd cut them into blocks with a hand saw, making Timmy a crude form of Lincoln Logs.

The logs were spread out on the floor and Adam stepped around them, not wanting to step on one with his bare feet.

A creaking from the floorboards above his head caused him to stop moving and listen. Small bits of dust floated from the ceiling as something heavy moved around on the first floor.

Adam moved across the room until he was at Paul's side. Shaking the man's shoulder gently, he frowned when all Paul did was grunt in his sleep and roll over. Adam reached for his shoulder and gave him another shake, this time putting some force into it.

Paul grunted again and sat up with a tired moan, bleary eyes looking around for signs of trouble. He was about to ask Adam what was wrong when Adam placed a finger over his lips.

"Shhh. There's someone upstairs," Adam whispered.

Paul's eyebrows went up in curiosity. "Oh, yeah? Alive or dead?"

Adam shrugged. "Don't know. You want me to go and ask?"

Paul brought his legs over the side of the cot, placing his feet on the floor. Scratching his head, he looked up at the ceiling, now hearing the heavy, plodding footsteps for himself.

"Nah. I say we do nothing. Whoever or whatever's up there doesn't know we're down here and the door at the top of the stairs is made of solid metal; nothing's getting down here unless I let it."

Adam nodded in the dark. "Okay, fine. Should we wake up Josey and Timmy?"

Paul shook his head and looked over at his wife and his newly adopted child.

"No, let them sleep. But be ready to keep them quiet if our friend upstairs decides to make too much noise and wakes them."

"Okay, sounds good," Adam said and moved to the middle of the room and back to his cot. Taking a moment, he got dressed, feeling better now that he had his pants on. A flutter of his dream came to his consciousness and he felt a chill slide down his spine. Then the memory was gone and he stood there wondering what had freaked him out. One of the blessings of bad dreams was that they usually didn't stick around after you woke up, and Adam had a feeling he didn't want to remember the one he'd just had.

The floorboards creaked some more and the sound of something falling to the floor above drifted down to the cellar. Adam thought it might have been a chair or some appliance from the countertops, carelessly thrown to the floor and forgotten.

Josey stirred in her slumber, but remained asleep. Next to her, Timmy slept the way only a young child could, the world around him irrelevant.

A loud crashing filled the cellar and Adam guessed it was the kitchen table or maybe even the refrigerator being thrown to the floor.

Josey sat up with terror in her eyes and Paul was there to comfort her. In hushed tones, he filled her in on what was happening. She nodded and carefully extricated herself from the bed and Timmy's arms. Then she moved to the workbench and retrieved one of the pistols. With the soft sound of the clip being ejected, she checked the load and skillfully snapped it back in, pulling the slide and preparing the weapon for battle . . . if it came to that.

Paul stood up and stretched. He'd already gotten dressed and had his trusty rifle next to him. He had wrapped the wooden stock in duct tape to try and repair the large crack it had received pummeling zombie skulls a week before.

Without realizing it, the three of them moved into the middle of the cellar and stood there looking up at the ceiling; waiting.

More crashes filtered down, making Timmy stir in his sleep. The three of them looked at each other, for the moment not knowing what they should do.

A thunderous crash rocked the cellar, causing dirt and dust to fall onto their heads.

"What the hell was that?" Adam asked.

Paul shrugged. "I have no idea, but if this keeps up, we're gonna have to do something or the whole house could fall in."

Timmy was up and crying, the noise startling him awake. Josey ran to him, and in soothing tones told him everything was fine, that he was safe. Adam listened, almost wishing she would do that to him; anything to block out the nightmare that had become their lives.

A second crash filled the cellar, and Paul moved to the door that led to the outside.

"What're you doing? Where're you going?" Josey called from the cot to Paul.

Paul opened the door and turned to Josey.

"Look, if I don't take care of whatever's going on up there it could end up fucking us over. If the gas is still on and the stove gets disconnected . . ." Paul trailed off, knowing Josey got the point he was trying to make.

Adam ran to the workbench and grabbed his father's .38, confident. "Wait, Paul, I'll come with you. You'll need someone to watch your back."

Paul grinned. "Thanks, man, that'd be great." He looked at Josey again. "You stay here and watch the boy. We'll be back in a minute."

Josey's lips grew tight. "Okay, but you be careful. I've spent enough time breaking you in; I don't want to lose you now."

He nodded, getting her meaning. "Don't worry, babe, I'll be back. You ready Adam?"

Adam jogged over to Paul. "Okay, let's get this over with." In answer, another crash filled the cellar and Timmy burrowed deeper into Josey's arms.

"If we come back and neither of us can dance, we didn't make it," Adam said. Nobody laughed. "Fine. Nevermind."

The two men opened the bulkhead and stepped out into the cool night air. There was a half moon out tonight, the light filtering through the clouds, bathing the area in anemic yellow light. Adam looked at Paul as he shifted his feet uncomfortably, studying his yard for dangers. His countenance showed a ghostly pallor from the moonlight.

"Keep to the shadows. Let's see if we can look through the windows to see what's happening."

Adam nodded. "You sure you don't want to just, you know, blunder in?"

Paul snorted. "Nah. Maybe next time."

The two men crept around the yard, wary of their surroundings. Every bush and shrub was a potential threat. They made it to the kitchen windows on the side of the house without a problem. Adam looked across the street at the van still embedded in the damaged house. The bodies of the supine zombies he and Paul had killed were shrouded in shadows, barely discernable from where he stood. *Could we use the van to escape?* He made a note to talk to Paul about it later. Paul's car was still in his driveway, but better to have more than less, his father had always said.

Thinking of his father gave him a pang of sadness. He brushed it aside, now was certainly not the time or the place to mourn his parents. Paul was trying to peek in one of the windows, reminding Adam of a Peeping Tom. He smiled to himself, but otherwise kept quiet.

"I can't see shit," Paul said, moving his head to try and see around the curtains.

"With those glasses? You should be able to see the future."

"It's too damn dark in there. I . . . what did you say?"

Another crash cut Adam off. "What in the hell is going on in there? It's like they're trying to destroy my house!" Paul hissed, aggravated.

"What do you want to do?" Adam asked quietly, trying to rein in his attitude.

"I think we'll just have to go inside and see what's what. You with me?"

Adam nodded quickly. "Yeah, I'm with you. I've been itching to blunder in since we came upstairs. Can we get this done? I've got to use the bathroom."

Paul chuckled. "Now that you mention it, I could go, too. It'll be nice not to have to go in a can. Tell you what, why don't we take turns and watch each other. Those bushes over there'll do."

Adam looked where Paul was pointing. In the middle of the yard was a circle of bushes, the flower buds just starting to bloom.

"Oh yeah. I hate those bushes anyway. You first?"

Paul answered by moving across the yard. "Yeah, that's fine. I've got to go bad."

Adam followed behind him but stopped a few feet away. He turned his back on Paul and watched the silent yard. Crashes filtered through the glass of the windows of the house. Adam grinned, knowing how annoyed Paul was by this.

Paul pulled down his pants and squatted in the bushes. He was so intent on pushing and watching the yard he didn't see the desiccated hand crawling out of the bush. It wrapped itself around his ankle. He was so busy grunting, he didn't feel the hand until it was secured firmly in place.

He grabbed some leaves and wiped himself. He stood and started to pull his pants up when his leg was pulled out from under him. He crashed face first into the grass. Spitting dirt, he rolled over to see something that was once human crawling out of the shrubs. More than half her face was missing, chewed or torn off. The smell of decay and rotted meat filled the yard as she crawled forward. Her mouth constantly opened and closed, her yellow teeth snapping on empty air.

Paul calmly called to Adam who was watching the yard and street carefully.

"A little help here, please?" Paul asked politely.

Adam turned and gave a start. He moved closer until he was standing next to the woman. She turned to look up at him, hissing and snapping her jaw, but then moved forward again, climbing up Paul's legs.

Paul's pants were still down and his penis lay between his legs like a worm. The woman spotted it and dove for the hanging meat.

Paul squealed and jerked back as the chomping mouth neared his crotch. Adam's left foot connected with her head, sending the zombie flying to the side.

Paul extricated himself and pulled his pants up.

"Paul, a ladies man?" Adam asked. Paul looked at the rotten teeth and shook his head.

The woman hissed at Paul and Adam and crawled toward them. Adam now saw that both her legs appeared to be broken, just useless stumps she dragged behind her. The two men stood back and looked at each other.

Paul held up a finger in a *wait a minute gesture* and darted to the corner of the yard. Adam stood there, waiting and watching as the dead lady tried to get to her feet. He kicked her in the chest, sending her sprawling onto her back. She flailed for a few seconds and rolled to her side, coming up on her elbows.

Inside the house, another crash filled the backyard, reminding him of that. He was about to call to Paul when the man reappeared out of the shadows, carrying a sledgehammer.

"Where the hell did you get that?" Adam asked.

"From the shed. I've got all my big tools in there. I figured this would do the job."

The woman hissed again and crawled towards them. Paul stepped up to her and brought the hammer over his head. With a grunt, he brought it down as hard as he could.

The hammer struck the back of the copse's head, driving her face into the dirt. The body jerked, then remained still. Paul pulled the hammer out of the caved-in skull. It came free with a slurping sound that had Adam thinking of his dream. He felt his stomach churning and quickly turned away.

Paul was already moving toward the house. Halfway across the yard he stopped.

"You coming? Or do you want to still go to the bathroom?" Paul asked.

Adam answered by moving across the yard, detouring wide around the body of the dead woman.

Suddenly he didn't have to go so badly.

CHAPTER 6

Reverend Bernie stood on his podium looking down at the twenty plus people sitting in the pews below him. He had a flock again. Parishioners to share the word of God with.

Over the past week people had arrived at his front doors. Their banging would draw him out of his prayers and he would quickly let them inside. Now, after only one week, he had more then two dozen people, and more continued to arrive every day.

There were few men in his new congregation; it was mostly women and children, but that was okay with him. Less macho brava-do he'd have to deal with. His new parishioners were thankful to be safe again. The Reverend had raided a few buildings in the area and managed to collect a decent supply of food and bottled water. All of the buildings around the church were empty of people, abandoned when the National Guard warned of the growing epidemic. Most of the people were told to go to rescue stations, where the living and dead were interred, although in different sections.

After the television had gone out in the recreation room, he had no way of knowing what was happening. In his few times of mental clarity, he wished those people well.

He thought back to one week before, after he had finished burn-ing all the zombies on the front steps. He'd worked quickly after that, not wanting to waste the time the Lord had given him. He hadn't had many visions while he worked, almost as if he knew they would only slow him down. He had retrieved all the chain-link fence from the back of the church and had brought it to the front steps and border-ing sidewalk.

Stepping out into the light of day with the smell of burning meat lingering on the breeze was one of the most frightening things he'd done in his forty-eight years on Earth.

But he had faith that God would see him through.

For the most part he was right, although it was mostly due to luck. The church was off the beaten path of the city, so there weren't as many zombies as in other areas. No houses meant no people for the undead to feed on, and so he was able to work relatively undisturbed.

He'd carried the metal fences to the front stairs and had stacked them up, building a narrow channel in front of the church. Before starting he had to dispose of the charred bodies. With a towel over his mouth and nose, he'd taken each blackened husk across the street and tossed them in a heap. When he was done, he was then able to build his fence in peace.

Once while he was working, the sun hot on his head, a zombie had wandered onto the street. Upon seeing him, the dead man had immediately started toward the Reverend, his legs moving like those of a baby learning his first steps.

At first, Rev. Bernie hadn't heard it, his attention focused on building the fence, but once the ghoul was closer, it kicked a bucket of screws over.

The tinkling of the can was enough to pull Rev. Bernie from his stupor. Turning, he stepped back at the sight of what could only be called an act of the devil himself coming towards him. The dead man's face was a rotted mass of maggots, his belly distended like an Ethiopian who was on the verge of dying from starvation.

He shook his head as the pitiful creature shambled forward. It reached out with skeletal arms to grab him, one hand missing. Where the right hand should have been there was nothing more then a jagged stump coated with black ichor.

The pitiful man was only a few feet away when Rev. Bernie calmly raised the hammer he was holding.

When the ghoul was close enough, he brought it down onto the man's forehead. Skull gave under the onslaught of metal and the zombie dropped to the sidewalk.

The man twitched on the ground, still trying to crawl toward the Reverend.

Rev. Bernie shook his head, pitying the poor bastard, then brought the hammer down again, cracking the skull and dropping the zombie to the pavement like a heavy bag of cement.

Breathing heavily, he made the sign of the cross in front of the corpse.

"May you find rest in death that you could not find in life," he said, for the moment clear-headed and his old self.

Then, like a breeze blowing a leaf, the madness returned to his eyes and he spit on the zombie, his face curling into a grimace.

"Demon spawn! Go back to Hell and tell your master I'll be sending him more soon enough!"

He dragged the body across the street and finished working. Hours later, when he was done, he stood on the stairs and admired his work. He now had a fenced area around his steps, with two doors, one in front of the other. He hoped people could gain access and be able to reach him without the undead getting them.

If it didn't work, he could always tweak the fence until it was the right set-up for maximum protection. He also knew if too many of the undead pushed on the fence it was possible his makeshift craftsmanship would collapse in a pile of metal and two by fours.

Sighing with the exertion of the day, he entered the church. The sun filtered into the room through the stained glass windows, giving them an eerie, preternatural glow.

Walking up the aisle, he stopped at the cross at the front of the church. While his was a Protestant church, the church was also used by a small Catholic congregation. Money was tight and even the Catholic Church had made sacrifices in the past years.

Jesus was on the cross, hanging as he always had. The statue began to shimmer and the head turned to look at him. Bernie knelt down on one knee, his gaze on the face of the statue.

"My Lord. I accomplished my task, just as you ordered," he said with respect.

The head nodded on the statue. "Excellent, my son, rise. You have done well, but the Rapture is still upon the world and if you do not want to be left behind, you must continue your work. First you must gather a congregation, and then you must collect some of Satan's minions and bring them to the back of the church. There you will keep them until they are needed."

Rev. Bernie looked up at the statue, the statue that was only talking in his mind, and nodded. "Of course, my Lord, but what are they for? Why do I need them?"

The face smiled down on him, filling him with love. "All in good time, my son, all in good time." Then the statue shimmered once again and became inanimate. Rev. Bernie stood up, blinking the tears from his eyes.

He knew what he had to do, his mission was clear. The good Lord had told him. All he had to do was have faith and the Lord would provide.

CHAPTER 7

With Paul in the lead, the two men crept closer to the house. The crashing had continued the entire time they'd been dealing with the woman zombie. Once Paul was able to peek in the living room window, he finally saw the source of the noise.

A hulking brute of a man staggered around the kitchen. Paul watched the man plow into one of the wall cabinets, sending it crashing to the floor in a heap of splinters and broken dinner plates.

It was only when the man turned toward the window that Paul saw the real reason for all the chaos and damage. The man had no eyes, only red, seeping holes in his face. The man stumbled close to the window and Paul backed away a step, startled. He had caught a glimpse of the man's complexion and either he needed a lot more sun or the man was dead.

"Well, who's in there? What did you see?" Adam asked from beside him.

"It's one of those dead bastards. Big one, too. He's got to be at least six-two, six-three, easy," Paul whispered.

"Shit, really? So what are we gonna do?" Adam asked.

Paul set his lips in a thin grimace. "What do you think we're gonna do? Ask him to play basketball? We've gotta go in there and kill him."

"Yeah, that's what I thought," Adam said.

The two men moved back through the yard and stopped by the back door. With a soft jingling, Paul found the key that fit in the steel lock on the door. The door opened with a soft squeak of rusty hinges. He winced at the creaking sound of the hinges and turned to Adam.

"Been meaning to get some oil on those. Guess now's too late, huh?"

Adam nodded. "Bob Villa you're not."

The crashing was louder now that they were in the house. They were standing in the shattered mess of the kitchen, the large zombie having wandered to the front of the house. Sounds of breaking items and crashing glass filled the air.

"Oh, man," Paul said. "Josey is gonna kill me when I tell her what this guy's done to our house."

"Let's worry about that later, huh? Once he's dead." Adam said, raising his gun.

Paul nodded and started forward, his feet crunching on the scattered debris lying on the tile floor. Paul looked down and saw one of the ceramic tiles was cracked thanks to the rampaging zombie. He idly thought about how he would fix it until he realized it really didn't matter anymore.

Paul stepped to the opening that separated the kitchen from the rest of the house. He was about to continue when the hulking ghoul suddenly appeared in the doorway. Before Paul could do or say anything, the zombie plowed into him, both of them falling to the floor in a tangle.

The zombie belched a fetid mix of dead air and decay, making Paul taste bile and want to vomit. Adam, by his side, jumped back startled, not prepared for the onslaught of dead muscle.

Paul could barely breathe with the weight of the body crushing his chest. All he could do was wheeze. He was staring into the face of death, the dead man still not fully aware that a free meal was directly below him.

Adam, forgetting about the gun in his hand, reached instead for the sledgehammer Paul had dropped. With his left hand, he started to bang it on the brute's back, trying to get the hulking mass of dead flesh to move before his friend suffocated.

Paul was struggling for every breath he could take from his compressed chest.

The dead man barely felt the hammer, but the bludgeoning did distract him enough for him to roll off Paul and reach out with his long arms for the source of his annoyance. Adam jumped away with a squeal. The zombie was almost twice as big as he. Even if the man had been alive and not a flesh-eating cannibal, Adam would still be scared shitless.

Paul was now on the floor, sucking in deep lungfuls of oxygen. The dead brute was swinging his arms, trying to find Adam. Once the tiny floating circles of light left Paul's vision, he looked around the floor for his rifle. He quickly found where it had fallen and retrieved it, flicked off the safety, and prepared to send the zombie back to Hell where it belonged.

Adam was still backing away from the walking corpse, struggling to just stay out of reach of the dead man's mammoth arms.

"Shoot him, will ya? Before he gets me!" Adam yelled. The zombie heard him and pinpointed his position by the sound of his voice. Adam saw this and muttered another curse.

Paul raised the rifle, trying to line up a shot, but the target wouldn't hold still. He was afraid if he missed, he might hit Adam instead. Adam's back hit the wall and he was out of time and room to move. If Paul didn't take a shot now, it would be too late for his friend.

"Adam, down!" Paul shouted.

Adam dropped. The dead brute's hands swiped empty air as Adam slid down the wall and hit the floor, broken glass cutting his hand.

Paul lined up the shot from not more then five feet away, and squeezed the trigger. The bullet flew from the rifle, striking the ghoul in the side of the head. Unfortunately the heavy skull plate was more then a match for the small caliber round and the shot grazed the skull, continuing onward and striking the far wall.

The zombie let out a guttural yell, sounding like a primordial creature. Adam cringed on the floor, all his courage deflating like a damaged hot air balloon.

Paul swore under his breath and racked the rifle, sending another bullet into the chamber. He lined up the shot, the roaring brute flailing around like a wild beast, and fired again. This time the bullet hit the ghoul's shoulder and the dead man continued charging around the room.

"Come on, man, hit him!" Adam screamed from the floor.

"What the hell do you think I'm trying to do?"

The blind man heard them talking and his head darted back and forth as he tried to zero in on the food so close to him. His nose flared frantically, almost as if he could smell them.

Then he stopped and turned to face Paul, and with two giant steps, crossed the floor until he was only inches from Paul's shocked face.

Paul stood perfectly still, knowing if he moved, he was dead. All the zombie had to do was grab him and those meat hooks for hands would tear him apart.

Adam saw this and forced himself to his feet on unsteady legs. Paul was standing perfectly still and Adam knew his friend's life was measured in seconds. Sucking in a deep breath, Adam picked up the revolver from where it had fallen and moved towards both of them. No matter how silent he tried to be, the crushed glass and debris crunched under his shoes, sounding like cannon shots to his ears.

Despite this, Adam made it to within two feet of the blind zombie. The dead man's nose twitched, catching Paul's scent. His head swiveled back and forth and then stopped, looking directly at Paul . . . even without eyes he had zeroed in on the man.

Just as the brute reached out to grab Paul's head in his giant hands, Adam stuck the barrel of the pistol, against his left ear.

"Hey, big guy. Listen to this," Adam said and squeezed the trigger on the .38.

The zombie's head rocked to the side as the bullet bounced around inside the skull, turning the brain to mush. The hulking brute stood there for almost a minute, swaying back and forth like a tree in the wind, as if the body didn't realize the brain was no more. Adam thought maybe if he should blow on the guy like they did in the cartoons, but the very dead corpse fell over, taking the last intact kitchen chair with it.

The two men stood there looking at each other, adrenaline and fear pumping through their bodies. Paul sagged to the floor and looked up at Adam. "Jesus, thanks buddy. That was quick thinking."

Adam leaned against the wall and slid down next to Paul, the gun in his shaking hand falling next to him as he released it.

"Just another day in zombie world," Adam said.

Paul chuckled at that. The zombie's hand twitched for a moment, causing both men to jump in their seats, but then the hand remained still. Just a few neurons not yet finished firing.

They looked at each other and Adam started to giggle. Before they knew it, both men were laughing hard and slapping each other on the back, the tension of the past half hour draining away like water down the drain. After a full five minutes, Paul stood up and took Adam's hand, helping him to his feet.

"Well, we should get this guy out of here before he stinks up the place. And we need to tell Josey we're still in one piece." Paul said, surveying the kitchen damage. If he ever came back to live upstairs, he wasn't relishing the cleanup he'd have to do.

Adam smiled. "I'll go tell her and then be back to help you, okay?"

"Sure, kid, but don't be too long. I'd hate to think what else is lurking around outside that might have heard all the noise."

With a wave, Adam took off out the back door, this time paying more attention. The yard was empty and he ran to the bulkhead doors.

Paul walked around the rest of the house, surveying all the damage the giant ghoul had made. When he reached the front door, he realized how the blind zombie had made it inside.

The door lock had been shattered, probably from when the National Guardsmen had checked the house for occupants, and the zombie had just stumbled inside. The door wasn't really built for security, anyway; it was mostly leaded glass with a few wood moldings. He'd always told Josey it didn't really matter. What was the point of having triple-hard doors when all a robber had to do was break a window?

Looking at the shattered remains of the door, he wished he'd gone with a standard heavy door. The zombies didn't seem to be bright enough to know to crawl through a window. In fact, it was like they couldn't reason at all. They appeared to be creatures of pure instinct.

He thought about that as he pushed the couch in front of the damaged door. Then he took a desk from the den and placed it on top of the couch. Hopefully, it would deter anymore visitors. *At least until we leave.*

Paul knew their food and water was dangerously low. It had been more than a week since the water had stopped flowing from the tap. He'd managed to suck what he could out of the pipes, but once their supplies were gone they would have to leave or start foraging. He wondered how those rescue stations he'd heard about on the television were doing. The news had reported that the nearest one was on the outskirts of the city. They could make it by vehicle in less then an hour, assuming the roads were clear.

Crunching footsteps behind him brought him out of his thoughts and he turned to see Adam step into the room.

He smiled at Paul. "Okay, Josey's cool. I told her we'd be down after we straightened up."

"That's good. Give me a hand with the stiff. Let's bring him out to the backyard. We'll drop him into my neighbor's yard. I never liked that guy anyway."

"Who? The zombie, or your neighbor?" Adam asked.

Paul frowned. "Ha-ha, very funny. Come on, let's get to work, smartass."

It took the two of them a little longer then they would have hoped. The sheer size of the ghoul was more then enough to tax their limited strength. Finally they got the corpse dragged into the backyard, But they'd only made it about half-way when Paul dropped his end. With a gasping sound he said, "Forget it, this is far enough. My back's killing me."

Adam agreed, but was too exhausted to answer, so he just nodded his head, happily dropping his own end. Once Paul caught his breath, he stood up, pain crossing his face from the strain on his back.

"Come on, let's lock up the back of the house and go back downstairs, I'm exhausted."

"Sounds good to me," Adam answered, starting back to the house.

Paul followed, but then stopped in the yard for a moment, listening. Adam saw this.

"What's up, something wrong?"

"No," Paul answered. "I just could have sworn I heard church bells."

Adam cocked his head, listening. "I don't hear anything."

Shrugging it off, Paul headed into the house to finish up. There was a soft cot waiting for him and he couldn't wait to get back into it.

In a nearby tree, a few birds screeched at one another, ignoring the two men entirely.

CHAPTER 8

Reverend Bernie stood in the bell tower of his church and continued to ring the large, two foot bell. The sound reverberated off the columns surrounding him and sent the vibration deep into his brain. He didn't mind. In fact, he found it quite pleasant.

While the bell filled his head with noise, there was no room for anything else. No voices in his head and no visions appearing before him. For just a little while, he felt whole.

Down below on the ground, the bell was doing its job. The living dead were slowly moving towards the church, like dogs being called for dinner.

For Rev. Bernie to complete the next phase of his plan he needed the undead; only then could he find his way to heaven. Jesus had already told him that he could still reach Heaven, if only he did what had to be done.

Far below him, inside the homemade fence, stood three of his parishioners. They were three of the few men he had taken in recently. When they had arrived, they'd been half starved and feverish. The Reverend had used the last of his aspirin to help get their temperatures down, and once the three men were feeling better, they had given their thanks and had said they would do whatever was required of them to help.

Now they were doing just that. Each of the men held a long pole with a noose on the end, similar to what a dog catcher would use. Their goal was to capture at least a score of zombies and bring them to the yard behind the church. Then his mission could begin in earnest.

Rev. Bernie stopped ringing the bell, its purpose fulfilled. More then a hundred of the undead were approaching the church. He could only pray he had reinforced the barrier enough to keep it from collapsing under the sheer weight of bodies.

The stench of death floated up to him and he turned his face in disgust. The Devil's warriors were a smelly bunch, he'd give them that much.

He watched from above as the first zombie reached the fence. The parishioner named Tom, easily identifiable by his Red Sox jacket even from up in the tower, reached down from the makeshift scaffold Rev. Bernie had made and looped the noose around the zombie's head.

Bernie could see from his vantage point that the undead creature had once been a housewife. The housecoat and curlers, plus the one pink slipper still on her right foot attested to it.

The moment the noose wrapped around her neck, she started to flail and hiss. Tom had a good hold of the stick and, after a moment, managed to pull her into the three-by-four foot corral. One of the other men pushed the gate closed, but not before having to push another walking corpse out of the opening.

The dead woman bounced off the sides of the fence, not under-standing what was happening. Rev. Bernie wondered if they felt fear and, despite the fact he knew he was doing God's work, felt a slight hesitation as pity filled his heart.

He quickly brushed it away. If he was to accomplish the goals ahead, he needed to be hard and unforgiving. He needed to remind himself that what was once flesh and blood was now nothing more than animated meat, filled with the Devil's essence.

He watched below while Tom dragged the woman into the open-ing in front of the door and pulled her up the stairs. The woman con-tinued to hiss, and claw-like hands reached for him, any part of him, so she could sink her teeth into his flesh. He was having none of it. Tom pulled her into the church and Rev. Bernie decided he should get down to the theatre to help.

Taking two stairs at a time, he moved down the circular staircase until he came out behind the theatre. Pushing through the large red curtain at the back of the podium, he came out just as Tom was halfway down the main aisle.

Tom didn't see Rev. Bernie; he was to busy struggling with the zombie. Rev. Bernie moved forward, and in a moment was standing next to Tom. He reached out his hands and grasped the pole below Tom's hands, helping to keep the dead woman steady.

"Okay, Reverend, I've got one. Now what," he breathed while struggling with the pole.

"Out back, through the side door. We can place her in the yard.

The rest we'll have to drop from the upstairs window or else risk them getting back in."

Tom grunted and pulled the dead woman towards the side doors. People in the aisles screamed and shrank away from the man and his captive. Children hid in their mother's skirts, already traumatized from the experiences that had brought them to the church.

Tom managed to get up the aisle and Rev. Bernie was ahead of him at the side door. Once he was close, Rev. Bernie threw open the door and Tom stepped into the courtyard. Tom let up on the noose and the woman slipped free. Before she could attack, he slipped back through the doors and Rev. Bernie slammed them shut. Muffled pounding of dead flesh could be heard as the zombie banged on the doors.

Tom shook his head. "I still don't get what we're doing here, Reverend, but as I already told you, I'll help in whatever you need."

Rev. Bernie placed a gentle hand on his shoulder. "My thanks, son. All will be made clear, I promise. All in good time."

Both men looked up as another man pulled another zombie down the aisle. This time the zombie was a small boy, no more then eleven or twelve. The boy was wearing a little league uniform, the shirt ripped above the left shoulder. Dried blood covered the area and stained the front of his chest.

The man pulling him, Philip, if Rev. Bernie remembered correctly, steered the zombie towards Tom and himself. Rev. Bernie moved to the stairs and pointed up.

"Bring the foul creature up there, Phillip. We'll drop it into the courtyard from the window at the top of the stairs." Phillip nodded, and with Tom's help, dragged the boy zombie up the stairs. Only the Reverend called him Phillip, as he preferred Phil.

Reaching the top, Tom opened the five-foot window. The woman zombie saw him and tried to scale the wall. Her hands would find purchase, but she would slip and fall back to the earth in a crumpled heap, her fingernails peeling back.

Tom stood back and Phil looked at him. "So what now?"

Tom walked wide around the boy zombie and when both men held the pole he took it from Phil.

"Now we do what the Reverend asked us to do." Tom loosened the noose and used the end of the pole to push the dead boy out the window. The boy lost his balance and fell backward out the opening, tumbling head over heels as he fell.

Tom and Phil both moved to the window to see what had

happened.

Below them, the dead boy was climbing to his feet. His head was at an unnatural angle and one arm was bent in the wrong direction.

Phil looked at Tom and frowned. "That's messed up, you know? How many more times do we have to do this?"

Tom stood back from the window. "At least eighteen more. Why?"

Phil shrugged. "Why? Because I don't want to get my ass chewed off by a zombie because some crazy priest asked me to, that's why."

Tom moved down the stairs, pausing at the second step. "I'd watch what you say, if I were you. The Reverend has saved a lot of people in here. They owe him their lives. They'd do anything for him, myself included."

Phil made a disgusted face. "What does that mean?"

Tom's face grew hard. "It means, that unless you want to end up in that courtyard, I'd keep your mouth shut, that's what." Then he continued down the stairs, the noose pole clacking on the wall.

Phil stood at the top of the stairs for another minute, wondering if the sanctuary he thought he'd found might just end up being as bad as the outside.

"Come on, Phil, get your ass down here, Roy needs help with the next one," Tom called from below. Phil sighed. What choice did he have? At least he was safe.

With a quick shake of his head, he headed down the stairs to help the men retrieve more zombies. He had no idea what the hell they were doing it for, but at the moment that was irrelevant.

With his footsteps echoing off the walls, he made it to the ground floor and joined Tom. Now together, the two men went outside, walking side by side. The dead were waiting and there was a lot of work to be done before the sun set that day.

The hours crawled by as the three men and Rev. Bernie captured zombie after zombie and tossed them into the courtyard. The dead didn't seem to care for sunlight and only the hungriest approached the church. The work was halfway done when things took a turn for the worse.

Roy had a large zombie in tow. The creature had once been a full grown man and Roy should have asked for help, but he didn't want to appear weak in front of the other men and had said he was fine, that he could handle the large ghoul.

After hours of dead captives being brought through the center aisle between the pews, the huddled people had started to calm down. More than a dozen zombies had been herded to the back courtyard without incident and the parishioners had dropped their guard.

An old man wandered too close to the zombie while it was being moved through the church. The zombie managed to get his hand around the old man's loose coat and before the old man or Roy could do anything more than shout, the zombie had pulled the old man within reach and sank its teeth into his throat.

The old man's screams echoed off the walls of the church, the acoustics perfect. In a heartbeat, the church was in chaos as people tried to get as far away as possible. In the chaos, Roy was knocked over and he dropped the pole, the zombie pulling free of its bindings.

With a mouth full of the old man's throat, the zombie looked for more meat.

Rev. Bernie walked up behind the zombie, looking like he was about to greet one of his parishioners, and whacked the living corpse over the head with a bust of Jesus.

The crack of heads echoed in the room, mingling with the screams and whimpers of the frightened people. Rev. Bernie struck twice more, the third time bringing the zombie to the carpeted floor. It twitched for a few times and laid still, black, once-living brains seeping from its cracked skull.

Roy moved closer and Rev. Bernie gestured to the corpse with a wave of his right hand.

"Remove that, and be more careful. There's no shame in asking for help," he said.

Roy nodded, ashamed of himself. "Yes, Reverend. I'm sorry." Roy looked at the old man, twitching on the floor of the church.

"What do we do with old Leroy?" he asked, quietly.

Rev. Bernie took one look at the old man and frowned. "He's been infected. Satan now runs through his veins. Take him and throw him in the courtyard with the others."

Roy was shocked, but when he saw the look in Rev. Bernie's eyes, he quickly assented and scooped up Leroy's body. With the back of the man's shoes whacking the steps, Roy dragged him up them until he was at the window overlooking the courtyard.

With a grunt and a heave, he tossed the old man out the window. Below, the zombies beset the man, tearing and ripping with nails and teeth.

One zombie managed to place its fingers inside the old man's mouth and with a yank, peeled the wrinkled face off. The zombie began devouring its prize while others tore into the man's stomach, pulling entrails out and gorging on them.

Spleen, kidney and appendix were all yanked free to be chewed and swallowed, blood dripping into the denuded ground to be trampled by dozens of feet.

Roy tasted bile in his mouth and quickly turned away. What the hell were they doing? Had the rest of them that had survived lost their humanity when the dead started to walk?

Rev. Bernie called to him from below, and after getting himself together, returned to help dispose of the large zombie still lying in the church.

Behind him, the sounds of feeding continued.

CHAPTER 9

Timmy was crying again, despite Josey's best efforts. For the past hour he'd been calling for his mother. Adam couldn't really blame him. He was a grown man and he missed his mother, as well. Thoughts of her lying dead in her bed less than twenty five feet away flooded into his head. He quickly shook them away.

Adam stood up from the table and walked over to Timmy. Kneeling down in front of him, he smiled.

"Hey, pal, I know this kind of sucks, but I tell you what. Why don't we play blocks together? I was hoping you could show me how to build a skyscraper."

Timmy's crying slowed as he thought about playing with Adam. Ever since Adam had taken Timmy out of the van, the two had become good friends. Out of the three adults, it was Adam who seemed to have made a connection with the boy. Adam didn't mind. Growing up, he'd always wanted a brother, but his parents had decided one child was enough. As the years went by, he had learned to adapt to being an only child, despite the fact that every friend he had ever known had at least one brother or sister.

Taking Timmy's hand, the two of them sat down in the middle of the cellar. Timmy's eyes were still red from crying, but otherwise he was fine, his mind now concentrating on stacking the blocks.

Adam looked up at Josey, still sitting on a cot. She mouthed the words, "Thank you," and then went to talk to Paul.

"We're almost out of food," Paul whispered to his wife as she moved up beside him.

"I know that. What are we going to do about it?" She inquired in the same low tone, not wanting to frighten Timmy.

"I was thinking Adam and I could check some of the other houses, see if they have anything in their kitchens."

She thought about it for a second, gazing out the window. The sun was just starting to set, the shadows growing longer. "What do you think it's like out there?"

Paul shrugged. "Your guess is as good as mine. Why?"

She looked at her shoes while she talked. "Since the power went out, we haven't heard anything about what's happening in the city and beyond. For all we know it's safe."

"Yeah, that's true, but it could also be nothing but infected people. What if that's the case?" Paul asked.

She nodded her head. "I know, but we can't stay here forever."

"Don't you think I know that," Paul hissed. "Look, if you've got a better idea, I'm willing to hear it."

She sighed, realizing they were arguing. "I'm sorry, Paul, it's just . . . I feel so helpless, you know?" She slumped down in a nearby chair.

He placed his hand on her lap and rubbed her leg. "Yeah, I know. I'm sorry, too. It's probably cabin fever. God, what I wouldn't give to be outside again."

As if to illustrate his statement, a pair of legs moved by the cellar window, followed by two more pairs.

The two of them went quiet and watched the legs shamble by. "Psst, Adam," Paul called.

Adam looked where Paul was pointing. He turned his head and his blood ran cold when he saw shadows walking by the window: the legs of the animated corpses occluding the sunlight.

Alive or dead?" he asked the room.

"Probably dead, look at how they're moving," Paul said.

Adam watched for a second and then nodded. "So, what?"

Paul shook his head. "So nothing. We do nothing. If they don't know we're here, then that's fine with me."

The blocks fell over with soft thump. The cement absorbed most of the sound. Still, the three adults felt their hearts jump into their throats. Minutes passed and the last of the shadows disappeared from the windows. All three breathed a sigh of relief. At least for now they were still safe.

The arrival of the zombies made Paul decide they needed to either find more supplies or leave the cellar. If the dead far outnumbered them, they would be permanently trapped and would eventually starve. He had done research on starvation. It wasn't a pleasant way to die. Better to eat a bullet than wither away while your stomach slowly ate itself from the inside out.

Paul stood, his mind made up.

"Adam, in the morning we need to search the surrounding houses for supplies. We need food and water."

Adam nodded grimly. "Suicide mission, sweet. Just you and me?"

Paul grinned. "Of course, and I wouldn't have it any other way."

Timmy's skyscraper fell over again and he mumbled his displeasure. Adam smiled at him and ruffled his hair.

"Don't worry, kid, if at first you don't succeed, try, try again."

<hr />

Adam was dreaming.

It had been over a week since his nightmare with the fishing boat and he had honestly thought he was adapting well to the new world, but the anticipation of knowing he had to venture outside again gnawed at him, like a belly full of rats.

Late in the night, sleep finally came, but it was a restless slumber. Every little creak of the house or shifting of a person in their cot would have his eyes open, searching the darkness for the source of the sound.

Finally, in the deepest hours of the night, he drifted off. No sooner was he asleep then visions of things undead flitted past his eyes, things that should stay deep down in the sub-conscious because once let out, they would threaten to envelop a person's very soul.

He fought them off, something inside him telling him he had the upper hand, but then he fell into an abyss. The gaping hole was too large to have an edge and Adam felt himself plummeting. He could feel wind blowing against his face, he tried to see, but in the utter darkness there was no light.

He closed his eyes against the dark and waited for the inevitable impact when his body found the bottom, but it didn't come.

The sensation of falling was gone and he felt something hard beneath him. Reaching out with his hands, he struck something in front of him, no more than a foot from his head. Running his hands along the soft fabric, he quickly realized he was in some sort of a box, the walls all lined with a soft, silky material.

He remembered he had a cigarette lighter in his pocket and thrust his hand deep, searching for it. Groping fingers found it and in another heartbeat he'd flicked the metal wheel. A small orange and red flame shot up from the plastic cylinder and for the first time he was able to actually see where he was.

He was in a coffin.

His breathing grew faint as he started to panic. Like everyone, he'd heard the urban myths and stories of people buried alive, of the bloody fingernail gouges on the inside of the coffin lid as the person tried to escape.

Little spots darted across his eyes and he realized he was hyperventilating. He closed his eyes and tried to maintain control. If he lost it in here, it would be over before it began, although he didn't see what he could do about it anyway.

The air grew stuffy, both he and the flame using up the oxygen.

He made up his mind . . . if he was going to die, then he had to at least try to escape.

Reaching up with his left hand, he pulled the fabric away from the lid of the coffin. The tearing cloth sounded ridiculously loud to him in the confined space. Bits of lint and dust drifted onto his face from the torn material and he blew it away, wiping his face with a shaking hand. Once the fabric was removed, he could see the cheap pine-wood slats that made up his coffin.

Evidently whoever placed him in here didn't go all out.

The screw in the corner was loose and he started to work at it with his finger. Despite the metal digging into his flesh, he managed to make some bloody progress.

An infinite time later, he cheered hoarsely when he managed to push the screw through to the top. The slat it had held was only a fraction loose, but that was enough for him to force his bleeding finger through. Ignoring the pain, he slipped his middle digit through the opening, the blood actually aiding him, a coppery lubricant he would have preferred to do without.

Once the first finger was through, he started to push a second and then a third. Eventually he managed to get his entire hand past the end of the slat, the other end of the plank lifting as he pried his hand like a wedge. Clusters of soil started to fall onto his face and he turned away, shaking off the dirt.

He could barely breathe now, the air almost gone. He imagined he was breathing nothing but carbon dioxide, sucking his own waste into his spent lungs.

He put the lighter back into his pocket, the warm top permeating the cloth of his pocket and warming his skin. He wedged his other hand into the opening.

Heaving, he pushed as hard as he could, and the slat gave way. More moist earth fell into the coffin and he had to turn his head away or risk suffocating under the onslaught of earth. He could smell the dirt and something else, something sweet that he just couldn't put his finger on.

Pushing his arms through, he was relieved to see the soil was loose, perhaps because he hadn't been here long enough for the earth to settle.

The slats separated while he worked his way up, the dirt constantly falling into his face. He would turn his head down and spit his mouth clear, but a second later it would be full again. Something wiggled by his face in the darkness and he repressed a shudder, not wanting to think about what it could be.

Slowly he made his way upward, or he thought he was moving up. For just a moment he imagined he was tunneling down. Deep into the earth until there would be no chance of escape, then his air would finally run out and he would suffocate, alone in the blackness.

Panic was setting in again and he struggled to breathe through gritted teeth, desperately trying to keep the loose soil out. His nose was full and he blew it out for the hundredth time since he'd started to claw his way out of his grave.

When he was ready to despair, his hand broke the surface. He wiggled it around for a moment, still not believing he'd made it.

His head broke free next and he pulled the rest of his body all the way out of the ground, a macabre imitation of being born, the earth standing in for a mother's womb.

He rolled onto his side and sucked in great lungfuls of air.

Adam looked up at the night sky and the moon shrouded in clouds. Looking around, he saw he was in a graveyard. Turning, he came face-to-face with the tombstone over his grave, the name Adam Walsh scribbled in what looked like red lipstick or crayon. The writing looked like a five-year-old had done it.

Adam stood, his wobbly legs not wanting to support him. Soon he had his balance and began to walk away from what should have been his final resting place.

Now that he was standing up and outside, he noticed he was wearing a suit, the black fabric now covered in dirt and grass stains. His backside felt cold and he felt back there, surprised to find his suit only covered his front. He thought maybe it was a mortuary trick for dressing a corpse before the service.

That is odd, he thought as he lurched across the graveyard. His legs didn't feel like they usually did, strong and sure, filled with the energy of youth. Instead, they felt like lead weights that almost had to be dragged when he moved them across the ground.

He spotted people in the distance and headed that way. Maybe they could shed some light on what had happened to him. When he was closer, he saw a man and a woman and a small boy standing at the edge of the graveyard's property line. The boy was hugging the woman and crying; Adam could hear the sobs as he moved closer. The man was patting the boy on the shoulder and Adam saw it was Paul, the moonlight reflecting off his glasses.

He raised his hand to them and called out, but no one responded. Moving faster, he called again. "Hey, guys, wait up! I'm here, I'm okay!" he yelled across the moss covered tombstones of long-forgotten residents.

Paul looked up then and his mouth turned to a frown, not at all pleased to see Adam. The woman turned to look and he saw it was Josey, and the boy was Timmy.

He called to them again, but they ran around the car they were standing next to, away from him.

For the life of him Adam couldn't imagine why.

He called again, this time holding out his hands in front of him, so Paul could see it was him, that he was all right. But Paul just cursed under his breath and spit into the grass.

Then to Adam's chagrin, Paul raised the shotgun he was holding and pointed it at him. Adam didn't understand, perhaps Paul couldn't see it was him in the shadows of the graveyard.

On stumbling legs, he moved closer until he was only a few feet from Paul and the car. Adam distinctly heard the sound of Paul pumping the shotgun and he asked him what the hell he was doing.

Paul answered by squeezing the trigger of the weapon.

The barrage of buckshot tore into his shoulder and took off half his face. Adam screamed with the pain and yelled for him to stop. Why was he shooting at him?
Paul answered him with another shot, this one taking off half of Adam's head.

Adam stumbled against the car, swirls of stars dancing in front of his eyes. He turned to face the glass of the driver's door of the car and saw his reflection staring back at him.

It was him, but yet it wasn't. He seemed to be wearing make-up and his complexion was ghostly pale where the make-up had been rubbed away.

A night crawler was poking out of his cheek, sniffing the air, then retreating back into the meat of his face. His eyes were sunken in to the point that he looked like a cadaver. And that's when it hit him.

He was dead!

It didn't make any sense and he turned to Paul, and fell to his knees. He raised his hand, a hand that was more like a claw than it should have been. He gargled something from his mouth, but now realized what he thought were words were nothing more than grunts and groans.

Kneeling on the ground, he looked up at the black opening of the shotgun. Behind it was the grim face of Paul.

"Sorry, buddy," Paul whispered and Adam thought he saw a tear rolling down his cheek. "But this is how it's gotta be."

Then Paul squeezed the trigger for the last time. Adam saw a bright flash of light and then nothing. He fell to the earth and lay still as his synapses shut down for good. He could still hear with his one ear, although sounds were muffled and far away.

Paul was bending over him, picking up his legs. He started to drag Adam back to the open grave, Josey and Timmy following.

While his body was bumped and dragged over the uneven ground, he heard Paul say in a serious tone, "I told you he'd come back."

Then he heard nothing and darkness descended for the last time, as he was returned to his grave for the last time.

The rocking continued and Adam fought it for as long as he could. His eyes snapped open and he was looking into the face of Paul. The man was smiling down at him in the dim light of the cellar.

"What, what's going on, where am I?" Adam gasped through dry lips.

"Wake up, buddy. You were having a dream, a bad one by the sound of it."

Adam blinked the sleep from his eyes and looked around the cellar. The sun was just starting to rise outside, its rays slowly chasing the shadows to the corners of the cellar. Josey and Timmy were still sleeping, the boy curled up in the woman's arms. Adam sat up and rubbed his eyes.

"What time is it?" He asked while stretching his arms, a yawn escaping his mouth. His breath smelled foul so he closed his mouth, not wanting to breathe it in Paul's face.

"About six. I've got to tell ya, I've been nervous all night, can't say I'm looking forward to going out there."

Adam nodded, his neck hurting from the way he'd slept. "Yeah, me too. I think that's why I was dreaming."

"Do you remember any of it?" Paul asked.

Adam shook his head. "Yeah . . . no, it's all kind of fuzzy. Maybe that's a good thing, you know?"

Paul smiled softly. "Yeah, kid, I know. Look, let's eat breakfast and get out there. By the end of the day we have either got to have enough supplies to last a while or we need to think about leaving. I've got to tell you, I'm not looking forward to the latter if it comes to it."

Adam stood up and yawned, his bladder screaming to be emptied. "Yeah, me either." He put on pants and went to the chemical toilet in the corner, the blanket hanging in front of it for privacy already pushed to the side. Once finished, he walked over to the card table. Josey was up and starting a meager breakfast of canned beans and crackers.

Timmy was still sleeping the sleep of the innocent.

Adam flashed the couple his best smile and sat down "So, what's for breakfast?"

"Eggs, bacon and fresh squeezed orange juice," Josey said, cracking a smile.

Josey handed him a plate of beans and the three ate in silence while the sun rose on another day in Hell.

CHAPTER 10

The first actual sacrifice wasn't planned. That's what Rev. Bernie kept telling himself.

It happened the day after the courtyard had been filled with undead. The chain-link fence had held up miraculously well, and once Roy, Phil and Tom had finished, they'd taken sharpened broom sticks with them to the fence. One at a time, using hammers, they spiked the zombies in the head. With their brains punctured, the zombies fell to the sidewalk, dead for good. But it was slow going; many times the wooden spike would become jammed in the skull, the bone seeming to act as a vise. But with a foot braced against the fence and a little muscle, the spike would come free.

Roy had lost count how many he had already put down, and there had to be more than fifty left. With sweat soaking his shirt, he moved in to take down another one. Next to him Phil continued complaining. At first he'd just grumbled to himself, but soon it had become a full-blown tirade.

Roy talked to Rev. Bernie about it, but the Reverend seemed unfazed. Roy told the Reverend that Phil was stirring dissent amongst the others, and if something wasn't done soon they would have a full-blown mutiny on their hands. Rev. Bernie had just patted Roy on the shoulder and smiled.

"The Lord will tell me what to do. Until then, let the man be," Rev. Bernie had said with a compassionate smile on his face.

Roy had sighed and returned to the messy job of destroying the zombies around the fence. Roy had never really been a leader; he'd always let others do the decision making. It wasn't that he was a cow-ard, far from it; he just preferred to let someone else give the orders. He preferred to be the second in command. But maybe this was the time when he should take the reins of power and run with them.

Now, as he spiked yet another zombie, he couldn't help wondering what the future held for him and his new friends.

———————•———••——•••———

Inside the church, Rev. Bernie had just finished a sermon. After the fiasco with the old man, he needed to placate his people. It had worked remarkably well . . . his parishioners just needed something to grasp onto, something to hope for.

When he was finished, he patted a few more shoulders and went to his chambers to rest. Sitting in his chair, visions of things he'd rather not face floating across his eyes. He closed them, but the images remained.

Opening his eyes, he looked at the statue across the room. At first the statue was still, but then it seemed to shimmer and dance before him, like the flames of a candle reflected from a mirror.

Jesus' face turned to look at him and smiled. He knelt down onto the floor and bowed his head. "My Lord, it is so good to see you. I was beginning to lose hope that you would visit me again."

The statue nodded. "Do not worry, my son. I will appear to you when I feel you need my guidance."

"What will you have me do, Lord? I've filled the courtyard with the Devil's minions like you instructed me to."

The head nodded slowly. "And you have done well. For you to truly show me your devotion, you must make a sacrifice in my name."

"A sacrifice?" He sputtered the two words, shocked.

The head frowned at Rev. Bernie. "Do you refuse?"

He shook his head no, vigorously. "No, my Lord, never."

"Excellent. You will know who and when at the appropriate time. Until then, continue as you have been."

"My Lord, may I ask why you need a sacrifice?"

"You may. Satan's minions are growing. Not only the undead are part of his army. There are some in your congregation that have become infected. They sow discontent and chaos wherever they walk. You must send them back to Hell. And what better way then to let Satan's own army dispose of them?"

Rev. Bernie bowed lower. "Of course, my Lord, how foolish of me to ask. Thy will be done." He looked up at the statue, but it was nothing more then a cement object again.

That was fine, he'd learned what he needed to and his faith was stronger than ever. A sacrifice would be made . . . now he just needed to discern who it would be.

Tom spiked the last zombie in front of the church. The smell was awful, the stench almost palpable. All three men had scarves across their lower faces to try to keep the odor at bay. It barely worked. Flies were everywhere, feeding on the meat and laying eggs while maggots crawled across the ground.

Breathing heavily, Tom looked to Roy. "What now?"

Roy surveyed the pile of corpses, some still vertical and some horizontal, in front of him. "Now we burn them."

"Burn them? Why the fuck didn't we do that before, instead of spending all day spiking them in the head?" Phil snarled at Roy.

Roy turned to face the man, their faces no more than inches from one another.

"Because we don't have enough fuel to get them all while they're moving around. This way they aren't moving and it will be easy to get all of them at the same time," Roy snapped back.

Phil backed down a little, but mumbled under his breath. "Still seems like a stupid idea."

Roy watched him for a moment, but when Phil stayed silent, he let it go. "All right, then, let's get the oil and finish this. I'm damn tired."

Tom agreed and the two men went inside. Phil stayed where he was, watching the fly-infested pile of corpses while the ones behind tried to crawl over the bodies of their brethren.

The bodies were stacked three feet high, higher in other places. Phil shook his head, wondering how in the name of God it had come to this.

While Phil watched the pile of bodies twitch in the sunlight, he wondered if maybe they were the lucky ones and he and his fellow survivors were the damned.

Letting out a breath he didn't realize he'd been holding, he turned and walked up the stairs.

Before the doors were completely closed behind him, Phil had his arms restrained by two men. He struggled for a moment, but gave up when he realized the hold the two men had on each side of him was vise-like; he was trapped.

"What the hell are you doing to me? Let me go!" he yelled. He looked at the faces of the people watching him from the pews, although he saw signs of compassion in some of the faces, most just watched, impassive.

"Bring him to the balcony," Rev. Bernie said from the front of the theatre. He was dressed in his best vestments, his arms held out in front of him.

The two men dragged Phil down the aisles, toward the front of the church. He struggled in vain, but their hold was true.He wasn't going anywhere they didn't want him to go. While he was being pulled to the front of the church, most of the faces in the pews looked down to the floor, not making eye contact with him. Mothers held their children close and the old simply looked away, pretending to study one of the many stained-glass windows lining the walls.

"What the hell is going on here?" Phil asked.

From his side, Roy squeezed his arm a little tighter. "I told you to shut up and keep your opinions to yourself," he hissed. "This is what you get for being an annoying fuck."

Phil was dragged up the stairs until he was overlooking the courtyard, fighting against his captors to no avail. The curtain that normally hung there was drawn aside so everyone could see. Phil looked down into the church at the people there. He saw no help coming his way.

By the time he was dragged to the open window overlooking the courtyard, he had guessed what was happening, although his mind refused to believe it. Why would the Reverend do this, what would be the reason? Sure, he had made some complaints, but he didn't deserve *this*.

The moans and the stench of the zombies below carried through the window and Phil started to panic.

"You can't do this! Someone help me, please. Make them stop!" Phil screamed into the church to the stone-faced people below.

No one helped.

Phil turned to Roy and smiled his most sincere smile, trying to reason with the man. "Come on, man, you can't be serious. Don't do this."

Roy grimaced. "Sorry, man, but this is what the Reverend wants, and he's the boss."

Phil put everything he had into his last struggles, but the men were holding him too tightly. Tom glanced down at Phil's boots. Phil was wearing a pair of motorcycle boots he used to wear when he would ride his Suzuki with his brother.

"Hey Roy, can I have his boots? It's not like he's gonna need them where he's goin'."

Roy shrugged. "Sure, don't matter to me."

Tom bent over and yanked one boot off after the other, another parishioner, a burly woman in her forties, took over holding Phil. With his new boots in hand, Tom stepped out of the way. "Thanks, Phil, I'm gonna enjoy these."

"You bastards, stealing my goddamn boots off of me before I'm even dead!" He spit into the Reverend's face and was rewarded with a punch in the kidneys from Tom. He cried out in pain and doubled over. They pulled him upright again. Vomit dribbled out of the side of his mouth and he saw fuzzy points of light around the edges of his vision.

Rev. Bernie silently wiped the spittle off his cheek and grinned. He made the sign of the cross in front of Phil, while Phil continued struggling.

"You have been infected with Satan's blood and must be cleansed. Satan's minions will accept you with their warm embrace or they will cast you out where you will journey to Heaven. Go with God, and may your sins be purified." The Reverend stepped back from the window and Phil was dragged ever closer to the open portal.

"What the fuck's the matter with you people? You're killing me for no goddamn reason! Please stop! I'm not infected!"

"Yeah, I know," Roy whispered into Phil's ear with a sneer on his lips.

Before Phil could say another word, he was pitched out into the courtyard, his arms pin-wheeling around him as he grasped empty air. His body seemed to float for a fraction of a second, floating like a balloon. Then he plummeted to the churned and muddy ground below. He landed on top of one of the zombies, both his and the ghoul's limbs tangling together in a heap of body parts.

Phil had just enough time to roll off the body and scream before the rest of the undead covered him with their hands and mouths. His shrieks filled the courtyard and even Roy had to look away. Rev. Bernie never stopped looking. His eyes flared with malice and insanity as he watched the man being ripped limb from limb. One last high pitched shriek left Phil's lips before his throat was ripped out, the scream reverberating off the walls of the courtyard. All that could be heard after was the sound of the mouths tearing and chewing as the dead slowly devoured the man alive.

There would be nothing left to become reanimated, the living corpses would see to that. The living dead were starving, the fresh meat revitalizing undead limbs. Nothing was left but some bloody rags, a few chewed bones and some hair from Phil's scalp. Everything else was devoured.

The zombies moved away from the red puddle left in the muddy dirt, each feasting on whatever gobbet of flesh it had managed to procure for itself.

Rev. Bernie slowly closed the window.

"The sacrifice is done. He is one with God now. Roy, have the bodies in the front of the church been burned yet?"

Roy moved closer to the Reverend, his face ghostly pale. "No, not yet Reverend. We were about to."

Rev. Bernie smiled; a smile that filled his face and eyes. "Excellent, my son. Your efforts will be rewarded in Heaven, I promise."

Roy nodded and looked out the window Phil had been tossed from, behind Rev. Bernie. The Reverend was framed by the window and the ghouls milling about below, like a messiah of the dead.

"That's great Reverend; I just hope it's not for a while, though."

Rev. Bernie laughed; his laughter filling the church and putting everyone at ease.

"I'm sure it won't be for many, many years," the Reverend replied and turned to the stairs. "I feel tired. I'll be in my chambers talking to Jesus. I'm sure he's pleased with what we have accomplished here today. Roy, please take care of things while I'm away."

"Sure, Reverend, no problem," Roy answered.

Rev. Bernie disappeared down the stairs, his footsteps fading away to leave Roy, Tom and the woman alone. Then two of them looked at Roy, wondering about the Reverend's last remarks. Before any of them could say anything, Roy waved them away.

"You heard the man, let's get to work!" he barked, giving each of them a steely gaze.

With a nod and a "yes sir," everyone filed down the stairs. There was a lot to deal with before the day was over and Roy was just the man for the job. He was indebted to the Reverend, but he wondered just how grounded in reality the holy man truly was. With a casual glance at the window, Roy grinned, thinking about how Phil had flown in the air for a second before falling like a rock. Hitching up his pants and fixing his shirt, he headed down the stairs.

After a moment, his footsteps also faded away to be lost in the echoes of the church.

CHAPTER 11

The bulkhead doors creaked as Paul opened them and he cringed at the sound. Sticking his head out above the steps, he looked out across his yard, then stepped out onto the overgrown lawn.

There was a stillness that was hard to describe. It was felt more than seen. Paul could feel the lightest of breezes caress his face, a hint of salt blowing from the ocean two miles away. The sun was bright that morning, the sky a clear blue with only a few clouds to mar the otherwise perfect view.

Adam stepped out of the stairwell and onto the grass. He glanced to the other end of the yard, the corpse of the woman and the brute of a man still lying where they had been left days before. Now the woman's corpse was barely identifiable as once being human. Insects had ravaged the body, feeding on the meat and what was left of the flesh. The blind zombie's corpse was fairing a little better, the larger portions of meat taking longer to disappear. Ants were everywhere, moving over the corpses as they slowly did their part to devour the bodies.

The only positive about the rotting cadavers was that, outside in the open, with the breeze blowing away from the men, the odor of decay wasn't as noticeable.

Adam had brought his father's revolver with him, feeling comfortable knowing the .38 was in his hand. Paul, wanting more firepower , had traded in the.22 rifle for a pump action shotgun. His pockets were full of shells, although he hoped he wouldn't need them.

Paul turned, ducked his head below the lip of the frame and looked back down the stairwell. Josey and Timmy stood there, Timmy pouting heavily. When the boy had heard the men were going outside, he'd asked if he could go, too. After being told no, he'd cried and said he just wanted to go out and play. It was Adam who explained in the simplest way he could think of that there were monsters outside that wanted to hurt him.

Timmy didn't want to hear it, but after a while the boy had given in. Especially after Adam had promised he would take the boy out to play if he was good.

If things were quiet after their foraging was finished, he figured he'd let the boy play by the bulkhead for a few minutes.

Paul waved to them. "Now don't freak out if you hear gunshots. It's just me and Adam killing the bad monsters," Paul said to Timmy.

"And then I can go out and play? Once the monsters are all gone?" Timmy asked so innocently it made Paul's heart break. Paul looked to Adam and Adam nodded back.

Paul nodded. "Yup, that's the plan. You take care of my wife now, okay?"

Timmy nodded and then Josey waved bye and closed the door. Paul did the same with the bulkhead and the two started for the side of the house, heading to the street out front.

With the sun shining down with a cheery luminance, the area didn't seem so imposing. They rounded the house and the two stood on Paul's front lawn. Adam looked over at his house a bit of nostalgia flooded through him. He let it flow for a moment and then pushed it away. He needed to stay sharp if he was going to see the end of the day alive.

Adam surveyed the street. The van was still in the house across the way, but Timmy's parents were nowhere to be found. The other houses were still, silent monuments to a fading mankind.

Adam spoke up. "So where are we shopping first?"

Paul was looking across the street to the house next to the van accident.

"Why don't we try that one? Mr. Mahoney lived there with his wife. He used to tell me over a beer that his wife always shopped too much. She liked to stock up on groceries. He used to say that if there was ever another war, he could live off what he had in his cupboards for a year."

"Okay then, what are we waiting for? Don't forget your coupons," Adam said and started across the street.

Paul followed, shotgun pointed at the sky. A few birds were singing in one of the nearby trees, the sound making the street feel almost normal. So far they hadn't encountered the undead.

"You think they sleep in the day?" Adam asked. "That's just great.

'Children of the night, what beautiful music they make'."

Paul shrugged. "Maybe. I don't think they like the sunlight that much, but if they know we're out here, I'm pretty sure they'll come out."

"Where do you think they are?" Adam asked. They had made it to the front walk of the house and were moving up it.

"Don't know. Probably went back into the houses. Maybe some memory remains after they come back and they return to what's familiar."

"Oh, good. Maybe they're all at the mall, then. Hey, you think the Mahoneys are zombies?" Adam whispered as the two men stood at the front door.

"Guess we'll find out. You ready?" Paul asked.

Adam shook his head. "No."

"Ain't that the truth," Paul said and reached for the brass door-knob. He expected the door to be locked and was surprised when it turned easily. The door opened inward on oiled hinges and the two men stepped into the house.

The shades were drawn on almost all the windows, casting the house in shadows. Small rays of sunlight snuck past the edges of the shades and illuminated parts of the floors and walls.

Paul was first, leading with the shotgun. He was relieved when the smell of death and decay didn't assault his nose. If there was something in the house with them, it was long rotted away.

The house was decorated in modern contemporary. A few oil paintings adorned the wall. One with Mrs. Mahoney in her wedding dress adorned the far wall in the living room.

A burgundy carpet covered the living room floor, with hardwood continuing into the dining room. In the middle of the room was a beautiful oak table that would easily sit eight. At the far end of the house, Paul could see the kitchen and a set of stairs, stained a dark red color; Paul thought it might have been cherry.

"Kitchen's that way," he whispered. Adam nodded and followed.

The kitchen was clear. A newspaper lay on the table, dated more than a month ago. There was a bowl with rotted fruit on the counter and a few dishes in the sink. A bowl of water with the name Mitzy on the side sat in the corner of the kitchen floor.

Paul looked at Adam and the younger man shrugged. "If there

was an animal in here, it's long dead," Paul said. "Why don't you see what's in the cabinets, I'll check upstairs."

"Okay, but watch your ass. You're too heavy for me to carry. Call if you need help," Adam as he went to the first cabinet.

Paul chuckled. "Shit, if I need help, believe me, you'll know it." Then he turned and started up the stairs, the wood creaking under his boots.

His finger was loose on the trigger of the shotgun. At the top landing he found himself in a small hallway with four doors. The first was half-open and he saw it was the bathroom. The tiles were a light shade of pink and he cringed, thinking of Mr. Mahoney. Evidently the wife had chosen the color of the bathroom.

Moving to the other doors, he slowly opened them one by one. The first two were spare bedrooms, the Mahoney's children having grown to adulthood and left the house. Now the rooms held neatly made beds and a few books stood on the nightstands. Paul idly wondered if Mr. Mahoney had ever had to spend a night in one of the spare rooms when he was in the dog house with the missus.

Turning the glass doorknob on the last door, Paul opened it a crack. Before he stepped into the room, he already knew what he was going to find. The air smelled of decay, but a decay that was old. The sour sweetness that filled the room drifted out into the hall.

Inside the room on the queen size bed were the Mahoneys. Or, what was left of them. They must have been dead for almost a month, since right after the outbreak started.

Mrs. Mahoney lay supine on the bed, her hands tied in front of her. The bedspread had been thrown to the floor and one of the nightstands was on its side. Mrs. Mahoney was missing the top of her head, although on closer inspection, Paul realized it was splattered on the headboard behind her.

Mr. Mahoney was there, as well.

He lay at the foot of the bed. The back of his head was missing, and an old W.W.2 revolver lay on the bed next to him. The bed had absorbed almost all of the blood; the viscous fluid now a large and dark maroon-colored stain.

It looked to Paul like Mr. Mahoney had given up and had taken his own life. Paul was surprised, though. The man had seemed like a fighter, not one to commit suicide.

A creaking of floorboards caused Paul to spin on his feet, shotgun coming up, ready to fire. Adam jumped back and put his hands in the air.

"Whoa there, hoss. It's just me. I finished downstairs and I thought I'd see what's up here." Adam looked at the bodies on the bed. "Dead, huh?"

Paul relaxed a little. "Yes, Captain Obvious. Very dead, a month at least. It looks like the house is empty."

Adam pointed to the other nightstand. "There's a cassette player," he said, bending over and picking it up. "It's set on record. You want to listen?"

Paul mulled it over. Should he? Was he invading a dead friend's privacy or was it left so someone like him would find it and learn what had happened here.

Before he could decide, Adam had rewound the tape and had hit play.

There was a moment of silence and for just a second Paul hoped maybe the tape was empty. Then a faint crackling sound started and a moment later he could hear the sound of someone wheezing. Adam set the cassette player on the bed and stepped back.

"*I don't quite know why I'm recording this,*" a hoarse voice said from the small speaker. "*Perhaps I just want to set the record straight about what someone might find when this is all over. I'm old and sick and I doubt I'd see the end to all this horror, even if I wasn't infected.*" That revelation had Paul looking back down at the male corpse lying on the bed.

"*Some nut bit my wife on the arm while she was out the other day. Luckily, there was a man there washing his car and he ran over and saved her. The police took the man away, I don't know what happened to him, and my wife came home. At first she was fine, but then she started to run a fever, so I put her to bed and let her sleep. I heard on the news what was happening, though I still didn't want to admit my Jodi was infected. That night she started to scream in her bed, waking me up. I turned on the light and I couldn't believe how pale she was. I tried to talk to her, but she was completely out of it. Her bedcovers had fallen off her and I reached over to pull them up, and she bit me. She only grazed my arm, but she managed to break the skin. It wasn't serious. I actually thought I might be okay.*" The sound of tinny coughing came from the small recorder.

Adam stepped away from the bed and went to the window and looked out on the street below.

"*I tied Jodi up so she wouldn't hurt herself, or me. I tried to call for help, but the phone was busy, nothing but recorded messages. The news said how hospitals had become deathtraps. I knew there was nowhere to go. Then my Jodi died. I saw the light go out in her eyes and watched as she slumped over. I thought that was it, hell, I prayed that was it, but within minutes she came back.*"

There was a silence and Paul wondered if that was the end of the tape. Then with an intake of breath, the old man continued.

"*Put a bullet in her head, like they said on the news. Said it was the only way to put them down, something to do with the brain stem. After that, I sat here in this room. I didn't really know what to do. Then I started to feel sick myself and I knew I had it, too. I didn't want to turn into one of them, so I decided to go out my way.*

"*I finished off the whiskey downstairs and now I'm good and drunk. There's pain shooting through my chest and stomach and I think if I don't do it soon, I might not be able to. If someone finds this and they know my children, tell them I'm sorry, but this was the best I could do. I know Jodi's waiting in Heaven for me. If there are any survivors when this mess is sorted out, I wish them well. Maybe they can do a better job the second time around. Can't talk anymore, my throat's sore and my head hurts somethin' awful. This is George Mahoney signin' off . . . seems a shame though, there's so much more to say . . .*" The sound of a gun being cocked floated through the tiny speaker. For a few precious heartbeats there was silence. Then a gunshot boomed from the recorder and the sound of something falling came next, followed by silence as the recorder finished its task, the taping of a dead room.

Adam was standing at the window, looking out on the street. Now he turned to Paul. "Jesus, that sucks." He looked down at the body of George Mahoney. "Poor bastard."

Paul retrieved the machine, turned it off and set it down. Then he picked it back up and flipped it over. He popped open the back and took out the batteries.

Adam watched him silently. Paul felt his eyes and stopped what he was doing.

"Yeah, I know it seems like a . . . desecration, but we need these batteries more than he does," he said. "Trust me, if we get stuck in the dark somewhere, you'll be glad I did it."

"I know, Paul, it just . . ." he trailed off.

Paul nodded. "I know. It's a different world now."

Putting the batteries in his pocket, he set the recorder down and picked up the handgun. He checked the weapon, and was pleased to see it still had four rounds left. Snapping the cylinder shut, he placed the gun in the small of his back. Hopefully they could find more ammo for it.

Paul headed for the door. "Come on, Adam, let's get out of here."

The two men stood in the kitchen, both feeling morose after

hearing the recording. Paul noticed a doggy door on the bottom of the back door and smiled. "Well at least we know what happened to the pet." Letting out a deep sigh, almost as if he was cleansing the bad feelings, Paul looked up at the cabinets, the wooden doors now hanging open.

"So what did you find down here? Was it a cornucopia of supplies?"

Adam shook his head and reached into the closest cabinet. "Well, there's a full cabinet with nothing but spices, and these two here have a lot of canned goods. Mostly lima beans and creamed corn, though. I did find a few cans of beef stew and a few bottles of prune juice."

Paul made a face. "Perfect, just what we need in a confined space."

"Oh, yeah. Total fartsville," Adam said. "Hey, maybe we can spice the zombies to death."

Paul sat down at the round table in the center of the room and sighed. "Not as much as I hoped for, but it's better than nothing. Let's find something to carry it with and bring it back to the house."

Adam nodded, walked away and disappeared into the living room. A minute later he returned carrying a small blanket. "We can use this like a knapsack," he said while laying the blanket on the kitchen table.

Paul just watched him, not saying a thing. His thoughts were to the couple upstairs, lying dead in their bed while he looted their house. He knew it was necessary, but it still wasn't a pleasant feeling.

Adam finished piling all the canned goods on the table, pulling the corners of the blanket together, he lifted his burden and slung it over his shoulder, testing the feel of it.

He noticed Paul deep in thought. "You all right?"

Paul looked up as if he had been released from a trance. "Huh, what? Oh, sorry, guess I zoned out for a moment. You ready to go?"

Adam repositioned the pack on his back. "Ready as ever. Let's go"

Paul stood up. Without realizing it, he pushed the kitchen chair back under the table, like a good visitor would. Then he headed toward the front door.

Opening the door a crack, he looked out onto the lonely street. Still quiet, nothing but a few birds chattering in the trees to break the silence.

Opening the door, he stepped out into the warm sunlight with Adam behind him.

Paul reached around Adam and closed the front door behind him, and with a glance to Adam, started down the front stairs.

At the bottom of the walk, he stopped and turned around to face the house. The cloth shade on the second floor window was open now, thanks to Adam. At least George would get to see the sunrise every morning.

With a sad smile on his lips, Paul turned and crossed the street, heading back to the cellar to deliver the canned goods to Josey with Adam trotting by his side.

CHAPTER 12

One week after the first sacrifice, Reverend Bernie stood at his podium, his parishioners sitting below him. Roy was now his second-hand man with Tom being the third. Roy had become a kind of enforcer. If the Reverend wanted it done, Roy would see that it happened.

Of all the people in the church, Roy was the most loyal. Rev. Bernie believed it was a flaw in the man's character. Some men just liked to be told what to do, and like a bulldog, they'd would do it.

That's exactly what Rev. Bernie thought of Roy, a bulldog. A tool to accomplish his goals. Over the past week a few more survivors had arrived. Some of them were troublemakers the moment they stepped through the doors of the church.

Some the Lord had told the Reverend to sacrifice, others Roy had made disappear on his own. When questions were asked, Roy would just say the people chose to move on, that they weren't happy in the church. That would usually placate any curiosity.

Rev. Bernie finished his sermon and stepped down from the podium. Roy stood off to the side and the Reverend waved the man to him. Roy snapped to attention and crossed the short distance between them.

"Yes, Reverend, what can I do for you?" Roy asked.

"The food supply, how are we doing?" Rev. Bernie asked. The two men were walking down the aisle of the theatre. Rev. Bernie would absently shake hands with some of the parishioners, but his mind was with Roy.

"Okay, I guess, but we could always use more. Why?"

"No reason. We are taking in more survivors from the Rapture everyday. We need the resources to feed them. How is latrine duty faring?"

Rev. Bernie was referring to the way in which they had managed to dispose of the urine and feces from all the people trapped in the church. Small trash buckets had been placed in two of the confessionals, and when they became full, someone would have to take the bucket outside and dump it.

There was now a growing pile of raw sewage growing on the street in front of the church. A few days before it had rained, washing some of the sewage away, but there was more added everyday. But the Reverend had to admit, compared to the smell of the undead, the pile of shit smelled downright fragrant.

"Latrine's fine, Reverend. Everything's running smoothly," Roy said beside him.

Rev. Bernie nodded. "Of course it is, thanks to you, my friend. When you reach Heaven you will be rewarded, you have my word. Now make sure I'm left undisturbed. I wish to go to my chambers and commune with God." Then he turned away from Roy, dismissing him, and walked to his chambers, waving to his parishioners as he went.

Roy watched the man go, thinking about his position in the church. His life before the dead had risen was nothing exceptional. He'd just been fired from his job as a truck driver, (he'd been caught sleeping on the job one too many times) and found out he was being denied unemployment.

His landlord was selling the house he was living in and he needed to vacate as soon as possible. He'd just found out his girlfriend was dumping him for his best friend.

Pretty much, his life had sucked.

But now, he was the second in command over forty people with more arriving everyday. Roy puffed his chest out and headed to the back of the church. For some, the end of the world had been a tragedy. For Roy, it had been the best thing to happen for a long time

---

Roy stepped into the back room where he and Tom had taken up residence. While the rest of the church had to sleep on the pews in the theatre, he and Tom got their own room.

Roy stopped when he stepped into the room. Tom was occupied.

He was sprawled on top of his bedroll on the floor, and as Roy watched him, he could see he wasn't alone. The body of a woman was struggling beneath the man, muffled cries escaping from the sheets.

"What the fuck are you doing, Tom?" Roy asked, sitting down in the room's only chair.

Tom craned his head over his shoulder to look at Roy. "What the fuck's it look like I'm doing? If you don't mind, I'd like a little privacy."

Roy sighed with impatience. "Yeah, whatever, but keep it down. I don't want the whole damn church on our asses."

Tom waved Roy away and continued his ministrations with the woman below him. "Fine, fine. Just go."

One of the perks of being in charge was that they could have any woman they wanted, whenever they wanted. If someone tried to complain, they might find themselves becoming a sacrifice. Roy had taken some advantage of the fruits of life, but Tom was a downright dog. It seemed every free moment the man had, he was giving it to some slut.

Not Roy though. He liked to take his time when he picked them. He liked the innocent ones . . . they screamed and struggled more.

With that in mind, Roy decided to go back to the theatre. There was a new recruit that had arrived a few days before. She had been alone and she wasn't bad looking; at least once the grime and blood was washed off.

Spitting in his hand and using it to slick back his greasy hair, he strutted out into the theatre to work his magic.

In the back room Tom continued ravishing the young woman. Her name was Evelyn Masters, but her friends called her Eve.

Eve's life had been going wonderfully before the zombie apocalypse. She had a boyfriend who loved her and friends that adored her. Her parents were strict, but not so strict she wasn't allowed to have any fun. She had just turned eighteen and was looking forward to going to Northeastern in Boston.

She had managed to procure a full scholarship, thanks to her strong academics.

Now, as she struggled under Tom, she still couldn't believe how it had all fallen apart.

Once the outbreak had spread to her town, she and her parents boarded up the windows of the house and hunkered down to wait out the worst of it. That plan didn't go so well. They weren't in the house for more then a week when the Army or the National Guard, she really wasn't sure which, showed up. All she knew was that they wore uniforms and had guns.

The soldiers kicked in the front door to her house and had taken both of her parents and her to a rescue camp.

The camp was located in a nearby high school football field. Tents had been erected on the trampled grass. When she arrived, she was given a number.

Despite the fact that they had been brought there to be rescued, it was easy to see it was a disaster. No one seemed to be in charge. Eve remembered the pictures taken from Louisiana after Hurricane Katrina, the hopeless faces of the people jammed into that sports arena as the flood waters continued to rise. That's what the camp reminded her of.

Soldiers stood around the fences that surrounded the camp, their rifles hanging at their sides. The worst part of the entire experience was when she found out that infected people were in the parking lot, surrounded by barbed wire.

Her father started complaining about that, along with some other men that she didn't know. They started demanding to talk to the man in charge and tried to explain that the infected people needed to be destroyed before they escaped and attacked the rest of them. The Major in charge refused to listen. He told her father and the others he had orders to capture as many as possible and only shoot when threatened. He said the government was hoping they'd find a cure and be able to return the infected people back to normal.

But her father wouldn't hear it. He continued stirring up trouble and gathering the other people in the camp.

Then, a week after she arrived, her father disappeared. No one knew where he was. When she asked one of the soldiers, he'd just smiled down at her, then grinned at buddy. Eve may have been young, but she was smart. The Major had made her father disappear so he wouldn't cause anymore trouble. After that the other men kept quiet, not wanting to share the same fate as her father.

Then her mother had taken ill. Whether it was from the low quality food or the water, she didn't know, but her mother had become seriously sick. She tried to get medicine, but the doctors and nurses could have cared less. It almost seemed like they didn't care, that they had already given up.

Eve managed to steal some aspirin when no one was looking and she gave it to her mother. It didn't help, though. Her mother's fever grew worse until it seemed like she was on fire. Eve did her best to keep her comfortable, but in the poor living conditions it was almost impossible.

A few days after her mother had taken ill, Eve woke to find that her mother had died in the night.

Once Eve had gotten over her shock, she went to find help. When she returned, her mother's shoes had been taken and the blanket she'd been in was gone.

The soldiers came and took her mother then. Behind the field, the soldiers had used a bulldozer tear a shallow hole in the ground. The giant scar became a death-pit. One after another the dead were tossed into the mass grave to be covered over when it was full.

She waited patiently for her chance to leave, and at the first opportunity she scurried under a loose part of the fence in the back of the field and had run for all she was worth with nothing but the clothes on her back.

She ran for almost an hour until her chest screamed with pain. When she finally stopped, she realized she was lost. Not knowing where to go and hearing the sounds of the undead around her, she hid in a dumpster for the night. She laid there shivering in the slime of the container, rats scurrying over her legs. She'd let filthy rodents do as they please, too scared to move and be discovered.

For the next two days she moved from place to place, finding what she could to eat from empty homes in the area. Whenever the undead were near, she would run away as fast as she could. The shambling, slouching ghouls were slow and she was always able to outdistance them.

Then she had seen the church. At first she figured it was abandoned, but then a man opened the door on the stone steps and walked out onto the sidewalk. He had a bucket with him and as she watched, the man dumped something brown and runny onto the street.

Before he went back inside, she ran as hard as she could and had stopped only when she hit the chain-link fence. At first the man thought she was a zombie, but after she spoke, pleaded for help, he opened the gate and let her in.

She had believed she was saved, that her troubles would be over. Instead, she found herself being attacked later that day by a man who hadn't bathed in over a month.

She continued to struggle and Tom squeezed her arms harder, making her cry out in pain.

"That hurts! Stop it, you pig. Get the fuck off me!" Eve screamed.

Tom rewarded her with a knee in the crotch for her troubles. "You better knock it off, bitch, or else I'll see to it the Reverend uses you for the next sacrifice."

Eve stopped fighting so hard. Since she arrived, she'd heard what happens sometimes, how the Reverend would pick someone to be thrown to his courtyard full of zombies. Eve knew she didn't want that to happen to her. The Reverend was obviously a nutcase, but he had enough people who did whatever he asked that he was still dangerous. And the pig on top of her now had the Reverend's ear; she knew that.

Deciding that fighting might only get her killed, she relaxed her limbs. Tom smiled at her.

"That's better. Don't worry, babe, I'll give you what you want." With a lecherous grin, he unzipped his pants and entered her. Eve closed her eyes and looked away, trying to think of something else, anything, to take her mind off what was happening between her legs.

The only good thing about her predicament was that Tom was quick. He hadn't thrust into her more than five times before he pulled out and came all over her stomach.

He grinned down at her, his breath smelling like garbage. "There ya go, babe. I even pulled out. Don't want you getting pregnant," he joked. "Clean yourself up and get out of here; oh yeah, and welcome to the family." Then he pulled up his pants and left; his laughter echoing down the hall after him.

Eve rolled over and cried, realizing she may be worse off than before.

Slowing her crying, she used an end of a dirty sheet to wipe her stomach clean. Then she stood up, straightened her clothes and went back out front to join the rest of the parishioners.

Despite the way she was feeling, she managed a wisp of a smile for show.

CHAPTER 13

After dropping off the canned goods with Josey, Paul and Adam continued exploring their neighborhood. So far the street had been clear of all movement, the undead curiously absent.

The second house they visited was a few doors down from Paul's. The front door had been kicked in and the place was a mess. Furniture was knocked over and pictures hung askew on the walls. After conducting a quick search of the premises, the two men relaxed.

"Empty," Paul said from the opening to the living room and dining room.

Adam had just returned from checking the second floor.

"Sure is. The drawers on the bureaus are hanging open. Looks like they left in a hurry."

Adam turned and walked into the kitchen. "Let's see what we got," he said opening the first cabinet he came to.

The cupboards were bare, nothing but a few stray cans at the back. The place had been picked clean.

"Oh. That. You think they took the food with them when they left?" Adam asked with his head inside a cabinet, his voice echoing slightly.

Paul shrugged. Adam couldn't see it. He realized this and spoke up. "It's possible, or maybe someone else came in here later and cleaned the place out. I can't believe we're the only ones left. You?"

Adam pulled his head out of the cabinet; wispy bits of a spider web had attached themselves to his hair. "I hope not. We ran out of shit to talk about days ago," he said. Paul pointed to his head and Adam brushed his hair clean. "Shit, that's gross," he said.

Paul looked around the kitchen. "Well, this place is a bust. What do you say we check the next one?"

Adam shrugged. "You lead, I'll follow, Kemosabe."

Paul grinned and turned to leave, Adam behind him with a small bag rattling with what he could find in the barren cabinets.

With Paul's shotgun leading the way, the two men stepped into the sunlight and quickly crossed the overgrown lawn that separated the next house from the one they had just left. Stepping over the blossoming flowers surrounded by weeds, they walked up the three brick stairs and opened the painted red front door of the next dwelling, once again pleased it was unlocked. It seemed people had left so fast they hadn't bothered to lock their doors, the military not giving them any time.

Entering the home, Paul and Adam quickly realized it was in the same state as the others. The only difference in this house was the splatter of blood coating the bathroom tiles, although no body could be found. Paul stood at the opening to the bathroom and stared at the stain, wondering what story it had to tell. He closed the door and walked away.

After a quick recon, they found nothing, the cabinets all empty. Adam found a half-full box of crackers and added it to the meager supplies already found.

"This house is a bust, too. We should try the next one," Paul said.

"You sure? We could just give up," Adam laughed.

Exiting the house, the two men crossed the knee-high grass and climbed the four steps that led to the painted and brown, wooden door of the two-level Victorian next door. Paul pulled the screen open and reached for the handle. They'd found so many houses empty that day, he'd relaxed his guard, the shotgun hanging lazily from his hand.

He stepped into this new house and knew things were going to be different. Paul stopped in his tracks and Adam walked into him, not realizing there was a problem. Before Adam could ask what was wrong, Paul was bringing up his shotgun, ready for the fight of his life.

As fast as Paul reacted, it still wasn't fast enough. The first of six, a man with no ears, lunged at Paul with his hands curled like claws. Behind Earless was a woman with one cheek, the other side of her face nothing but exposed gristle.

One Cheek dove at Paul as well, her mouth gnashing empty air as she prepared to sink her teeth into his flesh.

Paul brought up the shotgun and tried to step back and give himself some breathing room, but Adam had blocked his retreat. Adam's curse at Paul for his sudden stop was cut off when he was what the problem was. While Adam brought up his gun, Paul was kicking

Earless away from him. His boot came up and struck the dead man in the chest. Earless went backward, but that gave One Cheek more room to maneuver.

Paul danced away from One Cheek; her teeth snapping on empty air.

"Oh, what the *fuck*?" Adam screamed next to Paul.

"Shoot!" Paul screamed, the shotgun level with his chest.

Adam tried to shoot Earless in the face. The dead man stumbled at the last second, the bullet shattering his clavicle instead. The impact spun the dead man around like a top. Paul lined up the head and blew it into a dozen pieces, blood and brain matter flying everywhere.

Paul shot at One Cheek, the point-blank blast enough to almost sever her head from her shoulders. A sputter of blood shot from the neck wound and the corpse toppled over to the floor like a drunk at last call.

Paul swiveled on his boot heels and fired the shotgun, sending a barrage of death into the corner of the room. A zombie was struck in the chest, its body thrown backward. It shattered a window behind it and disappeared from sight, nothing but the fluttering curtain to mark its passage.

Adam ran to the side of the room, jumping over One Cheek's body, his left foot kicking the flopping head to the side. He wanted to give himself some space, not wanting to shoot or get shot by Paul. The three zombies left seemed to hesitate for a fraction of a second. They had two targets and didn't know which one to attack first.

Paul settled that decision for them.

Raising and pumping the shotgun in one smooth motion, he shot the middle ghoul in the chest, the impact knocking it back onto the couch it had been sitting on only seconds ago. It landed on the cushions, its feet rising off the floor for a moment before they settled back to the dirty carpet. No sooner did its feet hit the floor, then it was scrambling to get up, hungry for fresh meat.

Adam shot it in the head and the zombie's body went slack, its head sliding onto one of the cushions.

One of the last two wretches came at him. He fired his pistol and missed miserably, the ghoul lunging at him with a growl. Adam panicked, raising the weapon in front of him to protect his face.

Quite by accident, the barrel of the pistol became lodged in the zombie's mouth, its teeth chipping on the warm metal. With his eyes wide with both surprise and shock, Adam squeezed the trigger.

There was a muffled *Pop*! and the back of the zombie's head blew out across the room. The zombie fell to the floor, taking the revolver with it. Adam let out a yelp as his fingers bent in ways they were not meant to.

Paul was taking care of the last walking corpse. The ghoul had once been a teenager, maybe fifteen or sixteen. The dead girl wore a half shirt that said: *LOOK AT ME*. She had a belly button piecing that was all but lost in her bloated stomach and her too-tight jeans had rotten flesh seeping out of the top at the waist. Her filthy brown hair was tied back in a pony tail.

Paul hesitated for a fraction of a second, some small piece of compassion slowing him as he thought about this girl. This dead thing in front of him was once somebody's daughter, or sister.

The girl hissed and came at him, her white eyes were vacant, yet still seeing, her teeth clacking again and again. Paul stepped to his side and clubbed her in the back of the head. She went down, her own momentum pulling her along. Her legs flew into the air and she rolled over on the floor, mouth creased in a smile of yellow teeth.

Paul backed away from her, regaining his senses, and before the girl could regain her footing, he shot her in the head. Bone and brain splattered across the floor, the skull fragments leaving scratches in the hard wood.

Breathing heavily, Paul turned around in a circle, looking for more targets. His body was pumping adrenalin by the gallon, his senses hyper alert. He almost shot Adam when he saw him, but caught himself before squeezing the trigger.

Adam was wired, too. He'd just battled for his life and had somehow lived to tell about it. Now that it was over, he felt relief flooding into him and he couldn't stop shaking.

Paul walked the five feet that separated them and leaned against his friend. He gestured to the door with the barrel of the shotgun.

"What do you say we call it a day?" He said this in a soft whisper, his face red and his breathing coming hard and fast from his exertions.

Adam just nodded and gave a thumbs-up, too tired to speak. Both men headed for the door, exhausted.

Adam grabbed the bag of supplies he'd dropped when entering the house and the two men stumbled out into the sunlight.

They walked back to Paul's house like two soldiers returning home from the war. The house they vacated stood quiet until flies arrived and began feeding on the corpses. Their buzzing filled the room, sounding like a symphony of nature, while outside in the trees, a family of birds sang to one another, oblivious to the carnage that had just unfolded.

And possibly, even if they had known, they wouldn't have cared.

CHAPTER 14

Roy banged on the door to Reverend Bernie's chambers for the third time. But despite his best efforts, the Reverend wouldn't answer the door.

Roy was starting to worry. Had something happened to the man? Could he even now be laying on the floor suffering a heart attack or choking on a piece of food?

As these images floated through his head, Roy decided he had no choice but to push the door in. "Reverend, if you can hear me, I'm coming in," Roy called through the door. Then backing up a foot, he rammed his shoulder into the wood. The door gave easily, despite its thickness, the cheap locking mechanism snapping like tin.

Roy stumbled as he entered the room, but regained his balance before falling on his face. His eyes scanned the room quickly and he spotted the form of a man in black in the corner of the room.

Rev. Bernie was on his side curled up in a fetal position. Roy moved closer and heard weeping from the man and watched as his shoulders shuddered repeatedly. Not understanding what was happening; Roy turned him over and onto his back.

Tears flowed down the Reverend's cheeks and the man's upper lip trembled as he sobbed.

"Reverend, what's the matter, are you hurt?" Roy whispered. Tom appeared in the doorway and Roy looked up.

"Tom, good. Go get some water for the Reverend, I think he's sick," Roy ordered.

Tom nodded and was off, his footsteps fading away as he ran to the theatre.

Roy helped the prone man to a seating position. Rev. Bernie sat up and then slid backward until his body came against the wall.

Roy watched the man, trying to discern what was wrong with him.

The Reverend sat there, his face blank. His eyes seemed to stare at nothing and for a moment Roy wondered if the man was in shock. Maybe with everything that had happened, the Reverend had finally cracked under the pressure, well, more so than he already had.

Roy placed both his hands on the Reverend's shoulders and gently shook him. "Reverend, snap out of it, we need you," Roy said gently. When he ignored him, Roy shook him harder.

"Jesus Christ, man, wake the fuck up"" Roy snapped, slapping him across the face.

That seemed to break Rev. Bernie from his stupor. With glassed-over eyes, he looked up at Roy, as if seeing the man for the first time.

"He doesn't come to me anymore," Rev. Bernie whispered.

Roy sat back on his boot heels. "Who doesn't come to you? What are you talking about?"

Rev. Bernie's eyes brightened for a moment and he seemed his old self. "Jesus. Jesus doesn't talk to me, not since we sacrificed that man to Satan's minions."

"You mean Phil? Shit Reverend, the man was causing trouble, stirring up the others against you. I tell ya, you did the right thing."

Rev. Bernie shook his head. "No, you don't understand. Jesus would come to me in visions and tell me what to do. But he stopped. I've done something wrong."

Roy smiled with his most sincere smile. Unfortunately, Roy wasn't a handsome man and the smile would have sent any woman running for the hills. Despite this, it seemed to work and Rev. Bernie seemed to calm down a little more.

"Tell you what, Reverend, why don't you stay in here until Jesus comes back, I'll run things for you till then. How's that sound?"

Rev. Bernie barely heard him, and that was fine with Roy. Tom returned with a glass of water, but the Reverend wasn't interested.

"Just put it on the table," Roy ordered, standing up and backing away from the man. Reverend Bernie just sat there, staring at the statue of Jesus, as if he expected it to jump off its pedestal and dance around the room.

Roy took Tom by the arm and walked him out of the room. "I'll be back in a little while, Reverend. Until then, you just relax," Roy told him.

Rev. Bernie didn't react, just continued to stare at the statue.

Once the two men were out of the room, Roy closed the door. The door was left slightly ajar thanks to the broken lock.

"What's wrong with him? Is he sick?" Tom asked.

Roy shrugged his shoulders. "Beats me. Look, I'm no doctor, but if I had to guess, I'd say the guy's lost it."

"What do we do now?" Tom inquired.

Roy grinned from ear to ear. "We run this place."

Eve sat alone in one of the pews. Since she had been raped by Tom, she'd tried to stay as inconspicuous as possible. The last thing she needed was to catch the eye of another man.

Surrounding her was the new flock of the Reverend. Downtrodden faces looked at her, but quickly dismissed her when she averted her gaze.

There were all colors and nationalities in the pews. A Spanish family talking quietly in their native language sat behind her. She had looked over her shoulder once to get a better view of them, and the woman snapped at her. An elderly black couple sat next to her, but they refused to look at her. The same went for the rest of the people in the church.

They may have made it to the safety of the church, but they all acted as if they were already dead . . . beaten down and hopeless.

As Eve surveyed her surroundings, she wondered if they were right. Maybe they were already dead and they just didn't have the sense to lie down and die.

How much longer could they all survive huddled inside the church like prisoners? So far the Reverend had managed to keep everyone fed, but what would they all do when the search parties didn't return?

These ideas flooded her mind while she sat quietly in her pew. Her stomach was starting to growl and she knew she would have to eat soon. That would mean asking Roy or Tom.

Both Roy and Tom, under the Reverend's supervision, controlled the food and water. They decided when the people ate and they decided if the people ate.

She looked up when she saw both men coming out of the curtain on the side of the podium that led to the Reverend's chambers. They talked in hushed whispers and moved off to the front of the church.

Tom saw her and winked as he walked by. Eve felt a shudder of revulsion when he did it. Mentally she decided if she ever had the chance, she would slit Tom's throat from ear to ear for what he did to her.

The two men disappeared down a side hallway and were lost from sight.

Eve slumped in her pew, tired and exhausted. Just two of the many emotions she was feeling at the moment.

She looked up at the statue of Jesus situated above the podium and sighed. If he was true and he really did exist somewhere out in the ether of Heaven, then why was he allowing the extinction of the human race to move forward at such a brisk pace?

Shaking her head and deciding it was immaterial, she placed her head on her arm and closed her eyes. Sleep didn't come and all she saw were the horrors she'd experienced in the past few weeks, floating across her eyes like a movie.

In time her breathing slowed, and she managed to drift off into a light sleep, while around her, her fellow parishioners languished in misery.

CHAPTER 15

More than a week had passed since Paul and Adam had gone out looking for food and water, and almost all of the supplies from the Mahoney home had been used up.

They had covered more than a mile in every direction, but all they'd found were empty kitchens and destroyed homes. It was obvious someone else had been there before they had.

Signs of the undead were sporadic as they explored the abandoned houses. More than once they had to defend themselves or retreat and hide.

They found many houses empty and covered in blood, the remnants of human bodies scattered on lawns and sidewalks, painting a gory tale of what had happened.

Unlike Paul, who had gone to ground in his cellar, others had stayed above ground, deciding to stay in their homes until either help arrived or the government managed to regain control of the country. That had been their first and last mistake.

The two men had returned from their adventure tired and exhausted, their hopes for the moment squashed. Later that day, after a much-needed rest, Timmy's bright eyes, full of hope and wonder, had shook the two men from their sorrow and the two men had regained some of their lost spirit and now planned for the future.

The two men and Josey sat around the small table in the corner of the cellar. Timmy was on the floor, playing with his blocks. Paul set down a pencil he had been using to figure out how much longer their supplies would last, but one look at the shelf with the few cans of food on it and it was obvious he didn't need pencil and paper to tally the results.

If they were lucky and frugal, they'd have enough food for two more days. It was dark outside and one small candle flickered in the middle of the card table. The cellar windows had been covered to protect them from anyone who might happen to notice the illumination coming from the cellar of an abandoned house.

Since the day Adam and Paul had stumbled onto a nest of zombies, the street had been relatively quiet, with only a few wandering dead every now and then. Only once did they hear the rumble of a truck. They'd all run to the window, but by the time they made it, the vehicle was gone. Whether it was civilian or military was still a mystery to them.

On the floor at the edge of the circle of light the candle cast, Timmy stopped playing and watched his new guardians. He could sense their unease while they discussed what to do next.

"What choice do we have? We're gonna have to leave here. I know we're safe down here, but without food and water we'll starve," Paul said.

"Yeah, but we'll starve safely. Where would we go?" Adam asked.

"What about that rescue station on the other side of the city? Before the power went out, the television was telling people to go there," Josey suggested.

Paul frowned. "It's possible, but we have no idea what's happened since then, for all we know the place is gone, overrun by those *things*," he said.

Timmy stood up and walked over to the adults. "Are you guys talking about the monsters?" he asked sweetly, his eyes wide and full of life.

"Yeah, buddy, we were. Why?" Adam asked.

Timmy shrugged. "I don't know. I just want to know when they'll be gone so I can go outside and play again."

Josey held her arms out to the boy and Timmy moved towards her, hopping onto her lap. "Now, I told you about that. It could be a long time before the monsters are all gone. But guess what? We might have to leave here and go someplace else. If we do, you'll get to go outside. Would you like that?" She asked.

Timmy nodded. "Uh-huh. And will I get to see my Mommy and Daddy again?"

Josey went silent, not quite knowing how to answer him. A blatant lie just seemed so wrong, despite that it was for his protection.

It was Adam who answered the boy. "You bet, pal. In fact, they could be at the rescue station now, waiting for us."

Timmy smiled and clapped his hands. "Oh boy," he cheered. Then jumped to the floor and ran back to his blocks, a large smile on his face.

For the moment at least one person in their group was happy, Adam thought.

"That was cruel, Adam. What's going to happen when he finally finds out his parents are dead?" Josey asked.

Lowering his voice, Adam leaned closer to her. "Look, the kid might not even be alive in a month. The fact is, none of us might. If we leave here, we have no idea what's out there or how bad it is, so I say if we can keep the truth from him, then what the hell."

"He's got a point, hun'," Paul said from her side.

Josey threw her hands up in surrender. "Fine, all right, you win. We'll keep it a secret."

"Good. Now that that's settled, let's discuss what happens in a day. Because like it or not, there's no more food in the homes around us. All the homes in a half mile radius were picked clean. I guess we weren't the only ones that survived," Paul said.

"I wonder where they are? The other survivors, I mean," Adam said.

Paul shrugged. "Good question. I wouldn't mind meeting up with at least a few others. I know what I said about there being no safety in numbers, but a few more eyes when we're out there wouldn't be a bad thing."

"So how are we going to leave? We taking the car?" Josey asked Paul.

"Sure, don't see why not. Its got a full tank of gas and can fit us all easily. That okay with you, Adam?"

Adam leaned back in his chair and placed his hands behind his head. He stretched his body, and cracked his knuckles. "We don't have any jetpacks, so I guess it's fine with me," he said and went quiet.

Paul stood up, his chair screeching on the cold cement floor. "Then it's settled. I say we leave tomorrow morning after we have breakfast. We'll take the rest of our food and water and hope we find more on the road."

Both Adam and Josey nodded and the two shared a look of trepidation. It was a different world outside the cellar doors and they had no choice but to foray out into it.

The next morning Paul opened the bulkhead doors and stepped out into the sunlight. After a quick and meager breakfast, he'd decided to go outside and start the car. Then, if all was quiet, he would back it up into the backyard for easy loading of their weapons and supplies.

Sliding into the seat of his Ford Taurus, he slid the key into the ignition. Next to him on the seat was the Glock he had chosen to take with him.

Holding his breath, he turned the ignition to on, the dashboard lighting up and a ringing telling him to buckle up. He turned the key further to start the car.

The engine whirred for a moment as fuel flooded the fuel injection, then the engine caught, and with a surge of life, began to idle.

Paul looked around him, expecting a wave of undead bodies to come surging out of the nearby homes, but all remained quiet. With only the softly idling engine to break the silence, he let out the breath he was holding.

A small tree branch fell onto the hood of the car, and he jumped in his seat and reached for the Glock. A heartbeat later he realized what had happened, and with an embarrassed smile on his face, put the car in reverse and backed the car around the house. The rear bumper crushed the wild flowers and overgrown shrubs his wife had planted in the spring, but he was confident she wouldn't mind.

Placing the car in park, he stepped out, and after a quick look around, moved to the bulkhead. He briefly noticed one of the bodies lying at the end of the yard was nothing but bones and tattered clothes, the insects and elements doing their part to give the body back to the earth. Paul muttered a quick, "Ashes to ashes," and then turned to face the cellar stairs.

"Coast is clear," he called down the stairs. A second later Adam's head popped out of the shadows of the basement and he waved up to Paul.

"Okay, we're just gathering the rest of the stuff. You stay up there to make sure there aren't any surprises," Adam called up.

"Okay," he answered and set up watch near the front of the Taurus.

The sound of shoes on the cement stairs made him turn around and he saw Josey with her hands full of gear. Blankets, candles, flashlights and whatever else they thought they might need.

Adam followed her with the guns and ammunition. An old potato box served him well as he stumbled over the top step and walked up next to Paul.

"Where do you want me to put these?" While waiting for an answer he set the box down on the hood of the car.

Paul gestured to the back seat of the Taurus. "Right there will be good. I don't want them in the trunk if we need more firepower than what we have on our persons. We don't know how bad it's going to be once we leave this neighborhood."

Adam didn't answer, just picked up the box and opened the rear door of the car, placing the box inside.

Timmy flew up the cellar stairs, happy to finally be outside. He started running around the overgrown yard like he was a wind-up toy that had been wound a little too tight.

His hands were spread out in front of him and he pretended he was flying. The boy barely acknowledged the two corpses in the yard, just ecstatic to be outside in the sunshine again.

Paul watched him, not having the heart to tell him to stop. Although he had no children of his own, Josey's sister had two boys. Uncle Paul had played with them on many an occasion when they flew out to visit her in California.

Josey came out of the cellar with an armful of clothes and Paul wondered about her sister. Josey hadn't brought her up even once since they had barricaded themselves in the cellar. With the phones out, there would be no way of knowing whether she was alive or dead. Thinking about his nephews gave him a pang of grief as he imagined the boys being devoured by the undead.

Timmy tripped in the dirt, pulling Paul from his drifting thoughts and he took a step toward the boy. Before his second boot hit the dirt, the boy was up and running again. Paul admired the free spirit of the boy, watching him run circles around the car.

While Timmy was running around, his path brought him near the overgrown shrubs separating Paul's yard from his neighbors. Paul leaned calmly against the hood of his car watching the boy play. He turned to see what Josey was doing, looking away from Timmy for just a moment.

When he looked back, Timmy was standing perfectly still, his arms hanging by his sides like loose spaghetti.

Standing in front of the boy was a policeman. The man still wore his riot gear, including the shatterproof helmet and black leather gloves. The man's entire body was incased in his uniform.

Timmy was mesmerized, his eyes watching the now tarnished badge on the man's chest. The police officer stood perfectly still, his head looking down at the boy, studying him.

"Timmy, I need you to come here right now," Paul ordered the boy in a firm but serious tone. He wanted to scream at Timmy, yell at him to run, but he knew panic would do nothing but get the boy killed.

Timmy never stopped staring at the police officer's badge. "I don't want to. I want to talk to the policeman. Maybe he knows where my Mommy and Daddy are. Mommy told me policemen are good."

Paul picked up the Glock, holding it at waist level, not wanting to spook the boy.

"I promise you he doesn't know where your parents are. Now come here, right now!" Paul said this in a low voice, but with conviction. It worked, and Timmy turned his head to look at Paul.

"But . . ." the boy protested.

Paul shook his head and pointed at the ground in front of him. "No buts, get over here, now." He growled, but kept his voice level.

"Aww," Timmy said, still not moving, but closer to giving in. Adam stepped into the sunlight from the cellar.

He took in the situation at a glance and with a muffled, "Holy shit," pulled his .38 from the small of his back and prepared to shoot the policeman.

"No, don't do it," Paul snapped.

"Why the fuck not?" Adam asked, not understanding what was happening.

"The cop's got riot gear on, it's bulletproof. That jacket's got a Kevlar weave in it and that helmet would deflect a bullet easy. Just let me handle it."

Not knowing what else to do, Adam lowered his weapon and stood still. "Your rodeo."

Paul grunted. "Thanks, pilgrim."

He moved closer to Timmy and the officer, who was standing perfectly still. Paul couldn't see the man's face and tried to move closer. Timmy moved his eyes away from the officer's badge and looked up at his face.

That's when Timmy started to scream, and all hell broke loose.

CHAPTER 16

The policeman had been attacked while defending the city and had been bitten on the side of his own neck, one of the only places where his skin was exposed. Before his attacker could do any more, one of his fellow officers had killed the zombie. But it was too late. While his fellow policeman fought a losing battle against the undead, he bled out on the street.

Not long after, he rose and attacked the same officer who had tried to protect him, tearing the man's throat out in one bite, the bitter irony lost on everyone.

Once all the policemen had been taken down, some devoured, others reviving as fellow undead, he had wandered away looking for more food.

He'd stumbled into Paul's yard quite by accident, hearing the sounds of laughter from Timmy while the boy played.

When the policeman stepped into the yard and Timmy had stopped and looked at his badge with wide and trusting eyes, the dead policeman had paused. A residue of his past life crossed the front of his brain, memories of his own children, his son, about the same age as Timmy. He'd stood there, like a giant, towering over the boy, as these residual memories flooded his dead brain.

Then the boy screamed and new instincts overwhelmed defunct memories. The hunger inside him overrode everything else and the policeman reached out to capture Timmy in his dead hands and feed on his essence.

Paul ran up to him and smashed his gun into the zombie's face. The blow didn't do much, the face shield of the riot helmet all but stopping the blow. But it did deflect the dead cop's hands for a fraction of a second.

Paul pushed Timmy to the tall grass, the boy falling in a heap. The cop flailed out and stumbled backward, his right gloved hand striking Paul in the face.

Before Paul realized it, his glasses had been knocked from his face and his vision blurred like a blanket had descended over him.

Paul was almost blind without his glasses, the dead cop nothing but a fuzzy black shape in front of him. He heard Adam yelling from behind him, but he couldn't see where he was. To his side, Timmy was crying, his screams of fright filling the backyard with sound.

In front of him was an obelisk of dead meat that towered over him, prepared to substitute him for the boy. A shot rang out and Paul ducked instinctively. Adam had attempted to shoot the cop, but the bullet had just ricocheted harmlessly off the blood-stained helmet.

Paul heard Adam cursing and then felt himself being grabbed roughly. The smell of decaying meat filled his nostrils and he tried to break free, but the cop's embrace was solid.

Another shot rang out and the zombie cop's grip loosened for the fraction of a second as he shifted from the impact of the bullet on his Kevlar vest. Paul took advantage of the precious second he was given. Bringing his knees up to his chest, and placing the bottom of his feet against the policeman, he pushed. This might not have worked if Paul had been a tall man, but as he wasn't, and it worked perfectly.

His legs kicked out and sent him falling to the trampled grass, the dead cop's grip broken.

He heard another shot ring out and the muffled impact of the bullet. Paul frantically spread his hands around the grass, trying to find his eyeglasses or his Glock. He'd dropped the weapon when the cop's incredibly strong hands had grabbed his arms and now he knew it was his only hope.

He heard heavy footsteps behind him, a shadow blocking out the sun, and he rolled away, hoping to avoid the cop's path. A soft wheezing could be heard over the chaos and Paul desperately tried to make out something in the fog that was now his vision. He squinted as hard as he could, but his defective eyes wouldn't cooperate.

He could hear Josey's voice now, coming from his side. "Behind you!" she yelled, her face a mask of terror. Paul scrambled away, trying to put some distance from him and the dead cop.

"Where's Timmy, is he okay?" Paul asked while he crawled along on the grass on all fours.

"I've got him," Josey called from his side.

"Adam, I lost my glasses. I can't see shit. You've got to get in close and shoot it under the chin!"

98

"How the hell am I supposed to do that?" Adam said in a high pitched voice.

"Improvise!" Paul screamed and then let out a frightened shriek when he felt a hand wrap around his ankle. His hands reached out for something to stop him as he was pulled back, but found nothing.

"And for Christ's sake, hurry!" Paul yelled.

Adam panicked, not knowing what to do. The first thing Paul and him had established was to keep your distance from the undead. If they couldn't bite or grab you, your odds of surviving went up tenfold. But he knew there was only one thing he could do to save his friend.

Psyching himself up, he took two deep breaths and ran full speed at the dead cop. His arms were in the air and he flailed them above his head, screaming at the top of his lungs.

He plowed into the cop and the two of them fell to the ground in a heap.

Adam managed to stay on top, and before the cop could do more then snarl at him, he placed the .38 under the ghoul's chin, below the faceplate, and squeezed the trigger.

There was a muffled pop and the zombie cop stopped moving, his gloved hands falling to the side to lie still in the flattened grass. The helmet kept the skull from exploding outward and the body seemed to just stop, like a switch had been turned off. Red rivulets ran from under the helmet and dripped down the cop's ragged face to land in the dirt, where they were quickly absorbed back into the earth.

Adam stood up on trembling legs and backed away from the prone corpse. His boot stepped on something and he looked down to see Paul's glasses. Miraculously, nothing had happened to them but one of the lenses popped out of frame. Adam picked them up, sure he could fix them when he had a few minutes.

"Adam, what happened? Is he dead?" Paul asked from his side.

Adam nodded and then realizing Paul couldn't see him, spoke up. "Yeah, Paul he's dead. I got him," he breathed. "And I found your glasses. They'll be okay when I get a chance to fix them."

Paul's eyebrows went up in surprise. "No shit? Hey, that's great. I've got a spare set packed up in our stuff somewhere, just in case."

"If you two don't mind, we should go. With all that yelling and shooting we're sure to attract some more attention."

"She's right, Adam. Let's get loaded and get the hell out of here," Paul told him.

Adam nodded. Timmy stayed next to Josey, too afraid to be left alone. Paul waited by the stairs and took what supplies the others gave him and placed them in the trunk. Adam found the Glock and tossed it in with the rest of the weapons in the potato box. The dead cop had been missing his sidearm, so there was nothing to salvage from the battle but their lives, which was more than enough.

In no time they were finished and ready to leave. Josey locked the cellar door and Adam looked at her like she was crazy. She just shrugged.

"Sorry, force of habit," she smiled.

Paul was in the back with Timmy, the boy curled up tight against him. Adam was driving and Josey had the passenger seat. The engine was running and they were ready to go.

Paul looked out the window, with eyes that saw nothing but blurs. "Well, what are you waiting for, let's go"

"Which way?" Adam asked.

Josey had a map and she opened it. Her finger found where they were and where the closest rescue station was supposed to be.

"There," she said. "We need to take Route 2 all the way to the end. That will get us to the other side of the city."

Adam nodded quickly. "Sure, I know how to get there," he said and put the car in drive. The front tire spun in the mud, and for just a moment he thought they were stuck, but the front tire gripped some dry earth and the car started forward. Turning in the yard, he pulled out front and, just as Josey predicted, the street was lined with zombies from side to side.

Adam tried to stay calm, telling himself they were safe inside the three thousand pound vehicle. With his knuckles white on the steering wheel, he moved through the undead. Thumps sounded in the car, Adam twisting and turning through the ghouls. Hands slapped the windows and bloody faces slid across glass to fall away as the Taurus moved down the street. The front grille struck a body head-on, the face falling away, and the car bounced slightly as it rolled over the torso. Adam looked in his rearview mirror to see a crumpled mess of meat still trying to pull itself down the street after them. Only one hand was up to the task, the other limbs shattered from the undercarriage of the car.

You have to give the undead credit, Adam thought. They were persistent, if nothing else.

They left Paul and Adam's street behind and turned onto the main road. A few car wrecks were spread out, but nothing Adam couldn't maneuver around.

"Looks like we're home free," Adam said, leaning back in his seat.

"For now. Keep an eye out for trouble, living or dead." Paul looked at Josey who was fiddling with his glasses. "You got them fixed yet?" he asked, impatiently. He felt helpless without his glasses, needing to rely on everyone else.

"Almost there, relax," Josey said.

Paul could feel the steady rhythm of Timmy's breathing. The boy was sleeping, the day hitting him hard. Paul leaned back in his seat and closed his eyes. He felt exhausted too, and the day had barely started.

Adam was in the front humming a song and before she knew it Josey was singing too. Despite himself, Paul felt himself relaxing and before he realized it, he'd dozed off; the gentle swaying of the car more than enough to rock him to sleep.

Overhead, in the clear blue sky a crow paced the car, interested in the moving vehicle. It hadn't seen another vehicle in a while and its curiosity was peaked. It knew if it followed long enough, eventually the car would lead it to food. At least they always had in the past few months.

The car turned onto Route 2 and headed down the road. The rescue station was only a few miles away and they needed food. If everything went well, they would be safe in a few hours and everything would be fine.

If all went well.

CHAPTER 17

Route 2 was a mess of abandoned cars and wreckage. The first mile out of town had been clear, the highway empty, but once they grew closer to the city limits it became a maze of twisted metal and shredded bodies.

Paul was driving, his glasses firmly on his face once again. There was a piece of white tape holding the left lens in its frame, the metal twisted beyond repair. Paul maneuvered around another stranded vehicle and aimed the Taurus for the horizon.

The sides of the Taurus were scratched and dented from the few times he'd to literally push the car through the small openings between wrecks. The sound of scraping metal made his insides cringe until he finally accepted the reality that a new paint job just didn't matter anymore.

Timmy had just woken up from a deep sleep in the back seat, Josey sitting next to him. Adam was in the front seat with Paul, his eyes constantly scanning the road for signs of trouble.

Paul smiled. He and Adam had become a good team. "I'm hungry," Timmy said from the back.

Josey nodded and added, "Me, too, Paul. Maybe we can stop somewhere and stretch our legs."

The ride had taken much longer than expected because of the wrecks and detours they'd had to make. There were even a few times when Paul and Adam had to actually get out and push the abandoned cars out of the way to make room for the Taurus to squeeze by. They now had the aching muscles to prove it.

"I have to go to the bathroom, too," Timmy added.

Paul looked into the rearview mirror at his wife and grinned. "Okay, just give me a few minutes to find someplace that looks pretty safe."

Adam pointed out the window, the wind rustling his hair. "What about there?"

All eyes in the car turned to where Adam was gesturing. A gas station and attached convenience store. The perfect place to get fuel, cigarettes and milk for the family. The ultimate convenience.

Paul shrugged. "Sure, why not. Just let me and Adam check it out before you two get out of the car," Paul said to Josey and Timmy.

Paul pointed the nose of the Taurus to the exit that split off from the main highway. With the exception of two eighteen-wheelers sitting like a pair of dinosaurs, the lot was empty.

The car rolled up to the front doors, Adam looking for signs of trouble. He had his father's .38 in his hand as he slid out of the car and stood on the tarmac.

Paul put the car in park, and after setting the emergency brake, stepped out of the car to join Adam, carrying his shotgun.

The station had the feel of a miniature ghost town. Neither man could ever remember seeing this station or any other so deserted before. Even on Christmas there would be cars and trucks with people on their way to Grandma's house or to a friend's house.

Now there was nothing. The wind blew empty paper bags and Styrofoam cups around, the remnants of a dead culture swirling in the breeze.

Adam pointed with his chin to the glass doors of the station. "Want to go inside and check it out?"

Paul shrugged again. "Sure, let's go."

Adam reached for the door handle and Paul entered first, the shotgun in his hand. It had since been cleaned and reloaded and now had a patched gunstock, the epoxy giving the stock of the weapon a two-tone look.

Adam stepped in behind him and both men let their eyes roam across the inside of the station. Where once there had been a few aisles of must haves like candy, potato chips and popcorn, now there was nothing but knocked-over metal shelves and a few crumpled and torn boxes.

Paul stepped over a pile of Maxim and Cosmopolitans, the magazines thrown to the floor in someone's haste. All the food was gone, looted earlier by someone else.

"Shit," muttered Adam. "Nothing left."

Paul kicked an empty Pepsi bottle out of his path. "Maybe not. There's usually something left if you look hard enough. This place was ransacked quickly; it's possible something got left behind."

As if on cue, Paul's eyes caught a candy bar that was hidden under a pile of newspaper. Pushing the paper aside, he picked up the lone piece and waved it at Adam.

"See, I told you. Let's check the rest out and then go get Josey and Timmy," Paul said, rubbing his shoulder. He couldn't be sure, but he thought he might have pulled something when he and Adam had pushed a Toyota out of the way so the Taurus could fit.

Adam walked across the now somewhat open room and peeked into the glass doors that lined the back wall. Inside, on metal shelves were exploded milk containers and expired containers of yogurt. With the power out, the contents of the shelves had sprouted mold, looking like something out of a teenager's science project.

Adam walked by each door in turn until he stopped at the section that contained beer. More than ninety percent was gone, but there were still a few six-packs sitting on the bottom shelf. Perhaps in the looters rush to grab and run, the bottom shelf had been ignored?

Checking on Paul, who was digging through a pile of toilet paper, Adam opened the glass door and reached for a pack of beer. His taste buds were already tasting the wet, sweet liquid.

His hand wrapped around the opening in the top of the box and pulled it back. But as he started to pull, he felt something tug his wrist, and he looked down to see a zombie with its hand firmly wrapped around his arm.

He panicked immediately, caught off guard, and with a scream of terror, pulled back his arm. The zombie slipped through the shelf and was pulled out from its prison in one fluid motion. It fell to the floor and twisted as it tried to take a bite out of Adam.

Adam wiggled his arm, trying to break free, but its grip was like a clamp. The thing on the floor was barely recognizable as once being human. With no meat in the back of the store, the ghoul hadn't been able to replenish itself and it was nothing but a skeleton wrapped in dried skin, the head covered in tufts of white. In Adam's terror, he still wondered what the hell kept the thing alive and moving.

He continued to back up, dragging the animated skeleton behind him. Paul ran over to him and with one fluid motion, raised his foot and stomped down hard as he could on the ghoul.

Like a melon being flattened, the zombie's head seemed to deflate, only a small amount of blood and gore leaking out of the crushed skull. Intermingled with the blood and skull pieces were bits of gray matter.

Adam jumped away and the ghoul's arm snapped from its socket, the hand still firmly wrapped around his wrist. Bits of torn, dried skin drooped from the severed limb.

Adam jumped up and down, yelling. "Get it off, get it off, for Christ sakes, get it off me!" The dead arm flapped around him like the broken wing of a bird. Paul was trying to help, but the young man wouldn't stay still long enough for him to grab it.

"Hold still, damn it!" Paul yelled.

Adam slowed his movement and stopped jumping around.

Acting like he was Timmy's age, he held out his hand so Paul could pry the skeletal fingers loose. After a few seconds of pulling the arm with no luck, Paul decided to just break the fingers off. One after the other, the sound of breaking twigs echoed off the walls of the gas station until Adam was free.

Adam pulled his arm away the moment the last finger broke off and quickly checked his wrist for signs of scratched or broken skin.

He let out a deep breath and relief flooded through him when he saw his wrist was clean. Only a red mark where the hand had fastened onto him appeared on his pale, sun-deprived skin. Mentally, he decided he needed to get more sun; living underground wasn't for him.

Paul stood in front of Adam, his lips set in a grimace. Adam looked at him. "What? I just wanted some beer."

Paul sighed. "Fine, but pay more attention. I might not be there next time."

"Sure you will. You're my hero," Adam smirked, batting his eyes like a schoolgirl.

Paul chuckled at that. "Knock it off, you big idiot."

Paul turned away and moved to explore the back of the station. "I'm gonna check in back, you stay here by the front doors and check on the others. If I yell, then come running."

Adam saluted him military-style and went to the front door. Paul headed into the gloom of the back room, nothing but a small dirty window to let in the sunlight from outside. Shadows were everywhere as Paul slowly walked through the hallway.

The hall opened up into a back stockroom. It, too, was cleared out.

Paul was about to turn and leave when he saw a pile of empty boxes in the back of the room. Warily, he moved closer and knocked them aside with the barrel of the shotgun.

Behind the boxes was a door with a cheap padlock. Stepping closer, he tapped on the door. If there was something on the other side it was keeping its cool.

Deciding he should investigate further once Josey and Timmy

were safe in the store, he went back out front. Adam was leaning against the wall waving at Timmy.

"It looks safe, tell them to come in, but stay sharp," Paul said.

"Okay," Adam replied, and slipped out the door to the Taurus.

Paul saw him talking to Josey and gesturing to the station, then the back doors to the car opened and they stepped out. Adam brought Timmy to the side of the door and told him to pee on the wall. Adam had to go as well and he showed Timmy how to write his name on the red bricks. Josey just stood there and shook her head.

"Men," she muttered to herself. When Timmy and Adam finished, they went inside with Josey. Paul had just finished dragging the skeleton back to the glass doors at the rear of the station, and with a quick toss, threw it onto the metal shelf. The smell of sour milk and decay flooded his olfactory glands and he quickly closed the glass door. Wiping his hands together to clean them, he stood up and joined the others at the front.

"It's safe?" Josey asked. Her eyes dancing in their sockets as she looked around warily.

Paul nodded. "Yup, seems to be empty. What do you say we stay here for the rest of the day and tomorrow morning we'll start out fresh?"

Neither Adam nor Josey minded, and with a quick couple of trips to the car to retrieve blankets and more weapons, Paul moved the car to the side of the station and locked it for the rest of the day.

Stepping back into the station, Paul saw Timmy was already making himself at home. He was sliding on the smooth tiles in his socks, pretending he was ice skating. Josey had opened some paper towels and was cleaning up the brains from the zombie he'd put down. She sent Paul a glare that told him she wasn't happy about it. He flashed her a sheepish smile, apologizing.

Adam stood by the front doors, looking out at the empty lot. Paul turned to him and gestured beyond the glass, back at the highway.

"Think we'll have company?" Paul inquired while gazing out at the lonely parking lot.

Adam shrugged, the gesture becoming a habit among the two of them. With so many things now out of control in the world, how could it not?

"Don't know, but if we do, one of us should be ready. You go spend some time with your wife and I'll watch the road. Maybe later you can spell me for a while."

Paul slapped him on the back. "Sure, no problem. In fact, later there's something I want to show you in the back of the store. But it can wait." He left Adam and went to his wife's side. She was bent over, picking up the remains on the floor and he reached out with his right hand and goosed her playfully.

She squeaked and jumped up with a big smile on her face. She slapped his shoulder in the same playful manner.

"Oh you, cut that out. This isn't the time or the place."

He grinned back. "The way I see it, there never will be again. Now we need to make our own time and place." He called over to Adam. "Hey, Adam, I'm going to bring Josey in the back for ten minutes. Watch Timmy for a while, will ya?"

Adam smirked, understanding what he was asking. Adam waved them away. "Sure, go. Have fun. I'll watch the runt."

"Hey, I heard that. I'm not a runt," Timmy said next to of Adam.

"Sure you're not, kid. You're just waiting on a growth spurt," Adam quipped in reply.

Timmy stuck out his tongue and went back to sliding around on the floor.

Paul nodded thanks, took Josey's left hand in his and moved to the back of the station. As the two started walking over the debris to the back room, Paul stopped and pointed at her other hand, the one used to cleanup the brains of the ghoul.

"Before we do anything I really need you to wash that hand," he joked.

Josey looked around her feet and picked up an open container of baby wipes. Holding them up, she smiled.

"Way ahead of you, honey. Now come on, let's go. I'm feeling frisky."

Like teenagers, they ran into the back room, giggling to themselves like it was their first time. Timmy played on the floor and Adam kept watch. For the moment things were good. And if there was one thing they had all learned in the past few months was to take things one day at a time.

Tomorrow would arrive whether they liked it or not.

CHAPTER 18

Roy stood in the back of the church, watching the people who had become his subjects. No one but himself, Tom and a few others knew the truth.

The Reverend stood on the podium, his face drenched in sweat while the man struggled to give a quick sermon about the Rapture and Hell.

Reverend Bernie was still out of it, though. Only with Roy's support was he able to come out of his chambers every few days and give a short speech to the masses.

Usually Roy would tell him what to say, but sometimes the Reverend seemed to be his old self, full of fire and brimstone and damnation. But more and more he was nothing more than a wreck of a man, his mind flowing in and out of sanity.

With his mental faculties shattered, the Reverend had become nothing more than a puppet for Roy to control.

And control he had. Roy had already seen more than seven people sacrificed to the zombies kept in the courtyard. All were a threat to what he was trying to build inside the church. Most had been new arrivals, people who hadn't agreed with the way he ran things. Almost all had been men. Only one had been a woman.

After she had arrived a week ago, Roy had decided he wanted her for his own. The woman hadn't agreed. While he was forcing himself on her, she'd scratched him hard across the cheek. The wound had bled badly, and with hospitals a thing of the past, he had been worried about infection.

For her punishment, she'd been thrown to the zombies. He smiled as he remembered her screams for help, her wails as she was torn apart, her organs shown to her while being eaten as she stared in abject horror.

Bet she would have changed her mind now, if she'd been able to.

Over the past week a few other men had arrived. Some had gone with the flow, not caring how things were run, as long as they were safe and had food in their bellies. Some of those men had become part of his honor guard. The rest had been thrown to the zombies.

Roy was surprised how easy it had become to control the Reverend. Just a few whispers into his ear while he slept about who was an emissary for the Devil and the next morning he would point out the sacrifice, and off they would go.

Tom had spoken in private his distaste for the sacrifices, but once Roy explained he could now have all the pussy he would ever want, the man quickly changed his tune. Tom was selfish. As long as his needs were quenched, he was on Roy's side.

In fact, Tom had taken a liking to one specific girl. Roy thought her name was Eve or something like that. He also knew the girl thought Tom was a pig, but she knew better then to protest.

Yup, Roy thought, things were going better then he could have ever hoped possible. He still owed the Reverend a debt he could never repay from when the man had saved his life, but only a fool didn't take advantage of an opportunity when it came.

Roy looked to his side, his honor guard standing next to him. Some of the new men who had arrived had brought weapons with them and now almost all of his men were armed. He knew he could trust them not to mutiny because only he had the Reverend's ear, and the parishioners only listened to the Reverend.

But Roy knew once he had enough men he would change that.

Supply runs had been going smoothly. There was a grocery store less than a half mile away and it was still full of canned goods and boxes of food. The undead weren't interested in processed food . . . only live meat.

At night, outside the church, the mass of bodies would ebb and flow. When it seemed there were too many for the fence to hold, Roy would send a detail out to spike them in their heads. When there were too many corpses, he would have them burned where they lay. That was unpleasant, and the church would smell like burnt meat for a few days after a burning, the sweet odor enough to make any sane person want to gag.

Not Roy. He enjoyed the smell of the burning bodies. To him it was the smell of power. *His* power.

Roy snapped out of his daydreaming to see that the Reverend was finished with his sermon. The further the Reverend slipped into madness, the quicker Roy would make the sermons.

Roy and two guards moved up to the podium. Roy looked out on the people, more than a hundred now, and smiled.

"All right, people, the sermon is over. There are chores to be done. I want the buckets in the latrine emptied and the food that was brought in this morning needs to be sorted and prepared for dinner tonight."

He smiled at that. He and his guards always received the choicest goods. Just one of the benefits of being in power.

With an arm around the Reverend's shoulder, Roy helped the man off the podium and back to his chambers. While they all smelled due to lack of bathing, the Reverend was particularly ripe. The man was so out of it, he didn't even wash with a cloth, something that had become the new form of bathing in the church.

Pushing open the Reverend's chamber door, he helped the man onto the cot in the back of the room.

Rev. Bernie looked up at Roy, not really seeing him.

"Was my sermon satisfactory, my Lord?" He asked the air around him, not seeing Roy.

"Yes, Reverend, it was fine. Now rest and I'll check on you later," Roy said, leaving the room. A man stood at the door and Roy stopped to talk to him.

"You stay here, Steve, and make sure he stays put. No one in or out, standard rules."

Steve nodded. "Sure, Boss, no problem."

Roy smiled and slapped the man on the back. He was one of the new recruits and seemed promising. The man had no conscience. He took orders well and knew how to handle himself.

Walking down the hallway, Roy turned and went up the stairs that led to the window overlooking the courtyard.

He opened the window and looked down on the shambling corpses. When they saw him, they all moved below the window, like Pavlov's dogs, expecting a meal.

"Not today, you dead fucks, but don't worry. I'll have more for you soon."

From below came the sound of scraping hands as the zombies tried to climb the wall. The sound always made him cringe. One of the zombies scraped the wall so hard her fingernails bent back and ripped from her fingers. They fell off to the ground, to be lost in the churned up dirt under the shuffling feet.

His eyes scanned the courtyard floor, the denuded earth covered in scraps of cloth and bones from their victims.

The corner of his mouth curved up a little, just the hint of a smile. Oh yes, there would be plenty more before the week was out. Closing the window, he headed off to his quarters. He was horny and needed to take the edge off.

With a full blown smile now on his lips, he knew just who to call for. He was looking forward to the next half hour.

Stopping at the door for his quarters, he told the guard there who he wanted brought to him. The man nodded and disappeared. But he'd be back soon, and with company.

Roy stepped into his room and closed the door, his mind already thinking of the fun he'd be having in only a few minutes.

CHAPTER 19

Adam looked up as Paul and Josey walked out of the back room. Both seemed relaxed but sweaty. Adam grinned a little when Paul was standing next to him.

"Feel better?" he asked.

"You know it, brother. I can't remember the last time we were alone," Paul said, rubbing his chin in thought. "How's it been out here?"

Adam looked out onto the lonely highway. "Quiet, not one car. Where could everybody be?"

Paul shrugged. "Dead . . . or worse."

"What can be worse than dead?" Adam inquired.

Paul rubbed his nose with his finger, like he had an itch. "What's worse? How about being one of them?" He pointed to the glass doors in the back of the store, where he'd disposed of the skeleton zombie.

Adam stood quiet, thinking about what Paul said. Then he asked in a quiet voice, "Do you think they remember who they were? You know, before they died and came back."

Paul shrugged yet again. "Don't know, doubt it. You've seen how they act. Kind of stupid. It's a good thing, too."

"Why?"

"Because if they were smart then we'd all be royally fucked. As it is, at least we might have a chance."

Timmy ran up to them. "Would someone play with me? I'm bored," he said.

Paul patted Adam on the shoulder. "Go ahead if you want, I'll watch the door. Later, when he's done with you, I want to check something out in back."

"Okay, just let me know," Adam said. His conversation was cut short when Timmy pulled his hand to get him to move. Adam gave in and the two went across the room. Timmy had the idea to set up a couple of trashcans and use them as goals. He and Adam played soccer while Paul watched.

Josey came out of the back, her hair tussled and her face flushed from their bout of sex, and walked over to Paul. The package of paper towels Adam and Timmy were playing with as a soccer ball landed near her and she kicked it back their way, laughing merrily.

When she reached Paul, she stood on tiptoes and kissed him on the cheek.

"What was that for?" he asked, surprised.

"No reason," she smirked. "Just thought I'd say thank you. You were great."

He tried to look as heroic as possible and asked her, "Aren't I always?"

She patted his chest with her hands and smiled. "Sure dear, you bet." Then she walked away to see about wrangling up a meal for everyone.

Paul watched her walk away, considering her last remark. Then his eyes lit up when he realized she was mocking him.

"Hey," he said. "That's not funny." Josey just waved a hand while she walked away, the matter closed.

After a moment of watching her, he turned back to the glass doors and the highway. He was startled to see a car pulling into the lot. He moved to the side so as not to be seen and called to the others. "Hey, heads up, we got company!" He called across the store, his voice bouncing off the walls.

Adam stopped kicking the paper towel and ran over to him. "Timmy, go with Josey. We'll tell you when it's safe."

"But I don't want to, I want to keep playing," Timmy whined.

Adam gave the boy a look of iron. "Damn it, Timmy, do what I say!"

Timmy stopped his rebuttal, surprised to hear Adam talk to him like that. But it had the desired effect and he picked up his shoes and went to Josey. The two stayed in the rear of the store and waited for the all clear. Josey had one of the pistols in her hand just in case.

Adam ran next to Paul and had a look outside. An old Ford station wagon had just pulled up to the gas pumps directly in front of where Adam and Paul were hiding. Both men stayed quiet, watching.

A man stepped out of the car. He was in his mid-thirties and looked disheveled and ragged. His countenance was one of worry as he looked around the outside of the gas station.

The passenger door opened and a woman stepped out into the late afternoon sunlight. She, too, looked ragged. Worry lines creased her face while she looked around with quick, darting movements of her head. Whatever these people were, they were scared, Adam thought to himself.

"What do you think? They look harmless," Adam whispered.

Paul was so close to him, Adam could feel his breath on his neck. "Yeah, I know. Let's give it another minute. If they don't do anything stupid, then we'll go out and say hi," Paul told him.

The man and woman walked around the car and had what looked like a heated argument. The wind was blowing away from the gas station and with the glass doors shut; they couldn't hear what the couple was saying.

Then the man moved to the back door of the wagon and opened it. He reached inside and pulled the form of a small child out. From the pink dress the child wore, it was obvious he was holding a little girl.

The man carried her to the front of the car and gently laid her on the hood. The woman, probably the girl's mother, walked over to her and brushed the errant hair from the sleeping face.

Adam stood up from the crouch he was in. "They look harmless and they have a sick kid. I'm going out there."

Before Paul could stop him, Adam pushed open the doors and walked out into the sunlight. Adam breathed in the fresh air, relishing the wind blowing on his face. It felt good to be outside, no matter how short it might be.

He started to walk the ten yards that separated him from the couple. When he had covered half the distance, the man finally noticed him.

His eyes went wide and he turned to run back to the driver's door. Adam waved to them, calling out. "Wait, relax, I'm friendly. I just want to help!"

The man never hesitated.

Leaning into the station wagon, he came up with a small .45 pistol in his hand. Running back to his family, he aimed the gun at Adam.

"That's far enough! Don't come any closer or I'll shoot!"

Adam stopped where he was, both hands at his side. Even if he wanted to, he doubted he'd be able to retrieve his revolver from the back of his pants. He was also sure Paul was watching, and at any sign the man might shoot, he was sure Paul would take him out. Adam hoped it didn't come to that.

"All right, I stopped. Look, I just want to help. We just arrived a little while ago ourselves."

At the last word Adam spoke the man's eyes went wider, if that was possible. "Ourselves? You have others? How many, where are they?"

"Whoa, slow down. Listen friend, I just came out here to help you. You looked like you could use it. If you don't want it, then I can just go back inside and leave you be. But you should know my friend has a rifle pointed at you right now. If we wanted you dead, then you'd be dead already."

The man ducked lower, pulling his wife down with him, his eyes scanning the surroundings of the gas station more intently. His wife said something to him, but he just yelled at her to be quiet.

The man's shoulders seemed to slump just a little when he called back to Adam.

"I don't believe you, I think you're alone and you want our car."

Adam sighed. This was getting old real fast. "Fine, I'll give you proof. Now don't freak out," he called.

Adam turned to look at Paul and pointed to the side of the car, about three feet from the man's shoes. Adam made a motion with his hand, like he was pretending his fingers were a gun. Then he mouthed "bang, bang." Paul opened the door a crack and lined up the barrel of his rifle with the intended target.

A little to the left of the man's shoes, a puff of dirt shot up and the sound of the ricochet blended with the crack of the rifle. The man jumped and the woman screamed. Adam was ready to move, waiting for the distraction, and when the man looked away from him and ducked lower, he dove behind one of the gas pumps. He waited until the man had calmed down and snuck a peek around the side of the pump.

The man was covering the child with his body and the woman was hiding behind the station wagon. Adam stood up.

"See, no one wants to harm you. We have food inside and water if you want to join us."

The man seemed to deflate as he looked up. "Really? You really don't want trouble?"

Adam nodded. "Of course not, why would you think that?"

"Because that's how it is now. There hasn't been a single person that didn't mean us harm since those *things* appeared."

"Well, we're harmless. Why don't you put that gun away and we'll get your wife and child inside. They are your family, right?"

The man nodded. He walked closer to Adam, the gun hanging

loose in his hand.

Adam watched the weapon warily, in case the man was somehow pretending. The man saw Adam staring and turned the weapon in his grip so he could hand it to Adam. "Don't worry about this," he said looking down at the weapon. "It's empty. Has been for quite a while."

Adam let out a deep breath, one he hadn't realized he'd been holding. "Really, wow. You got balls, mister."

The man shrugged and gave Adam the faintest hint of a smile. "A bluff was all I had. It worked for a while, didn't it?"

Adam grinned back. "Yeah, I guess it did." He reached out and took the weapon from the man's hand. Then turned to Paul and waved the all clear. Paul warily opened the glass doors and stepped out into the light. With his rifle still ready, he walked out and joined the two men.

Adam was the first to speak. "Relax, Paul, the gun was empty."

"No shit? Jesus buddy, that's a good way to get yourself killed," Paul said, looking the man up and down.

"Not like I had a choice. I had to at least try to defend my family."

Adam held out his hand. "Well, you're among friends now, so relax. I'm Adam and this is Paul."

The man shook Adam's hand. "Nice to meet you. I'm Carl Foranti and that's my wife Claire. She's with our daughter Alicia," he said, pointing to the woman and child.

Paul gestured to the little girl on the hood of the station wagon. "What's wrong with your kid? She sick?"

Carl nodded. "Uh, yeah, she is, seems like the flu. She's always been a sick one, not that her mother would ever admit that. But we haven't been able to find any antibiotics. The hospitals are deathtraps, you know."

Paul nodded. "Yeah, we heard. We've got aspirin inside if you want. It's not much, but it's better than nothing."

Carl smiled from ear to ear. "That would be great, thanks. You don't know how good it is to meet someone who doesn't want to kill you, you know?"

Paul and Adam looked at each other and then at Carl.

"Yeah, we think we know what you mean, now let's help you get . . . Alicia is it?" Paul asked.

Carl nodded and Paul continued. "Okay, let's get Alicia inside and see what we can do for her. Once she's feeling better, we have a child of our own she can play with."

"Oh, hey that's great," Carl said, walking back to the wagon. "It's okay, honey, they're friends," Carl told Claire.

"Really?" she asked. "We're safe here?"

Adam nodded. "Well, as safe as anywhere can be nowadays, but yeah, you're safe with us."

Claire seemed to slump against the car as the tension she'd been feeling left her, then she picked up Alicia and carried her towards the gas station.

Paul and Adam led them into through the glass doors and Josey helped make a bed for the sick child. While Claire walked with the girl, the child's pale arm slid from under the blanket she was wrapped in, an obvious bite mark on her skin.

Before anyone could spot the wound, Claire pulled the arm back inside the blanket and smiled when Josey helped her lay the child down on the bedding.

"Thank you so much for your help," Claire said to Josey., who nodded.

"Of course. You think it's the flu?"

Claire nodded slightly and looked away. "Yes, I do. She'll be better soon, I know it." Her eyes started to tear up as the woman looked down at her sleeping daughter. "She has to."

Josey patted Claire's arm for support, stood up and walked away.

On the bedclothes, the girl grew paler and her breathing grew shallower as the infection continued to ravage her body.

CHAPTER 20

After Claire tucked Alicia in on a makeshift bed and made as comfortable as possible, she joined the other adults.

Timmy was close by, sleeping. After being cooped up in the small cellar for so long, the boy had finally tired himself out running and jumping. Now all the adults sat in a circle near the front door. Paul faced the doorway, his eyes always checking the highway for more visitors.

Carl told the story of how he and his family had arrived at the gas station. After the National Guard had come through their neighborhood to evacuate all the residents, they had holed up in their home, just as Paul had.

They'd hid in the attic, and after the soldiers were gone, they'd returned to the first and second floors of their house.

That was their first mistake, Carl told Adam, Paul and Josey. About two weeks after the Guard left the first walking corpses had arrived outside the house.

In the beginning, they were relatively harmless. Until more arrived, and once the walking dead knew there was life inside the house, they attacked in force.

Carl quickly found out it was a hopeless endeavor, even though he had barricaded the doors and windows. The sheer weight of the undead was enough to break the hastily nailed-down wood. The family was trapped on the second floor and the undead tried to climb over the furniture Carl and Claire had thrown down the stairs. The barrier held at first, but in less than a day it had started to loosen.

The dead were hungry and the Forantis were the only source of food for miles.

When Carl realized it was only a matter of time before the ravenous ghouls broke through the furniture, he climbed out onto the roof carrying nothing but his pistol. With his wife and daughter in tow, he slowly shimmied down the lattice work on the side of the house and managed to land on top of the garage roof. From there, he forced open the roof vent and his family crawled through the hole and fell onto the storage loft in the garage.

Carl kept an extra set of car keys in a drawer in the garage, just in case he accidentally locked his keys in the car. Now those keys were his family's salvation. Once everyone piled into the car, he hit the garage door opener but all he got was an empty click. No power.

Doing something Carl never thought he would ever do in his life-time, he revved the engine and plowed through the garage door, shattering the wood and sending zombies flying across his driveway.

The station wagon hit the street and he floored it, leaving his house and possessions behind. Since that day, they'd been on the road, stopping and hiding when and where they could. A few times they'd come across other survivors. These people were ruthless and had tried to kill Carl and rape Claire. Carl had shot a man earlier that day in order to escape with his family. That was something else he had never thought he would ever do in his lifetime, shooting another man.

That was why he was so paranoid when he'd met Adam and was very glad he had been wrong. When Carl's story was over, he thought about the one piece he left out.

With Alicia and Claire at his side, they had entered a small one family home looking for food. The inside was shrouded in darkness as night fell outside, and they moved through the shadows to the kitchen. Claire had told Alicia to sit at the kitchen table while she and Carl rummaged through the cabinets. They had been in luck, the cupboards more than half-full.

While they took item after item from the cabinets, Alicia sat quietly.

Then she saw a boy about her own age at the end of the hallway. Before Claire could stop her, she ran toward the boy, excited to have someone to play with. Carl turned at Claire's scream and saw Alicia standing in front of the small boy, his head was wreathed in shadows and Alicia holding out her hand to say hi. Carl had moved as fast as his legs would carry him. He grabbed one of the kitchen chairs and darted down the hallway to grab his child. The smell of death emanating from the tiny corpse confirmed what he was already dreading.

The boy took a step forward, his face illuminated by a ray of moonlight from a side window. The boy was very dead. His eyes were sunken into his head and his lips were pulled back tight against his gums. There was a deep wound on the boy's throat that glistened red and black in the feeble light, and his skin was covered in blotches.

Carl charged at the dead boy and swung the chair from over his head. As the chair came crashing down, the boy's head darted at Alicia, his mouth open unnaturally wide to take a bite out of her tender young flesh. Carl was there and he crushed the boy, but not before the dead boy's teeth managed to graze Alicia's arm. The skin broke just before his head was smashed to the ground.

After that, Carl scooped Alicia in his arms, and with Claire grabbing whatever she could carry, they ran out of the house as if demons were chasing them. Once in the station wagon, he floored the gas pedal and the vehicle screamed into the night on a trail of exhaust smoke.

Carl knew he could never tell anyone what had happened.

"Wow, that was some story. And the whole time you've been on the road, you've only seen a few other people?" Paul asked from his side, shaking him out of memory.

Carl nodded. "Yup, I guess the National Guard took everybody."

"You mean everyone that hasn't turned," Adam said.

"Turned? What do you mean?" Claire asked.

"You mean you don't know?" Josey asked her.

Claire shook her head. "No, what, I don't understand."

"Didn't you watch the news? They were talking about it right up until the power went out," Adam told the confused couple.

Carl raised his hands. "Once we knew we were staying in our house, I stopped watching. I mean, what else could they tell us? Then the power cut out and it didn't matter. Why, what do you know that we don't?"

"What we know," Paul said, "is the reason why this infection is out of control, why so many people are nothing but walking corpses. If you get bit by them, you die. But then you come back as one of them. That's why their numbers are so high. Every time they kill one of us, we become like them."

"At least until we're all gone," Adam finished.

"Oh, Adam, what a horrible thing to say," Josey said.

Adam turned to look at her. "Why? It's the truth. If things keep going like they are, humanity will be extinguished. Long live Humanicus Deadicus."

"We'll stop it before then, Adam. Quit being so morbid," Paul told him.

Adam stood up, now looking down on the others. "Stop it? Shit,

Paul, wake up! There's no stopping it. If there was, we wouldn't be sitting in the middle of a ransacked gas station with no power. What's happening now is like when God sent the flood to wipe us out, except this time there's no damn Ark. This time we're all gonna drown. The sooner you guys accept that, the better off we'll all be." He turned and walked to the back room.

Josey moved to call to Adam, but Paul stopped her with a touch of his hand.

"Let him be, babe. He's just tired and scared like the rest of us. This was his way of blowing off some steam," Paul said gently.

"Okay, but in a little while you go check on him. Okay?" Josey asked.

Paul nodded and then turned to watch the front of the station again. The sun was just starting to set, painting the sky a beautiful shade of orange with a touch of red. Claire sat next to him, quietly eating from their meager supplies of canned goods and Carl was looking at his little girl with a touch of fear in his eyes. He noticed Paul looking his way and quickly changed his expression.

While the sun continued to set, the four of them sat in the circle in silence, each lost in thoughts of what was to become of them all.

Adam sat on a crate in the back. No sooner had he sat down then he was up again. The adrenalin was pumping and he just wanted to hit something. He paced. What was the matter with them? Didn't they realize what was happening? He sat back down again and crossed his arms over his chest.

His angry breathing came fast, but as he sat there alone, his breathing calmed and his heart slowed in his chest.

Soon he was back to his old self. Now, as he thought back to how he'd acted and what he'd said, he felt a little stupid, definitely embarrassed.

He was about to go back out front and apologize when he noticed the door. It had a cheap-looking padlock. Adam searched the room for some kind of tool to use as a pry bar. He found something in the back corner mixed in with some brooms: a long piece of pipe.

Adam carried it to the door and jammed it into the small gap between the lock and the wood. With a few grunts, he managed to loosen it a little. On the third try, he yanked it out with a screech of torn screws, each of the small fasteners falling to the dusty floor as they were slowly pulled from the wood.

With sweat glistening on his brow, he opened the door, expecting anything. What he got was a storeroom full of cigarettes and candy.

From floor to ceiling the small closet was lined with shelves. On those shelves were every brand of cigarettes he could think of and a few he'd never heard of.

Too bad he didn't smoke. But then again, it's not like he needed to worry about the smokes killing him anymore. Hell, that was the least of his problems.

On the floor, in open boxes were colorful packages of a dozen candy bars. He saw Hershey's, Kit Kat and Butterfingers.

With a smile on his lips, he grabbed a handful of each and carried them out front. If he had to return and apologize for his ravings, at least he could go back bearing gifts. Dropping bars behind him as he left the back room, he strolled out front to see his friends.

He expected to see them relaxing around the circle they had made earlier. He exited the back room and with a gasp, dropped the candy and reached for his weapon.

Things were definitely not the way he'd left them.

CHAPTER 21

Five minutes earlier, Alicia had gasped her last breath. The death rattle carried to Claire and the woman left the circle to check on her daughter.

Claire looked down at Alicia's face. Her eyes followed the soft curve of her cheeks and the small cleft in her chin. Claire smiled as she admired her beautiful daughter. Someday she would turn into a beautiful woman.

Suddenly, Alicia's eyes snapped open. The girl remained perfectly still, but her eyes moved left and right as the girl tried to discern where she was.

Claire let out a gasp of emotion.

"Oh my God, she's awake," Claire said out loud. The others turned to look. From where they sat, Alicia's eyes were hidden.

The sun had set and one candle sat in the middle of the circle. The flickering flame cast deep shadows across the inside of the gas station, filling every corner with ghosts of movement.

Claire's eyes went wide as Alicia's mouth tried to move, but instead her teeth began to grind, the upper scraping the lower teeth, the sound like sandpaper to her ear.

Claire bent over, sliding her hands under her child's body and raising her to a sitting position. The candle flame danced in Alicia's eyes, making her demonic.

Claire hugged Alicia to her body, her eyes welling up with tears. If Alicia was awake, then the worst was over. Her fever had broken!

Alicia's head was hidden from view from the others, so none of them saw when Alicia's jaw opened to the point of dislocating. Her head bent back, and like a snake attacking its prey, she latched onto Claire's throat, ripping and chewing in one smooth motion.

Claire tried to let out a scream , but only managed to fall over.

Josey, Paul and Carl all jumped to their feet, wondering what was happening. In the corner of the room, Timmy woke up and started staring at her, not knowing what was happening.

"What the hell is wrong, what's going on?" Paul yelled to the room, his head turning every which way.

"I don't know," Carl said, already moving to Claire's side.

"Josey, see to Timmy," Paul told her. With a curt nod, Josey was across the room, hugging Timmy to her breast and telling him things were okay.

Things were most definitely not okay.

Alicia had pushed Claire to the floor while she continued ripping chunks of flesh from her neck. Claire's carotid artery had been severed and then her jugular, a massive amount of blood to fountaining out of her. Within seconds, the time it took Carl to reach her side, her heart was already pumping its last, the fountain nothing more then a trickle.

Carl stood over what was once his family, his face frozen in shock. The sounds of Alicia feeding filled the room.

Carl broke from his stupor, leaned down and grabbed his daughter with both hands. He threw her lightly across the room, away from Claire. The girl landed in a heap of limbs, but was soon on her feet again.

Carl knelt down to see to Claire, but it was heartbreakingly obvious she was dead.

Carl looked up to see Adam step into the room from the back. He dropped something he was carrying behind him and pulled his handgun from his back. He waved it around, not quite knowing who to shoot or what to do.

Then Carl turned his head and saw Paul with his shotgun. The man was lining up his little girl in his sights.

Carl jumped to his feet and darted between Paul and Alicia. He thrust his hands in front of him and yelled at Paul. "Wait! Don't shoot her!"

Paul lowered the weapon a fraction of an inch.

"Don't shoot? She just killed your wife!" Paul yelled back, pointing to Claire's body.

Carl shook his head back and forth vehemently. "I don't care! She's still my little girl. Let me handle it. I promise she won't hurt anyone else."

Paul's mouth turned into a grimace. "You better fuckin' believe it. If she takes one step towards my wife or Timmy, she's done."

Carl nodded quickly. "Fair enough. Just let me handle it." Carl picked up a roll of packaging tape, one of many on the floor of the station. Then, like a cowboy rustling a wild bull, he circled around and knocked Alicia to the floor. With his knee on her back, he hogtied her with the tape and stepped back, breathing heavily, his cheeks wet with tears.

Adam finally figured out what had happened. He gestured with the tip of his .38 at Claire's body on the floor, surrounded by a pool of blood.

"What about her? Any second she's gonna come back. We need to put a bullet in her head, quick," Adam said, the .38 aimed at Claire, waiting for her to return.

Carl ran over to Paul and Adam, tape still in his hand. "No, wait, I'll take care of her, too!" With tears in his eyes he turned Claire over and wrapped her hands in tape, then stood up and looked down at his wife. She was just starting to twitch, the infection taking over her dead nervous system and jumpstarting her body.

"So what do we do now?" Adam asked from Paul's side.

Paul looked at Adam, the candle flame fluttering from the movement of the air. "What else can we do? We need to put them down."

Carl moved closer to Paul and Adam. "You're not shooting my family," he breathed heavily. "They're all I have."

Paul placed a hand on his shoulder, sympathetically. "I know, Carl, and I'm sorry, but your family's gone. Those two," he said pointing at the zombies, "are not your family. Not anymore."

Carl shook his head back and forth, faster and faster. "No, you can't, I won't let you."

"Shit, man, it's not like you have a choice," Adam said quietly. "If we don't, they'll just try to attack us. And if they break free you know what will happen. We still have Timmy to think about."

Carl looked across the room at the boy cradled in Josey's arms. He watched them for almost a minute. Then his shoulders lowered in resignation, realizing the futility of what he wanted. He turned to Adam and Paul, his eyes becoming hard, a determined set to his jaw.

"We'll go, we'll leave right now. All three of us. Then you'll be safe."

Paul's eyes went wide. "What? You can't be serious."

Carl held his ground, his eyes looking back and forth at the two men. "Yes, I'm serious. I'll leave. And I'll take my family with me. What we do after that is none of your fucking concern." His voice was hard as he said these last words and his hand brought up his .45.

The .45 Paul had loaded.

Paul held up his hands in surrender. "Fine, all right. You win. If you want to take them, then go. We won't stop you. But we won't help you either," Paul said.

Carl looked at Adam, the young man nodding in agreement.

"Go man, and quick," Adam told him.

"All right, then," Carl said and turned to see to his family.

❖❖❖❖❖

First Carl went to Alicia.

He picked up the small living dead girl, after making sure she couldn't bite him, and carried her through the front door. He walked to his station wagon, the girl on his back like a sack of potatoes. Opening the rear door of the wagon, he set her inside gently. By the light of the moon, Adam and Paul could see the girl's mouth constantly trying to snap at Carl. Once she was inside, Carl closed the door and walked back to the gas station. His face was set in stone while he worked at his grim task.

Claire was harder to manage. She had returned while Carl had been bringing Alicia to the station wagon and was now thrashing about, only her bonds keeping her from everyone in the gas station. She was a full-grown adult and, try as he could, Carl wouldn't able to carry her without getting bit. Finally, he picked up the packaging tape and wrapped it around Claire's mouth. The entire time, Claire continued wiggling and trying to bite him, her mouth just wanting to taste his flesh.

Throwing the tape away, he picked her up in the classic fireman's carry and took her out of the gas station.

His dead wife's feet were kicking as she struggled to free herself the entire time. Once he was at the station wagon, he opened the door and slid her inside. The slamming of the door announced the finality of his decision.

Walking back to the front doors of the gas station, Paul waited patiently, a shotgun resting in the crook of his arm. Adam waited beside him, Carl's few belongings held out to the man.

"I think you're crazy, but good luck," Adam told him.

Carl shot him a hint of a smile. "Yeah, thanks," he said.

"You're a goddamn fool. You know that, don't you? The first chance they get, they'll rip you apart," Paul said with a disgusted look on his face.

Carl shrugged. "Maybe, maybe not. They're my family. Without them, I really don't want to go on."

Paul looked at the man and then spit on the ground. Then he slipped back inside the station.

Adam and Carl stood there in the night, nothing but a few crickets to mar the silence. Adam held out his hand to Carl. "Sorry things went down like they did, man. I hope you do all right."

"Yeah, me too. Listen, when your friend there calms down, ask him a question for me, will you?"

Adam nodded that he would.

"Ask him what he'd do if it was his wife who got bit. Somehow, I doubt he'd just shoot her in the head and be done with it. Just ask him, all right?"

"Yeah, man, I will."

Carl nodded slightly, and with his belongings in hand, turned and walked to his vehicle. He climbed into the station wagon and started the engine. The car headed off out of the lot, Claire and Alicia kicking and bouncing in the back like wild animals. He didn't look back once.

With the wagon driving away, Paul stepped back outside and stood next to Adam.

"He's a goddamn idiot. The first chance those ghouls get, they'll rip his throat out," he said flatly.

Adam stood in the dark, thinking quietly. "Perhaps. Either way, he's with his family. It may be creepy, but I understand what he's doing."

Paul turned and looked at Adam who was watching the receding tail lights disappear down the highway. "Then you're an idiot, too." Without saying another word, Paul turned back inside the station.

Adam ignored him. It was easy to feel that way when you still had your wife. Adam had lost his family already. He sympathized with Carl.

He had already decided not to ask Paul the question, because the truth was, some questions couldn't be answered until they were right in your face.

Letting out a sigh, he turned and entered the gas station. Outside in the night the crickets continued their symphony to an undead world.

CHAPTER 22

With Carl gone, they were left to clean up his mess.

Paul had already decided that at first light they, too, would be moving on, but there were still many hours until the sunrise. Josey opened more than a dozen rolls of paper towels to cover Claire's blood. The smell of copper filled the room and Adam used every can of Lysol to try to dampen the odor. Then he retrieved all the candy bars and added them to their supplies by the front door.

Timmy was still shaken up. He never left Josey's side, following her like a chick to a mother hen.

Once the place was moderately clean, the three adults and Timmy sat by the front door and relaxed. While the three of them would usually have plenty to say to one another, after the events with Carl and his family, there was a pall of gloom hovering over them.

For the rest of the night, not much was spoken until it was finally time to get some much-needed rest. The next morning would see them at the city limits and no one had any idea of what they might find.

With a few mumbled goodnights, everyone settled down for a restless sleep.

For some the night was more restless than others. Paul tossed and turned in his bedroll and Adam lay next to him. Josey had agreed to take watch for a few hours, the dark highway beyond the clear glass her only company. Timmy curled up next to her, and after a restless hour, he too, drifted off to sleep.

Paul shook in his sleep, a dream forming from his subconscious.

He awoke to the sound of snoring, Adam still sleeping soundly next to him.

Josey had come up to him in the dark and nuzzled his ear. He smiled to himself, knowing what she wanted. Her hand slid under the blankets and started to massage him. Despite the events of the day, he found himself rising to the occasion. They kissed passionately, her mouth tasting sweet from the candy bar she'd had. His hand slid under her shirt and caressed her right breast, his fingers squeezing her pert nipple. He was now rock hard, his hips thrusting upward in expectation of what would happen next. But Josey had other ideas. Although he couldn't see her in the dark, he saw the glint of a smile from her teeth just before she slid down his torso and her head disappeared under the covers. Her mouth opened, accepting him inside her wet mouth. He let out a sigh of pleasure and thrust upward. He was in Heaven.

With eyes closed he let out pleasured sighs until from beneath the sheets came a gurgling sound, then a moan. He was about to ask if she was all right when he felt a sharp pain and tugging on his groin and heard a tearing sound, like pork ribs being separated by hand. The pain grew in intensity and he let out a scream.

Throwing the blankets off, in the moonlight he saw a monster. Josey's face was distorted into a rotted, decayed human skull. The dead eyes were filled with a malevolence that went beyond human understanding.

Her mouth was curled up into a deformed rictus of a smile, but the thing that had Paul's blood running cold and had his heart stopped in his chest, was what was in it.

Still flapping, the blood pumping out of it, was his penis.

Only the ripped and jagged end extruded from her mouth, looking like a macabre flower. He looked down at his crotch and let out another bloodcurdling scream. Blood shot from the wound and seeped into the bedroll below him. With each pump of his heart, the blood spread more, until he thought he would drown in a lake of crimson.

His vision grew dim and he thought he was going to faint. But then he saw a light. He wondered if this was the fabled light he had heard about when people had near death experiences.

He felt himself floating towards the luminance, until he felt something wet on his cheek. At first he thought it was his imagination, but then he felt it again.

Slowly, he opened his eyes to see the sun coming up, its brilliance flooding through the glass doors of the station. He had to close his eyes and turn away, his pupils adjusting to the sharp glare.

He looked up to see Timmy standing over him. The boy had a candy bar in one hand and an overflowing cup of water in the other. Every time he bit into the candy bar, the cup would tip a little, allowing the fluid to drip onto Paul's face. After the third time, Paul sat up, wiping his forehead dry with his blanket.

"Hey, kid, how about going over there and finishing that?" he asked politely.

"Sure," Timmy said around a mouthful of Snickers bar. He walked away, sloshing clear liquid on the floor as he went. Paul sat up and rubbed his face, feeling the week's worth of stubble there.

Josey came up and knelt beside him. Paul jumped back, startled at the first sight of her. She clearly saw something was wrong in his expression and placed her hand on his leg.

"You all right? You look like you've seen a ghost."

Paul nodded and forced a grin. "Yeah, babe I'm fine. Just had a nightmare, that's all."

Her eyebrows went up in interest. "Oh really, what about?"

He shook his head and changed the subject by getting up.

"Doesn't matter. Look, are we ready to go? All I want to do is take a piss, then I want to be out of here."

Adam called from the front door. "Fine with me, man. We've been waiting for you to get up. If you didn't wake up on your own in another half hour, I was planning on kicking you awake," Adam joked.

Paul turned to him and smiled. "If you tried, you'd have to hop around after I put that same foot up your ass," he quipped back.

Adam grinned and turned back to the glass doors.

Josey spoke up then, busy wrapping up the bedroll. "Will you two stop it? I don't want Timmy hearing that kind of language."

Both men mumbled apologies while Paul slid his pants on. He had a serious case of morning wood and seeing the tent in his underwear gave him the chills, thinking about his nightmare.

Josey noticed his hard-on also, and slid over to him, her hand idly touching his stomach.

"Hey, handsome, I can take care of that for you, if you want," her voice was seductive, her eyes passionate.

Paul swallowed hard, the dream right in front of his eyes, his penis flopping in her mouth like a half-dead fish.

"Ah, well, uhm, thanks, babe, but that's okay, really. I'm fine right now. Look, I'm gonna hit the john, I'll be back." Paul then quickly stepped out of her embrace and almost ran to the back room where the bathroom was.

Josey stood there, not understanding, her hands on her hips. Paul had always wanted sex whenever she did. Usually more often.

"Now that's weird. What's got into him?" She muttered, then shrugged and got back to work picking up what they were taking with them.

Paul slid across the floor in his boots on something wet, regained his balance, then hobbled off to the bathroom, trying his best to forget his nightmare.

The moment he reached the bathroom, the smell of urine and fecal matter assaulted his nose. The bowl was already half-full and he had to make a point to look away and hold his breath. If they had decided to stay any longer at the gas station, they would have had to start going outside. He sighed while zipping up his pants. The plumbing was dry here, as well. He'd managed only one flush when they had first arrived, but once the tank was empty, the toilet became inoperable.

Closing the door on the small lavatory, he was pleased to never have to step into its smelly interior again.

He walked out into the open front of the convenience store and saw that his wife and Adam were ready to go. Timmy was sliding off in the corner, trying to get in some last minute mock ice skating.

Paul strolled over. When he was next to Josey she handed him his shotgun.

"Thanks, hon.' Okay then, if we're ready to leave then let's get the hell out of here."

Adam grinned. "I hear that. Come on, Timmy we're going to the city!" Adam called to the boy.

After a few "awws" and "can't we stay longer?" Timmy gave in and followed the adults to the car. The boy wasn't looking to being stuck inside the car for a few hours again.

Before they climbed inside the Taurus, which Josey had pulled to the front of the gas station while Paul was using the bathroom, Adam handed Timmy a stack of comic books. "Here, kid, I found these last night behind the cash register."

Timmy's eyes went wide. "Oh, wow, cool!" he exclaimed, taking the comics and jumping into the car.

From the back seat Josey grinned at him. "Thanks, Adam. That should keep him happy for at least a little while," she said.

"Sure, glad to help," he replied while getting in.

Paul hitched up his pants and with one last look at the gas station, got into the driver's seat of the Taurus and started the engine. Without another look, he stepped on the gas pedal and left the building behind.

Within less than a minute the car was nothing but a dot on the horizon, the red taillights glowing softly, until those too faded away into the distance.

Outside the gas station, near the glass doors, refuse continued to swirl around the building, man's leftovers floating on the wind and catching in the openings on the gas pumps.

One newspaper hit the pump open, the title page splashed across the top.

In dark bold letters it read: *CITY EVACUATED AFTER BEING OVERRUN, QUARANTINE NOW IN EFFECT.*

Then a sharp gust of wind caught the paper and pulled it off the gas pumps. It fluttered in the air, almost dancing, until a cross-current caught it, taking it away to be lost with the rest of the floating trash.

CHAPTER 23

"I'm telling you, if we don't put a stop to it, he'll kill us all!" Stewart said from the podium. Below him in the pews, heads nodded in agreement.

"We hear ya, Stewart, but what can we do? He has an armed force of men behind him," a small man in the second row asked.

"We have to get the drop on him when he least expects it. The Reverend is nothing more than his puppet now," Stewart answered back.

"But what if we fail? Roy will feed us to the zombies." That from a woman's voice near the back of the theatre.

Stewart nodded. "He'll probably do that anyway. At least to the men. He's trying to make his own harem in here. Shit, since I got here two weeks ago, I've seen five men get sacrificed to the zombies . . . and for what? So he can have a different woman every night! I say enough is enough!"

Murmurs of agreement echoed off the ornate walls.

Then, from the back of the theatre, Roy's voice bellowed to the front.

"But what will you do when he finds out what you're planning?" Roy asked as he walked down the center aisle.

Stewart became speechless when he realized it was Roy. Behind him were Tom and Steve, and four other men had moved to the sides of the theatre to watch the parishioners, just in case someone wanted to be a hero.

Stewart remained motionless, his eyes on the Glock 9mm in Roy's hand. One of his men had found it on a dead cop's hip and had given it to Roy when they had returned from a supply run.

The weapon only held half a clip, but that was more than enough to keep the people in line.

"I asked you a question, Stewart: what would you do if I found out?"

Stewart's mouth opened and closed, but nothing came out. Reaching the podium, Roy stepped next to the man and put his arm around Stewart's shoulders.

"I'll tell you what you'd do, since you don't want to answer me. You'd take a walk upstairs with me." Roy leaned in close to Stewart and lowered his voice so only he could hear. "If you don't come with me, your wife and daughter will feed the zombies tonight."

Stewart looked down at his family in the front row. He knew that Roy would do it, too. He was that cold-hearted. Stewart nodded slightly and stepped away from the podium. Roy took his place.

"My friends, Stewart has just told me he was wrong and takes back everything he just said. Isn't that right, Stewart?" The frightened man nodded, his eyes never leaving his shoes.

Roy clapped his hands together "Excellent. Let this be a lesson to the rest of you. You never know where I'll be." Roy looked out at the faces of the men and women in the seats. "Now let's put this behind us and get back to work. Outside on the sidewalk are the supplies we found. Let's get them inside and inventoried." He snapped his fingers. "Tell you what. We found a case of peaches today; I want them opened up for dessert at supper. That'll be nice, won't it?"

The heads in the pews nodded politely and Roy smiled. They didn't have to like him, they just had to fear him.

"All right then. Stewart and I have a date upstairs, excuse us, all right?" Then he nodded to Tom who grabbed Stewart by his right arm and dragged him away. Stewart started to whimper as he looked at his family for the last time. His wife mouthed the words "I love you" with tears in her eyes, his children crying softly in her bosom, then he was through the curtain and being pushed up the stairs.

Roy and Steve followed and soon the four of them were standing over the balcony that looked down onto the courtyard. Roy opened the glass window and pulled Stewart out with him so that they were hovering over the ghouls below. Tom gripped the doomed man's arms so he couldn't try to run, while Steve stood nearby just in case.

Stewart was crying now, tears flowing down his cheeks unhindered. Roy relished the fear the man gave off.

"Oh, Stewart, relax, it won't be so bad. Just a few seconds of pain and then an eternity of blackness. Unless you believe in God. Then I guess you'll go to Heaven, or maybe Hell. I doubt that, though. Seems to me we're already in Hell."

Stewart was praying now, mumbling under his breath. He jerked and broke free of Tom and tried to make a run for it. Steve clubbed him over the head with the rifle as he passed. Stewart dropped to the floor like a sack of potatoes, dazed and confused.

Roy shook his head. "All right, enough of this shit. Toss that fucker in the yard and let's be done with it. After this, I don't think we'll have to worry about anyone else getting any ideas."

Steve nodded, and with Tom's help, they picked up the dazed man and carried him to the edge. The zombies moaned below, hands upraised, trying to reach the meat above them. Roy smiled. They wouldn't be disappointed, he thought.

With a heave, the men tossed Stewart out into the open air. He plunged like a rock to land on top of a zombie in a bloody tuxedo. The dead man was flattened by the weight of Stewart and both lay prone in the dirt.

Stewart's head popped up when he realized where he was. He heard shambling footsteps behind him and turned his head to see the horde of zombies charging, hands in front of them, fingers curling and uncurling, jaws gnashing empty air.

He screamed and tried to back away, but shrieked in pain and realized his left leg wouldn't' work. Looking down, he saw the white of bone sticking through his pants leg at his knee.

Scrambling on the ground with his one good leg, he desperately tried to escape the hungry undead. The ghouls fell on him, ravenous, ripping and biting through his clothes. He screamed with pain and he saw small pinpoints of fire as his synapses shut down, overloaded from the excruciating pain. Hands ripped his stomach open, pulling intestines out like a magician's scarf trick. Jaws ripped flesh away, leaving his arms connected by nothing but gristle. Legs were separated and taken away to be consumed.

Stewart disappeared a little at a time while Roy watched from above. Tom and Steve had to turn away, both looking like they were about to vomit.

Roy chuckled at that. "Pussies. And you call yourselves men. Go on, get out of here. We'll talk at supper."

Both men took off, each going a different direction. Roy looked down at the remains of another adversary. He would be very surprised if he'd get any more trouble from the parishioners. At least until some new asshole showed up and decided he didn't like the way Roy ran things.

Closing the window, Roy walked away. There were a few more

things to attend to before dinner. Like breaking in Stewart's pretty wife. There was a guard at the end of the hallway and Roy gave him instructions to fetch the woman. She would already be devastated from the loss of her husband. And now he would take her only minutes after his death, thus making his victory even sweeter.

With a smile of things to come, he headed for the stairs to finish supervising the organization of the supplies personally.

Eve sat in the fifth row of pews and watched Roy catch Stewart in his act of mutiny. Her stomach heaved when she saw Tom with him. She ducked down low, not wanting to be seen by the pig. Tom had taken a shine to her and he now raped her almost daily. She had learned to accept it. It wasn't as bad as the first time, but it was still rape.

His wife and daughter started to cry and her heart went out to them, but only so much. They were all suffering one way or another.

But the fact remained, it was moderately safe here in the church. Even the men were safe as long as they just obeyed Roy. True, he was an evil man, but he did feed them and he kept the zombies at bay. She sighed and crawled out of the pew, stepping on a few feet as she went. She apologized and went to help with the supplies.

One of her duties was to keep track of the food they had and how long it would last on a day to day basis. In the real world she'd been the secretary of an accountant, so Roy thought it only natural to put her in charge of counting and organizing.

Considering she'd have access to the food whenever she wanted, she had decided to just go with it and do what he asked. Joining the others by the doors of the church, she got to work while deep down in her head, she thought of ways to kill Tom.

But for now, all she could do was wait. Maybe in time someone would arrive and help her, help them all. She had to have hope. If she didn't, then she might as well jump off the balcony into the courtyard and end it now.

An old man handed her a case of beans and Eve wrote in her notebook, adding it to the list. She let her work distract her.

CHAPTER 24

Route 2 was a wasteland of shattered and broken automobiles.

Two miles out of the city, the road was choked on both sides with metal for as far as the eye could see. The highway was deathly quiet, the only sound breaking the stillness was the Taurus as it slowed to a stop, gravel crunching under the tires.

Paul parked the Taurus on the side of the rode out of force of habit and slammed the transmission into park.

"Will you look at that. There must be a thousand cars out here," he said, looking through the dirty windshield across the sea of metal.

"Must have been when everyone tried to evacuate the city," Adam said next to him.

"Maybe this is a bad idea," Josey said from the backseat. "What if there's nothing but dead people? We'll be overwhelmed in no time with no transportation."

"Look," Paul said, "we still don't know what's really happened, just what the news said before the power kicked out. Why don't we go, and if it looks bad then we'll just turn around and come back here."

"Where will we go then?" Josey asked.

Paul shrugged. "Honey, I have no idea. But before we go live in the mountains for the rest of our lives, I'd like to at least make sure civilization is screwed."

Adam sat next to Paul quietly, listening to his reasoning. It made a kind of sense. When they had saved Timmy and been out foraging, they'd only seen a handful of the undead.

Squeezing the grip on his .38, he set his jaw and looked at Paul. "Let's do it. If there are too many zombies, we can just blow them to Hell and retreat. They don't move fast, we should be able to outrun them easily."

"All right, that's my boy," Paul said, slapping him on the back.

"Come on, everyone, let's get the stuff out of the trunk and get moving. I want to be at the rescue station before it gets dark."

Everyone climbed out of the car and started to gather their gear. Paul slung the shotgun over his shoulder, carrying the rifle in his hand. Adam carried his .38, the weapon the only real thing he had left of his father. Josey carried the Glock that Paul had given her, the weapon light enough for her small hands to use.

Paul carried the extra ammunition as well as a few miscellaneous items in a small knapsack. Paul had given Adam a hunting knife, the seven inch blade a good weapon in an emergency. Paul carried one of his own an inch longer, strapped to his belt by a few laces of leather and it would slap against his thigh while he walked.

He didn't mind. Every time he'd feel it bounce off his leg, he felt more secure knowing it was there. Even Timmy carried a small knife Paul had given him, a Swiss Army knife. After showing Timmy how to open the small knife and the added extras, like the can opener and scissors, Paul had instructed him to put it away and leave it in his pocket.

Timmy had beamed with pride and happiness, feeling like one of the adults, and hid it away in one of his pockets.

Twenty minutes later they were walking up the middle of the highway, weaving in and out of the maze of iron. Almost all of the cars were empty, most with their doors still open and the keys in the ignition. The ones that weren't empty held dried corpses, dead for weeks.

"Looks like people just up and left," Adam said, shutting a mini-van door as he walked by it.

"Yeah, creepy isn't it? They must have just decided to walk." Paul said, kicking a soda can that lay in his path.

"But where did everyone go?" Josey asked. "And why did they try to get into the city?

"That's a good question. Some might have tried to get back, probably to get to loved ones. Others tried to get out and go to the suburbs," Paul suggested.

Paul slowed his pace as they walked by a station wagon similar to Carl's and glanced inside the interior. In the back seat of the abandoned vehicle, was a car seat and diaper bag. Otherwise the interior was empty. Paul caught a flash of red on the back seat and reached inside to see what it was. A choo-choo train lay on its side by the car seat, forgotten and discarded by the parents in their haste to leave.

"You want this?" he asked the boy, holding the train so Timmy could see it.

Timmy made a face like he'd eaten something sour. "No, I'm not a baby. That's for babies," he said disgusted.

"Timmy, that's not nice," Josey scolded him.

Timmy looked up at her, his face still sour. "Sorry, Auntie Josey, but it's true. I used to play with stuff like that when I was small, but I'm grown up now."

Paul chuckled at that. "All right, all right, it's fine. You don't have to take it if you don't want it." He chucked it back through the open window of the station wagon. The toy bounced off the seat and fell to the floor, forgotten once again.

"Come on, let's move. We've got a lot of ground to cover before dark," Paul said.

They started walking again, the sun high over their heads and only a few clouds to break the perfect blue. A crow hovered overhead, darting and soaring in the air currents. It banked to the right and dove earthward, disappearing amidst the cars littering the highway in front of them.

Adam slowed for a moment, raising his hand for the others to stop. "Wait, I thought I saw movement in that car up ahead."

Everyone stopped and waited, not seeing what Adam had. "Stay here with them," Adam told Paul. He began walking toward the supposed disturbance.

The car was five vehicles in front of him, and while he walked, his eyes swept the interiors of the other cars he passed. He half-expected something to jump out at him at any moment. He imagined claws and teeth ready to shred his flesh to the bone.

He slowed his walking and readied his weapon.

Adam saw movement again and raised the .38, but hesitated when a crow turned to look at him through the dirty glass, cawing at him noisily at its interrupted meal.

Adam stepped closer to see the desiccated corpse slumped against the driver's door of the car, now nothing more than a skeleton from being exposed to the elements. The crow was still trying to find a few tasty morsels. The corpse was still dressed in a business suit, a briefcase sitting on the next seat. A cell phone sat on the dash, part of its casing melted from the heat of the sun amplified through the glass. Letting out the breath he was holding, Adam turned to wave the others onward.

"It's okay, just a bird eating on a body. By the looks of it, it's been dead a long time."

The others started towards him, and he continued walking. There was a delivery truck on his left, taller then he was and when he walked by it, something grabbed his head and pull him down. The stench of rotten meat filled his nose and he gagged from the smell.

He looked up at the face of a dead man.

He screamed in shock, his eyes widening in horror as the pus covered head dove down at his exposed throat, blocking out the sunlight.

Adam could only scream louder.

CHAPTER 25

Paul saw Adam thrown to the tarmac and mounted by something. The thing had two arms, two legs and a head, but that was where the resemblance to anything human ended.

Paul brought his rifle to his shoulder and lined up the misshapen head of the ghoul. The shot was tough. The zombie's head moved around and Adam was trying to push the body off. Paul knew if he didn't take the shot, Adam was a goner, so with a silent prayer, he squeezed the trigger.

The bullet struck the ghoul in the neck, causing the body to lift up. Ignoring the shot, the animated corpse moved to dive back down and tear Adam's throat out.

Adam reached down for the hunting knife Paul had given him. He pulled the blade free of its sheath, and brought it around in an arc, jamming the knife into the zombie's ear.

The monster jerked and pinkish fluid dripped out around the blade as Adam forced it in. The zombie went slack, falling onto Adam and keeping him pinned to the street.

"Little help?" Adam called, sucking in a lungful of rank air. It was one of the sweetest breaths he'd taken in a long while, fetid corpse aroma or not.

Paul trotted up to him, slowing when he got close. After checking the surrounding vehicles for other dangers, alive or dead, he leaned down and pulled the corpse off Adam, who rolled to his side and vomited. The awful stench so close to his nose was too much for his stomach now that the danger had passed. Climbing to his feet, he wiped his mouth on the back of his sleeve and grinned at Paul.

"Thanks man, I owe you one."

Paul waved it off. "Don't worry about it. Just make sure you're there to return the favor."

"Done," Adam said, picking up his .38. He gave it a quick once over, satisfied that it wasn't damaged.

Josey and Timmy caught up quickly. "You all right, Adam?" Josey asked, patting him on his arm.

He nodded yes. "Yeah, I'll be fine. He just wanted to dance more than I did, that's all."

Paul climbed onto the hood of a beat-up Honda and looked over their route. They only had just over a mile to cover and should make it to the rescue station by nightfall. He slowly scanned the vehicles in front of him, looking for signs of movement.

Deciding the highway was empty; he hopped down to the asphalt with a slapping of boot soles.

"Looks clear up ahead, no movement. Guess you were just unlucky, running into this guy," Paul said, nudging the corpse with his foot.

"Yeah, that's me, Mister Unlucky. Come on, let's go. I don't think I want to hang around here." He turned and started up the highway, more aware of his surroundings.

The group of four made slow progress. On both sides of the highway, and especially outside the guard rail, the land sloped down into a gulley. Even if they'd wanted to, they couldn't use it to travel. The terrain was way too uneven and loose, a sprained ankle waiting to happen. The only way into the city was by the highway.

The sun had reached its zenith and was starting to descend when the group finally made it to the city limits.

"My feet hurt, I want to sit down," Timmy said from the middle of the group.

Paul turned and looked at the boy. He was moving like he was on automatic, face slack from exhaustion. It had been a hard walk. Stressful. Every time they had come up to a large bus or delivery truck, they had to make sure what happened to Adam didn't happen again.

Adam turned to see the boy dragging and stopped walking, waiting for him to catch up. When he had, Adam crouched down so his face was even with Timmy's.

"Tired, huh?" Adam asked, with an easy grin.

Timmy nodded. "Yeah, my feet are killing me. I want to take a rest. I'm hungry, too."

Adam thought it over and then his eyes lit up with an idea. "What about if I carry you for a while? Could we keep going then?"

Timmy's face seemed to relax a little. "You mean like a piggy back ride?"

Adam nodded. "Uh-huh, exactly."

He turned around so Timmy could hop on his back. Timmy didn't hesitate, jumping onto Adam like a monkey, making him stumble a bit. Once he got his hands under Timmy's legs and shifted the boy's weight he started walking again.

When he caught up to Paul, he nudged him with an elbow. "Hey, I can't shoot like this. Keep a lookout, okay?"

Paul grimaced. "What the hell do you think I've been doing all day, watching for the red-breasted robin?" With a frown he moved ahead, giving Adam his back.

Josey caught up with Adam and smiled. "Don't worry about him, Adam. I've been married to him for twelve years and I know him. When he gets tired, he gets grouchy."

Adam looked at Paul's back and then Josey. "Shit, Josey, I'm tired, too. We all are. No reason to be a dick."

She nodded. "Once we stop to rest he'll be better. You'll see." With a smile to Timmy, she sped up to walk with her husband. On reaching him, she slid her arm into his and for a moment it looked like he was going to shrug her off, but Josey gave him a look that no man would say no to, and gave in. The two walked hand in hand down the abandoned highway with Adam and Timmy bringing up the rear.

The skyline of the city was ahead, the outline of the buildings looking like cubist mountain ranges.

Thin columns of smoke came from a few of the shorter buildings, definite signs of life. Others had shattered windows as high up as the twentieth floor. With the sun reflecting off the other buildings' glass eyes, the ones that gave off no reflection stuck out the most. They were black holes that absorbed the sunlight, cavern mouths on the face of a mountain.

An hour later they reached the end of the highway, the road splintering to carry commuters to different areas of the city while the main highway continued through the middle to points south. So far there had been no sign of people, living or dead, and the city loomed over them, smothering with its silence.

A group of pigeons took wing when the survivors walked off the highway ,their wings flapping in harmony as they flew off as one.

Staying in the middle of the street, the group continued onward. Now buildings were on either side of them and the feeling of being watched settled in, making the backs of their necks tingle.

Paul pointed to a side street. "If we go down there and take a right, that will bring us to the football stadium where they set up the rescue station," he whispered.

Both Adam and Josey nodded, following him.

Passing the mouth of an alley, they saw figures in the shadows. The group started to jog, exhaustion forgotten, nearby danger acting as fuel for aching muscles.

Something banged behind them and Adam turned quickly, looking for it. A soda can rolled across the street.

The wind maybe? He shrugged.

Ten slow and watchful minutes later, they reached the stadium. Blocking the street were two National Guard trucks with a military Hummer on the sidewalk. The trucks were parked at an angle to each other and the doors were wide open.

Paul moved closer while Adam set Timmy down. They had no idea what was going to happen and he wanted his hands free.

Paul climbed up into the first truck, checking the inside. He moved around to the back and saw crates of supplies, mostly ammunition and first aid gear. He looked around for food and found none. He jumped down and walked back to the others.

"Not much in there. There's ammo, but not for anything we're carrying."

"Any food? Or, I dunno . . . dancing girls?" Adam asked.

Paul shook his head. "Could check the other truck, but . . . " he left the rest hanging while he looked around. "I doubt it. Looks like a ghost town."

Adam glanced around him, not happy out in the open. "Well, let's keep going. Maybe there's someone in the camp, but if they left the trucks unmanned, it doesn't look too good," Adam said.

One at a time, they climbed over the bumpers of the trucks and filed down the street. In front of them was the football stadium, gates hanging wide open, the field full of large tents. Next to it was the high school. The large two-level brick structure stood quiet as they made their way toward the tents.

Nothing moved as they made their way closer. The silence was thick, heavy. When they got closer, they saw dozens of shapes spread out on the denuded football field.

Adam put his hand to his mouth. He could see they were bodies. Hundreds of bodies, spread out on the torn up grass and churned soil, all silent and unmoving. Some wore green Army uniforms.

"What happened here?" Josey whispered, surveying the carnage.

"Now that's a good question," Paul answered, scanning the unmoving forms. He kept expecting them to jump up and attack, but all was quiet.

Dead.

Paul stepped quietly between the gates. He spotted a shallow ravine at the end and a bulldozer sitting by itself, abandoned. He turned toward it, the others following. Timmy was as close to Josey as he could get. She rubbed his hair and whispered to him things would be fine. The boy tried to keep his eyes closed, not wanting to see all the field of death. Adam saw this and frowned, wishing the boy didn't have to be a witness to all of this.

Paul stalked up to the edge of the shallow ravine and looked down into what could only be called a death pit. Hundreds of bodies lay in distorted positions in the five foot wide tear in the earth, thrown there like garbage. The drone of buzzing insects filled the area, rats scurrying around the bodies, feasting on this hideous horn o'plenty.

Paul looked over the lip into the bottom of the ravine and saw it was partly full of water. Green slime that spread over every inch of the pool's surface, broken here and there by limbs. Flies were everywhere, laying eggs and feeding on the corpses.

The smell was unbearable.

Paul caught movement. He turned and saw that some of the bloated corpses still moved. Dazed, he was about to climb down and help the wounded . Adam grabbed his arm and held on strong.

"Paul, don't. Take a closer look," Adam said, pointing to the bodies.

Paul stopped and looked again. This time he studied the faces more carefully and saw they were all slack-jawed and vacant. Eyes were milky white and no sounds came out of the pit but guttural moans. These weren't survivors from the camp. They were trapped in the pit by their shattered limbs. All they could do was moan and twitch. Their days of feeding were over.

Paul walked away from the edge, kneeling down and lowering his head. "What the hell happened here? All those dead people. Jesus Christ, it must have been horrible."

"You don't know the half of it friend," said a voice from behind the bulldozer.

Paul and Adam turned as one and swung their weapons up at the bulldozer. The man there had both his arms out to his sides and empty as he walked closer. In his front waistband was some a pistol, but Paul couldn't make out what it was. The man continued closer, not minding the two guns aimed at him. An M-16 was slung over his shoulder.

He was a pudgy man in his late forties or early fifties. He wore a Yankees baseball cap on over a mustache out of the Old West. Below that, the man's yellow teeth stood out as he smiled at the three adults and child.

Six feet from the group, he stopped. He reached into the chest pocket of the coveralls he wore. Adam and Paul tensed, but the man pulled out a small package of tobacco. They kept their weapons up.

The man pulled a pinch from the package and then tucked it under his lip. He spit into the mud at his feet.

"Hi, my name's Johnson. Peter Johnson. You mind telling me what the hell you people are doing here?"

Paul blinked at the man, not believing what he'd just heard, like they were trespassing or something. "Motherfucker," he said under his breath.

Josey walked up and held out her hand.

"Hello, I'm Josey Walker and this is my husband, Paul. That's Adam and this here's Timmy," she finished, rubbing Timmy's shoulder.

Peter looked down at Timmy and smiled, his teeth now stained brown from the chew. "Howdy, Timmy, it's nice to meet you."

Timmy waved slightly and moved closer to Josey. She shrugged at Peter and smiled apologetically.

"Sorry, he's shy."

Peter nodded, "Yup, don't blame him really. This is a dangerous place to be. You people need to get out of here."

"Dangerous?" Adam asked. He'd lowered the revolver, not realizing it. The man seemed harmless.

Peter looked up at the setting sun. "Too late for that," he said, pointing. "Once the sun goes down they come out in force. Guess they don't like it much."

"That's bullshit. We've seen them out during the day," Paul snapped.

Peter nodded. "Sure you have. Some go out, but most of them wait for nightfall. One of the doctors that was here before everything fell apart said it had something to do with the sensitivity to the light. The dead can't focus their pupils like you or me so they like the darkness better."

"If I may ask, what are you still doing here if it's so dangerous?" Josey asked.

Peter spit out a brown glob of chew again and scratched his head, taking off his baseball cap to show a head that was quickly losing ground against baldness. Placing the cap carefully back on his head, he looked at them all.

"That's a long story, and this isn't the place to tell it. Look, I can't invite you to stay long-term, I don't have the food. I do have the room though, so I can offer you shelter for the night. But in the morning . . ." He left it at that.

Paul nodded understanding and finally lowered his rifle.

"Thanks, Peter. That would be great and we have our own supplies. In fact, we'll be happy to share them in," Paul said.

Peter shifted his stance in the mud, looking around, checking to make sure it was clear.

"Well, I don't think that'll be necessary, but let's worry about that later. Come on then, follow me. I've got a place inside the school.." He spit into the mud a final time, turned and began walking toward the school. Adam looked to Paul and Josey, waiting to see what was next. It was Josey who started first, following the man's footsteps in the mud, Timmy at her side.

Paul gave Adam his patented shrug. "Where else are we gonna go?"

Adam grunted and started walking, his boots sinking into the mud. "I guess, After what he said, I really don't want to be out here when the sun goes down. I doubt they have cable, though"

Paul chuckled, "Amen, brother. Amen."

Picking up their pace the friends caught up with Josey and followed Peter off the field. Behind them, the flies continued to feed in the mass grave.

Deep in the bowels of the city, the dead were coming out of their hiding places, their wails echoing among the empty buildings. The sound was one of desperate hunger.

Paul, Adam and Josey all heard waking dead and quickly picked up their pace. The sooner they were under cover and behind locked doors, the better.

CHAPTER 26

Peter led the survivors through the fire doors at the north side of the school. Once everyone was inside, he closed the door, making sure to hear the click of the latch catching. Satisfied the door was secure, he waved them on and started down the long, open hallway.

Footsteps echoed off the ceramic tile walls as they moved down the corridor. Glass cases showed upcoming school events that would never be held. A banner reading *GO WILDCATS* hung over the opening to the gym, and beneath it pamphlets listing the schools basketball schedule littered the floor. On the wall near the end of the hallway hung pictures drawn by younger students, the stick figures and box homes sitting under round suns rendered in heartbreaking crayon.

Peter strolled through the open door of the gym and stopped. The group stopped behind him, waiting to see what was next.

Peter pointed to the middle of the gym at a large campfire and scattered bedrolls. Two people were at the circle, one woman and an old man.

At the sound of their footsteps, the old man and woman looked up. They waited patiently while Peter escorted the group to the circle.

"Ellie, I found some more people wandering outside. Figured I'd bring them back with me," Peter said to the woman.

Ellie moved away from the cook fire, wiped her hand on the dirty apron she was wearing and held it out for each one of the group. After introductions were made, she turned and started working again. The old man ignored them.

A five-gallon kettle hung over the fire by metal poles lashed together with steel wire. Soup was simmering, the smell enough to make the survivor's stomachs rumble. A long piece of heating duct had been hung down from the ceiling, the smoke and fumes from the fire flowing up and out into the crude exhaust vent. Paul marveled at their ingenuity.

"I'm hungry," Timmy said, smelling the food.

Josey shushed him. "Hush, Timmy, we'll eat when it's time."

Peter laughed. "That's all right. I reckon we can bend our routine a bit." He leaned down and looked Timmy in the eye. "I doubt he'll take that long to eat."

Josey was looking around the room, looking at the doorways at the ends of the gymnasium. Peter noticed her curiosity and asked her. "Something wrong, ma'am?"

"No, but I was wondering about the bathroom. With everything that's happened since we headed out this morning, I never had a chance to, uhm, you know."

Ellie spoke up. "I know what you mean, hun'. These men just whip it out whenever they want. They have no idea what it's like for us girls." She pointed to a door on the other side of the gym. "That's the bathroom. We got running water and soap if you want to clean up."

Josey's face brightened. "Really? Running water?"

Peter nodded. "Yup. We lost power, but the waters still running. So far, anyway. It might be just what's left in the pipes, but one can hope."

Josey looked down at Timmy. "Come on, Timmy, you're coming with me. You could use a good washing up," she said, pulling the child by his sleeve.

"Aww, I hate baths," Timmy protested. But he was no match for Josey and as she dragged him across the gym he soon gave in and walked.

Peter held his hand out to the chairs around the fire.

"Have a seat, gents, rest a while. If you want to trade for some food, I'm sure we can accommodate you. Food's been scarce. Supermarkets and corner stores have already been looted, but we're managing."

Two men walked through the doors at the front of the gym. Adam and Paul watched them as they strode over the scuffed Parquet floor. They wore dirty clothes and dirtier faces. It looked like they hadn't bathed in weeks.

Peter smiled at the sight of them and waved them over.

"Ah, my boys are back.. Paul, Adam, these are my sons, Will and John." Peter looked at his sons. "Boys, these are some friends, Paul and Adam."

Both young men grunted a hello and then slumped down onto chairs. Paul looked hard at their M-16s.

Peter saw Paul checking out the rifles and grinned. "You like them,

Paul? We found them after all the Guardsmen left. Most of them were slaughtered, the rest grabbed what they could and retreated. Don't know where to, but they left us some goodies."

Ellie was ladling soup into cracked ceramic bowls. Steam rose from each bowl, the fragrance of the contents making Paul's stomach rumble harder. She was picky with the contents of the guest's stew, only picking choice bits of meat from the kettle. Paul noticed but didn't care.

Adam took his bowl with a smile, licking his lips. The soup was piping hot and Adam blew on it. Ellie handed them spoons.

While Paul waited for his food to cool, he watched Ellie work. She was in her mid-forties, her figure good, but not a perfect ten. Still, Paul couldn't help but admire the female form.

Ellie was off to the side of the fire, taking something out of a galvanized bucket. She noticed Paul looking and quickly covered the bucket again. Then she moved back to stirring the stew.

Paul sat there watching her, something itching at the back of his head, but he just couldn't put his finger on it. He stood up and walked over to the stew, examining it more closely. Peter tensed in his chair.

Paul picked up the ladle and placed it into the stew. A few vegetables floated on top and the stew was filmed, greasy. He stirred the pot and he felt something hard at the bottom. Prying up with the ladle, he brought up a bone.

It broke the surface of the stew and Paul's breath caught in his throat. Floating in the middle of the stew was a human femur. A hand popped up, a silver ring still on the second finger. He dropped the ladle and turned away.

Adam was still holding his first spoonful of stew to his nose, waiting for it to cool and savoring the aroma. Paul dropped the ladle and yelled at Adam. "Oh, Jesus, Adam, don't!"

Adam snapped to attention, confused.

Peter and his sons drew their guns, and before Paul or Adam could do more than blink, they had weapons trained on them.

The old man near Paul calmly pulled an old revolver from the inside of his jacket, his toothless smile covering his face from ear to ear, a few cackles and chuckles escaping his dry and cracked lips.

Peter shook his head. "Well, looks like you found out our little secret. That's too bad. We could've just kilt you in your sleep tonight, nice and peaceful. Hell, you probably wouldn't have felt anything. Now we gotta do it the hard way. Both of you, go over there by the fire, and no sudden moves."

Adam stood up and followed Paul. Adam's revolver was still on the floor by his seat and Paul's shotgun and rifle were leaning against his chair. Their weapons were only a few feet away, but it might was well have been miles.

One of the sons spoke up. "What are we gonna do with them, Dad? We gonna kill them here?"

Peter shook his head. "No, we'll take them to the cafeteria. There's a drain there. Once we cut 'em up, clean 'em, then we'll bring 'em back here."

Adam looked at Peter, then at Paul, then at Peter again.

"Will someone tell me what the fuck is going on?"

Paul gestured with his chin to the kettle still simmering over the fire. "The stew has got human parts in it. They're fucking cannibals!" Paul spit.

Peter shouted, angry. "Don't you fucking judge us, you prick! We were starving and the place was picked clean. The goddamn Guard left and took everything with them. The school cafeteria stockrooms were empty and we were starving. I don't know about you, but I don't see any apple trees in the city. We did what we had to do to survive." Peter's eyes seemed to flare with just a touch of madness. "And guess what? Once we tried it, we decided it wasn't half bad. You know that joke, it tastes like chicken? Well, they're wrong. Tastes more like rabbit."

The two sons and the old man chuckled at that. Paul didn't know if he wanted to heave or go crazy.

Peter pointed to the doors leading out of the gym. "Boys, take them to the kitchen. I'll be there in a minute. We'll gut them and hang them to smoke."

One second, John was grinning and gesturing for the two men to get moving, the next his head was exploding into a hundred shards and blood was spraying across the bedrolls on the floor, a gunshot echoing in the gym.

For one-half of one heartbeat everyone stood perfectly still. Paul turned and picked the kettle up, his skin searing to the sides of the kettle. He swung back around and threw the contents at Peter. The man put up his hands to protect his face, but the steaming liquid passed over and through them. Peter let out a shriek that shook the rafters.

Adam pulled his hunting knife from his waist and hurled it at Will, the blade spinning in the air. The heavy pommel cracked his nose, and Will squeezed the trigger of the M-16 while it was pointed at the old man. The bullets stitched him from waist to neck and he fell over dead, landing in a heap on the floor.

Adam leaped for his revolver, hitting the floor hard. His breath knocked out, he rolled over and sent a round through Will's chest. The bullet pulverized the man's heart, shredding muscle severing spine. He was dead before he fell.

Ellie, ignored, leaned over and threw away a blanket to reveal another M-16 under the heavy cloth. She picked it up and aimed at Paul's back, ready to revenge her husband.

A black hole appeared in her forehead. She stood there for a moment, rifle in hand, looking as if she would squeeze the trigger, but then her knees crumpled and she fell face-down into the fire.

Breathing heavily, Paul dropped the kettle. His hands were killing him, the flesh burned and raw.

Adam was looking around, searching out targets, still with no idea what had just happened. Paul looked across the gym to see Josey standing at the bathroom door, gun in hand and Timmy behind her. He waved to her, signaling that it was all clear. Taking Timmy by the hand, she started across the gym, the barrel of her Glock still smoking in her hand.

Paul looked over at Peter. The man was rolling around on the floor, mewling in agony. Paul reached down and pulled the man's hands from his face. Peter stared back with eyes that were now pure white. They looked like two small eggs had been jammed into the sockets in place of his eyes.

"Oh, Jesus Christ, you fucks. I'll kill you, you bastards!" he yelled across the gym.

Paul kicked the man in the stomach and the swearing stopped.

"Shut the fuck up, you piece of shit, before I put a bullet in your head," Paul said, very quietly. He saw Timmy standing with Josey.

Paul pointed to Ellie, still burning in the camp fire. "Adam, pull her out of there and put her out, will you?"

Adam did as requested, holding his nose as he did it. When she was out of the flames, he threw a blanket over the blackened and charred corpse and stepped away.

Adam looked over at Paul. "What are we gonna do with him?" he asked, pointing at Peter.

Paul stared down at the man who had just tried to kill him and his family. Then his eyebrows went up a little as an idea hit him.

He looked at both Josey and Adam and smiled malevolently. "We'll give him what he deserves."

The sun had set and darkness suffused every corner of the school-yard. With the city power out and no lights to compete, the stars sparkled from above, looking like a twinkling canvas of fireflies. The outline of the city's buildings only just stood out against the night sky.

The doors to the north side of the school flew open. From the dark hole, a figure flew and hit the landing, rolled down the stone steps. His hands came out in front of him to break his fall, managing only to break two fingers. The soft snap of bone carried only as far as his own ears.

The school doors slammed shut, leaving him all alone in the darkened lot. Not that it mattered. Peter would forever be surrounded by night. He was blind, his eyes scalded beyond repair.

Peter turned around and climbed the stairs with his hands held out, tripping in his haste. His broken fingers throbbed, but he was too angry to feel it. He punched and kicked at the door, and when he'd worn himself out he cursed at it until he was hoarse.

It was useless. Peter slumped to the landing and wept. It had all fallen apart in one night. His family was dead and he was blind.

An hour passed and the man finally stood up. Revenge—living long enough to get it—was the only thing on his mind.

He stumbled back down the steps and stood quiet for a moment, listening. Now bereft of eyes, he was much more aware of sounds. He started walking, unsure where he was going. His foot bumped something and he bent over to feel what it was. His hands ran over what felt like a long pipe, perhaps from the end of the chain-link fence that surrounded the parking lot.

He picked it up for a walking stick.

Peter didn't want to get lost. He thought about the school. Perhaps he could find another opening and sneak back in? Paul and Adam had just got there, and they didn't know the school like he did.

He started off towards the back of the school, as best as he could tell, careful not to tap the wall and give himself away. In two minutes he was hopelessly lost. He continued moving, the pipe tapping his way down what he figured to be the street.

Peter continued into the city, oblivious. He stopped when he heard something scraping off to his right. His head turned that way and he strained to catch the sound again. He heard it again, more scraping . . . or was it shuffling?

His heartbeat pounded in his ears, breath rasping in and out of his throat.

The scent of decay. Rotten meat left out in the sun too long. Road kill lying on the hot asphalt on a summer day.

His head darted from left to right as he tried to hear what was happening. He couldn't make anything out. Every bump became a footstep, the breeze a cold breath on the back of his neck.

Panicking, he started to swing the pipe around him, hoping to hit something, anything.

"Stay the fuck back, I'm warning you!" he yelled. The city remained silent.

He started to back up, hoping to retrace his steps and escape from whatever danger he had walked into. He hadn't taken more than four steps backward when he came up against something.

The redolence of death became stronger. On all sides, he could now hear a soft shuffling sound. A sound of leather rubbing against leather came to him, making him think of when his sons would wear corduroy pants to school. Thinking of his sons and his wife sent a wave of grief over him, causing him to lose focus for a moment.

The smell grew worse and the sound grew louder, and he swung his head from side to side, trying to pinpoint the source of the noise. But it didn't matter. He was blind and whatever was happening could be happening no more than an inch from his face.

He fell to his knees and cried, accepting his hopelessness. He should have begged Paul to put a bullet in his head.

At least it would have been quick.

The pipe fell from lifeless fingers, the metal clanging loudly, and rolled away.

As the ghouls surrounded him, he kept his head low. Only a few tears managed their way from his seared tear ducts and he marveled at how they stung his scalded, tender cheeks.

Peter's screams filled the street as the dead swarmed him. They echoed off the giant obelisks and then faded away forever.

Minutes passed and the screams finally stopped, replaced by the infinite stillness of night.

The doors to the school were open again and Paul stood there, listening to the screams. His jaw was taut but there was no emotion in his eyes. He waited, cleaning his eyeglasses on his shirt. His hands were covered in white bandages, spots of red seeping through the material.

Once the screams faded away to nothing, he stepped back and closed the doors again. One soft click and silence again reigned supreme.

CHAPTER 27

Eve stood in the bell tower and studied the landscape below, her blonde hair blowing in the wind. Her left thumb idly turned the silver ring on her finger. Tom had given it to her, made her wear it. It was his way of claiming her. Every second she wore it, her hand felt like it was on fire. She wanted to throw it off the tower and be rid of it, but she knew that as soon as she did, she may as well leap after it. She was stuck with the ring and the pig who gave it to her.

The few streets she could see that bordered the church property were devoid of life or movement. More than two dozen crumpled and bloated forms lay here and there across the sidewalks. All of them had been cut down by Roy or his henchmen on one of their outings.

The sun was just starting to set, the crimson sky reminding her of diluted blood. A cold breeze blew from the north, making her shiver in her light cotton dress.

She stood silently, watching the area below. Someone seeing her from a nearby building may have been reminded of a woman waiting for her mariner husband to return from the sea, but that would be the furthest thing from the truth.

She was waiting for someone, but not with any kind of hope that they would return. Quite the opposite. She prayed with every fiber of her being that the foraging party would never return.

The minutes crept by and darkness lay its cloak on the city. Below her, the undead came out of their holes to search for food.

The daytime belonged to the humans now, the zombies shying away from direct sunlight. The foraging teams would leave at sunrise and return by sunset, usually with a truck-bed full of food and water.

The city was deserted, with the exception of a few isolated enclaves in buildings on the other side of the vast metropolis. Roy had already given an inkling of his plans for these other survivors. When he had enough men, he wanted to find these groups and absorb them into his flock.

Eve knew it wouldn't be enough to make the man happy. He was a greedy, evil, man who would always want more, no matter how much he was able to gather and hold.

A scream sounded from somewhere deep inside the city as the undead found another soul to claim as one of their own. The scream was faint, probably more than a mile away, only the emptiness of the streets allowing the sound to carry to her at all. She said a soft prayer for the poor soul who was probably by now beyond caring.

She looked down at her hands. Once soft and smooth, they were now scraped and callused from the manual labor she'd been conscripted to. She wasn't alone in that. All the other people who were once "parishioners," now nothing more than prisoners that had to work hard if they wanted to live. Everything had to be done by hand. Thankfully, one of the supply runs brought back some hand-powered tools, like a washboard with wringer for laundry, and an old sewing machine operated by foot pedals.

She looked up at the sound of an engine. A large Suburban had appeared. It was speeding up the street like the demons of Hell were on its tail. She knew why they were rushing. If the team didn't unload and get inside the chain-link barricade before the undead appeared, they would be trapped outside its protection until morning.

A zombie stumbled into the road with hands spread wide. The SUV never slowed. The front grill struck the animated corpse dead center. The impact ripped the head from the torso, pieces flying in opposite directions. A few splotches of red covered the windshield from the destruction of the corpse. The SUV's windshield wipers came on and it and continued moving.

Eve saw the SUV screech to a halt in front of the church. Two men jumped out of the back and two came out of the front. Their movements were frantic and uncoordinated as panic gnawed at them.

While they were offloading cardboard boxes the doors to the church were flung wide, so hard they struck the sides of the church loudly.

Roy strode down the stairs, followed by three more men and a woman. Her name was Kate and she was as hard as any one of the men surrounding her. When she had first arrived, one of them had tried to rape her. Roy had watched and laughed as she was dragged to the back of the church.

Less than two minutes later a shriek came from back there. Then the man came running out, cradling his broken arm against his body. He was bleeding from the side of his head where his left ear was flapping. When Kate had stepped out from the back, she had something red between her teeth.

She walked up the center aisle and stopped in front of Roy. She spit out the piece of ear at Roy's feet. Roy looked at Kate, her mouth and chin covered in blood, and let out a laugh that had given everybody chills.

Since that day, she had been by Roy's side, his new right hand woman. Eve knew that Tom wasn't pleased to have been replaced by Kate, and that little nugget of information filled her with pleasure.

Eve watched Roy and his men spread out and open the makeshift gate. With controlled chaos the supplies were transferred to inside the fence. A few of the undead had ventured near the SUV and a couple of well placed shots disposed of them.

When the supplies were finally offloaded the SUV was driven around the side of the church. There was a rope ladder hanging from a side window. Once the driver had secured the vehicle, he would climb up through the sunroof of the SUV and climb the rope to safety. It had worked well so far and they had suffered no casualties.

Eve watched Tom moving about down below. He'd been one of the men that had just returned and her heart sank when she saw he was unharmed. She wanted nothing more than to see the man ripped to pieces by an army of the undead. The man had taken to raping her every night as and every day,. In his eyes, she was his property for life and he could do what he liked with her, whenever he wanted to. He had even inferred that he might start loaning her out to some of the other men for barter.

While she was looking down below at the flutter of activity, Tom turned his head up and saw her. For one brief moment their eyes locked and Tom blew her a kiss. He gave her a smile that told her what he had planned.

Fighting off a shiver, she stepped away from the edge of the tower and started back down the long, winding metal stairs. She would be needed to help inventory the new supplies and she knew what would happen if she displeased Roy.

With only the faintest spark of hope still burning in her chest that she and the others would be saved, she continued downward, her footsteps reverberating in the confines of the stone hall, sounding to her like her own broken heartbeat echoing off the walls.

CHAPTER 28

Paul walked into the gymnasium, his boots barely making a sound.

He stopped and looked down at the campfire. It was still burning, even after the crone fell into it. The flames crackled, the wood popped and hissed.

Josey and Adam were watching Paul, waiting for him to say something. More than thirty seconds of dead silence went by until Paul spoke.

"It's done. I heard his screams," he said quietly.

Josey moved next to her husband and hugged him. Paul stood perfectly still, not reciprocating. Josey squeezed harder and held out her hand for Timmy to come into the embrace. The boy had been standing out of the way, crying silently. Now he started to sob, running into Josey's open arms. The three of them stood very still. Over a minute passed and then Paul's shoulder slumped and he gave in. He hugged his wife and let out a deep sigh.

"Oh my God, Josey, what have I become?" he asked softly.

Josey shook her head against his shoulder. "You're still the same man I fell in love with all those years ago. You did what had to be done. He was an animal, he deserved what he got," she said.

She pushed away from him and looked over her shoulder at Adam. Adam was standing there, feeling like a fifth wheel, not quite knowing what to do.

Josey separated herself from Paul and walked over to Adam. She hugged him too and kissed him on the cheek.

"You okay?" she asked him.

Adam smiled, half-heartedly. "Yeah, I'm fine. It's just that happened so damn quick, you know? I mean, one second we were eating with some new friends and the next one of them gets his head blown off and I'm fighting for my life." He moved closer to Paul, until he was no more than a foot from him.

"Paul, since I started hanging out with you, my life has sure gotten more interesting."

Adam said the last sentence with such sincerity that Paul started to chuckle. Chuckles became giggles. Paul bent over and started laughing so hard spittle fell from his mouth. Josey caught it as well and soon was laughing, too. Timmy didn't get what was happening, but joined in and was soon laughing alongside the adults.

The three of them stood around Adam, laughing up a storm, releasing their pent up worries. While they laughed and clapped their hands, enjoying the release, Adam stood watching them, dumbfounded.

His mouth went down into a frown and he scratched his head and said, "What'd I say?"

That only got him more laughter and he frowned, for the life of him just not getting what was so fucking funny.

When everyone had calmed down and the laughter had dwindled to slight titters, they got to work cleaning up the gym. Adam and Paul dragged the bodies out of the gym and left them in a side hall. They weren't worried about disposing of the corpses, as in the morning they'd be leaving. Paul grimaced every time he had to use his hands and the white bandages were slowly turning a dark red. Adam saw this and nodded at them.

"Hurts?"

Paul snickered. "Like a motherfucker. I need to change the bandages." The two walked back to the campfire and Paul called to Josey. "Hey, honey, we need to change my hands again."

She frowned. "What did I tell you about that? You need to rest so they can heal," she said, exasperated.

He just smiled and gave her a puppy dog look. "Sorry, but there's things to do."

She shook her head. "That's no excuse. We need you fit when we leave here. Come on, let's go," she said walking away.

Paul followed and then called to Timmy. "Hey kid, you want to keep us company?"

Timmy looked at Paul and then turned away. "No, I'm good, I want to stay with Adam and help him clean up."

"Suit yourself," Paul said and walked away, his boot steps echoing off the polished wood floors.

While Paul and Josey went to the nurse's office to wrap his hands again, Adam continued cleaning up the gym. All he was doing was throwing blankets and other articles of clothing onto the messes, figuring that would be good enough for one night.

Once he was done with that, he took all their stuff—and some of the cleaner blankets that hadn't been splattered with blood—and moved everything across the gym. Timmy helped carry items closer to the door where they'd entered.

The two didn't talk much, but just concentrated on the work at hand.

Finally, once all the packs and blankets were laid out, Adam sat down in one of the chairs. "God, that feels good," he said, stretching his legs out in front of him. Timmy stood next to him, grinning.

Adam looked back. "What's so funny?"

"That you're tired. It's because you're old, isn't it. Old people get tired quicker then young people like me."

Adam's eyes opened a little more. "Oh, really, you think I'm old. Tell me, Timmy, just how old do you think I am?"

Timmy's brow furrowed in concentration as if he was trying to figure out the meaning of life, then he grinned. "I don't know, twenty-five?"

"Twenty five? Jesus kid, I'm only eighteen. Now you want to know who's old? Paul is old. He's in his *forties*."

Timmy took a step back. "Wow, now that's old. I can't believe he can still walk! His bones must be so tired."

Paul and Josey arrived unannounced. Paul scanned the faces of Adam and Timmy. "I thought I heard my name. What were you guys talking about?"

Adam and Timmy looked at each other and they both burst out laughing. Josey had caught the tail end of the conversation and squeezed her husband's shoulder. "They think you're old, dear," she said.

Paul's face lit up with surprise. "Oh, really? Well, I guess I am." He sat down on one of the chairs and stretched out. "I'm going to sit right here while Adam makes me dinner. Us old timers need our rest." Then he closed his eyes and relaxed, finished working.

Adam sighed and stood up. "All right, fine. But you owe me."

Paul answered by pretending he was snoring. As the minutes went by, Paul relaxed some more and before he knew it, he was drifting off into a nap, his hands throbbing in the background of his slumber.

⋯•◦●◦•⋯

For the rest of the night they relaxed. They ate, they drank deeply from the schools still-flowing tap. Secure in the gymnasium, they all went to sleep at the same time, figuring no watch was needed.

The next morning Paul's hands hurt like hell and they decided to stay in the school one more day. They spent the day exploring, but quickly found that the entire building had been cleaned out. All the extras from the nurse's office were quickly packed away for future use, including all the bandages they could find.

Luckily, there were two bottles of aspirin in one of the bottom drawers of a cabinet, which Paul pocketed immediately after taking four pills in one swallow.

Adam found the supply locker for the gym and took out a basketball. At the other end of the gym, away from the bloody blankets and spilled human stew, the four of them played and enjoyed just being able to run and jump. After the cramped space of Paul's cellar, the school was like a castle. Unfortunately, there was still no food, so no matter what had happened or how safe they were, they knew they would have to move on.

The second night Paul and Josey snuck off to have some alone time. While they were gone, Timmy read by the light of a candle from a book he'd found in a classroom.

The book was about Vincent Van Gogh, a famous painter who lived in the 1800's. Timmy didn't know who he was, but the book had lots of pictures he could look at. Adam laid back and listened while Timmy wove a tale of the painter and described some of the paintings in the book.

The second book was more fun. It was about a world of dragons and black knights and warriors who battled both.

When the child was finished with the second book, Adam sat up and saw that Timmy's eyes were heavy.

"Come on, kid, time for bed," Adam said.

"Oh, man, I don't believe it. Even with monsters everywhere I still have a bedtime. It's no fair," he whined.

Adam chuckled. "Timmy, let me share something with you. Whether there are monsters running around or just plain regular people like you and me, life is never fair. The trick is to bend the cards in your favor."

162

Adam stopped talking, realizing Timmy had all ready drifted off to sleep. Adam leaned back. Making sure both his revolver and his newly-acquired M-16 were next to him, he closed his eyes and let sleep take him.

Adam dreamed again this night, Timmy's second story in the forefront of his mind. His dreams were of castles and knights and fair-haired maidens that needed to be rescued by him as he rode on his white stallion. Images of dragons to be slain and empires to build floated across his mind, keeping at bay the demons and monsters who wanted to rise and fill him with dread.

He slept so soundly, he didn't wake when Paul and Josey returned. They curled up together and fell asleep quickly, both tired and sweaty from their exertions.

That night, the four survivors slept easy in the empty school, while in the streets surrounding, the dead walked, hunting for prey and ruling the night.

CHAPTER 29

Timmy was gently shaking Adam, but the older boy wouldn't wake. Timmy frowned, not pleased that he wouldn't get up, so he stood up and walked over to Josey.

"Auntie Josey, could I have some water, please?" Josey nodded and poured him a half cup of tepid water from one of the water bottles near her. The others were in the bathroom where they were waiting to be topped off before the four of them left the school.

Timmy walked back to Adam, and with a mischievous smile, poured the liquid onto Adam's face.

Adam shot up to a sitting position, his head swinging left and right. Water droplets flew from his face and soaked into the sheets.

"What the f—" he stopped himself when he realized Timmy had just doused him.

His face turned into a scowl. "Timmy! What the hell did you do that for?" he yelled, upset.

Timmy just shrugged, like he'd seen both Paul and Adam do on many an occasion.

"Sorry, Adam. Paul told me to wake you up and you weren't budging."

Adam wiped his face with one of the sheets he was laying on. "Well, you didn't have to pour water on me. Jesus, now I'm all wet."

Paul walked over to Adam and sat on a nearby chair, a steaming cup of instant coffee in his bandaged hand.

Chuckling softly, he rubbed Timmy's hair and looked at Adam. "Sorry about that Adam, but you've got to give the kid an A for effort. That was pretty clever."

Adam stood up, the blankets falling away. "Yeah, clever. Easy to say when you're not the one who's all wet."

Josey handed Adam a mug of coffee. "Oh, quit being such a baby. We're all ready to go and you were snoring away. It was time to get up. Look at it this way, at least now you've had your bath, too."

Adam took the coffee and smiled at her insincerely. "Very funny. I've got to go to the bathroom."

Adam walked out of the gym to the bathroom a few doors down. Memories of high school flooded back to him as he walked into the lavatory. The five urinals lined up on the wall and the three stalls on the opposite side glistened in the light of the sun. The window's grating cover layered the room in criss-crossing lines, giving the room a prison feel.

Adam used the first urinal and after three good shakes, returned to the gymnasium.

He walked into the gym and saw that Josey hadn't been kidding. They were almost packed and ready to go.

"Christ, how'm I supposed to breakfast in bed if you've packed up the bed?"

"No time, I want to get moving. The sun's up, and if what Peter said is true, then we need to be behind some walls before dark tonight." Paul threw Adam a small, stale package of cookies and a candy bar. "Here, munch on this while we walk."

Adam mumbled under his breath about having to rush, but in short order he was dressed and ready to move out.

With Paul in the lead, they walked down the lonely hallway one last time and out the main doors of the school. The sun was warm on their faces and Paul decided to return to the rescue station, and from there they'd decide where to go. They hadn't really checked the area out very well, having been sidetracked when Peter popped up.

Paul figured they'd give the place a quick once over and move on, maybe taking one of the National Guard trucks or Hummers that had been left behind.

Walking single file, they moved off down the street. Adam was munching on cookies and every now and then Timmy would pull on his shirt and hold out his hand.

Reluctantly, Adam would give him a cookie and then ignore the boy. He was still mad at Timmy for the water incident.

The streets were empty once more, zombies nowhere to be seen. They took a meandering route to get a better lay of the land, curving around the field next to the school and following the surrounding roads. In less than an hour, they were back at the football field again.

Paul wandered over to the bulldozer where he'd seen Peter the other day. Climbing up into the cab, he saw the wires were all pulled from the dashboard. It looked as if Peter might have been trying to hotwire the machine.

Paul glanced into the death pit one last time, the bodies exactly as when he'd left, the same ones twitching and moaning, flies and maggots covering everything.

Repressing a shudder, he joined the others where they nervously waited for him.

"Anything?" Adam asked when Paul was closer.

Paul shook his head. "Nothing. The dash of the dozer's ripped apart, don't know why. Though it doesn't really matter." Paul looked out across the denuded field at the few tents still standing. "Let's check those tents out, maybe there's still something in there."

He started off, the others following. In the past two days, the field had dried some, the mud not as wet as before. Paul entered the first tent without hesitation.

Adam looked down and saw what looked like the remnants of a human arm near the opening to the tent. He turned to Josey and Timmy and shot them a smile.

"Why don't you guys hang back and keep an eye out for trouble," Adam suggested.

Josey had seen the arm and knew what Adam meant. Timmy had seen more death and violence than any nine year old boy ever should. She nodded and moved away from the tent opening, asking Timmy to go for a walk with her. Timmy frowned, knowing something was up, but did as he was asked.

When they'd moved away from the opening, Adam joined Paul inside the tent . Tables were set up every two feet, most of them covered in dried blood. Stained surgical instruments were scattered everywhere, as bloody clothes draped on anything with a corner. The clothes hung from every surface as if they were thrown without a care.

On the last surgical table lay a prone form covered by a maroon-splattered sheet.

With his the tip of the M-16's barrel, Paul lifted the corner of the sheet. He let it drop right back down. He turned away and leaned over another table, trying not to vomit.

He heaved a little as he tried to keep it down. After a moment, he stood back up and looked at Adam.

Adam's eyebrows were up in a questioning gaze and he asked, "What's under the sheet?"

Paul waved his hand in a "be my guest motion," and then backed up a few steps to give Adam room.

Adam looked at the sheet and then at Paul, wondering if he was better off not knowing. Then his curiosity got the better of him and he moved closer.

The figure under the sheet couldn't have been more than three feet long, Adam figured as he moved closer.

With a shaking hand, he reached out and pulled the sheet off of the figure. As the sheet slipped to the wet earth at his feet, he already wished he could go back in time and change his mind. Despite all the things he'd seen in the past month and a half, some things were still better unseen.

On the stainless steel gurney laid the remains of a little girl. If Adam had to guess, she couldn't have been more than five or six. Her hair was filthy and caked with blood. There were teddy bear clips in her hair.

Except for her blessedly closed eyelids, the face was gone.

Below her head, her neck was nonexistent. The skin had been peeled away until there was nothing left but a few tendons and the white spinal cord.

Her chest had been opened in a clean, V-shaped incision. Whoever had done this had either been a doctor, or at least had had surgical training. The girl's arms and legs had been severed and lay beside the torso in their appropriate places.

Adam looked away, not believing what he had seen. The sheer barbarity of what lay in front of him made him grip the M-16 tight enough to make the grip creak. His knuckles showed white as he stared at the once-human form.

"Jesus, Paul, what sick fuck would do this to someone? I mean, it's a little girl for Christ sakes."

"I don't know, and I don't want to know," Paul said. "Come on, let's get the hell out of here before I lose my breakfast. I'm just barely keeping it down as it is."

Adam swallowed hard and grabbed a sheet from another gurney. He wanted to cover the abomination that represented everything that was wrong with humanity.

Laying the sheet on the small body, he jumped back two feet in the air and let out a yelp of surprise when the eyes of the little girl snapped open and stared at him.

"Holy shit, she's still alive!" he screamed.

Paul turned from the opening of the tent and quickly ran back. The queasy feeling was gone, the sheer shock of seeing those eyes move wiping it away.

The white eyeballs moved back and forth from Paul to Adam as they scanned the room. Without a mouth or throat, the girl couldn't do anything but blink at them.

Adam stared at those eyes, feeling horrified.

Slowly he leaned closer, realizing he wasn't in danger.

"Jesus Christ, who did this to you?" he asked the girl. The eyes just blinked back.

Adam stood and turned to Paul. "We've got to do something, man. We can't leave her like this it's . . . it's . . . it's inhuman."

Paul nodded, knowing what to do. "You go outside and stay with Josey and Timmy, tell them everything's fine. And for God's sake, don't tell them what we found here. Now go," Paul said, pushing him away to the opening of the tent. With a brief look over his shoulder and a shudder, Adam did as Paul asked.

Paul stood alone in the tent. He looked down at the eyes of the girl as they moved erratically back and forth. He knew the girl was a zombie. There could be no way she could still be moving otherwise. Still, to experiment on children just seemed evil, even if they were undead.

He backed away from the tiny head and raised the M-16. The eyes still swung back and forth in their sockets, as if the girl was trying to see where Paul had gone to.

Flicking off the safety, Paul squeezed the trigger once, the crack of the shot echoing inside the tent.

What was left of the head was pulverized by the shot. With the echo of the gun blast still in his ears, he picked the sheet up from the dirt floor and draped it over the small corpse.

The rear tent flap opened suddenly, and a man pushing a gurney stared at Paul in shock. Stepping around the gurney, his eyes went wide when he saw Paul and the shattered corpse's head bleeding out under the sheet.

"Just what the hell do you think you're doing?" he demanded. Paul swung the muzzle towards him, but didn't squeeze the trigger.

The man was wearing a filthy white lab coat, covered in dirt and gore. His hair was a tangled mess of brown and his cheeks were streaked with dried blood.

Paul lowered his rifle and stared at the man in front of him, not quite knowing what to make of him.

The man ran up to the table, took off the sheet, and looked down at was left of the girl zombie's head. Nothing but bits of gristle and a few shards of bone remained. The man turned and moved close enough that Paul could smell his breath. It was foul with an aftertaste of garlic.

"Why did you do that? Do you have any idea how long it took me to dissect that specimen?"

Paul blinked, still not believing what was happening. Paul looked straight into the man's eyes and didn't see sanity anywhere inside the wide pupils.

Paul shook off his surprise and pointed at the corpse of the child, keeping the barrel of his rifle pointed at the crazy man.

"Specimen? You did that?"

The man nodded vigorously. "Yes, I did. And now thanks to you, hours of work have been wasted."

Paul looked at the man and then the corpse. "Why, why would you do that to a human body? A little girl?"

The small ones are easier to manage," the man in the coat said, trying to brush his hair with his filthy hand.

The man seemed to get a hold of himself, the wild look in his eyes subsiding. "I'm a research scientist. Was. I was one of a dozen men sent here to investigate the source of this outbreak, perhaps find a cure."

Paul looked around the disheveled, chaotic room and then back at the scientist.

"Where's everyone else? Where's your support staff?"

The man looked down at his shoes, as if thinking of a response. He backed up a step from Paul and leaned against a gurney. His hand landed on a particularly nasty piece of bloody gristle . . . he didn't seem to notice.

"Well, that's a long story."

Paul grimaced. "Give me the abridged version," he said, fingering his rifle.

The scientist nodded and in quick words started his tale.

"My name is Doctor Albert Hopkins. The military . . . um, *recruited* me to try to find a cure. I was with a group of other scientists whose only mission was to find out what had happened to the human race. The National Guard had placed infected people in a steel cage next to the football field in hopes of finding a cure and saving them.

"Well, they got loose and tore down their barricade. They

descended on the entire camp like the wrath of God. I saw my colleagues ripped to pieces and eaten in front of my very eyes. Some were only partially eaten and once infected, they too revived and attacked.

"When the National Guard realized it was hopeless, they bugged out, leaving us to fend for ourselves. I hid in a small chest freezer. I stayed there for almost two days, living on the ice attached to the walls. I could still hear the carnage outside my little prison.

"When I finally opened my small haven, I found the camp deserted. I believe the infected migrate as they look for food. It's an instinctual thing that harks back to when man was nothing but an animal living in caves.

"Once I knew I was safe, I continued my research. I was alone, but I was determined to find the antibody that would reverse this plague."

Paul nodded slightly. "So, no one knows you're here, there's no power, and you're cutting up corpses on your own."

"Well, that's rather crudely put, I must say, but I suppose you have the gist of it."

On the gurney Hopkins had been wheeling in, something twitched under the sheet. Shifting his aim, Paul stepped back. "What's under the sheet, Professor?"

"Hmm? Oh, nothing really, just another experiment. It doesn't concern you. Oh and it's Doctor, actually."

Paul's mouth curved into a frown. "Why don't you let me decide that, huh? Doctor?" Paul gestured with the rifle for Hopkins to move over to the gurney. With downcast eyes, Hopkins did as requested.

"You know, my friend, this is really all beyond your understanding. I've had to go to the extreme trying to solve this quandary."

"Uh-huh. Pull off the sheet, Doctor," he ordered the man.

Hopkins slid the sheet off the twitching form.

Paul gasped.

On the gurney was what was left of a black woman in her early twenties. IV's were connected to her arms. Her torso was exposed to the air, the V-shaped incision plainly visible to Paul. Her arms and legs were tied down and as Paul stared in horror, the woman's face turned to him. Pain-filled eyes returned his stare.

Her mouth opened and while the voice was soft, it was plainly understandable. "Help me . . . please . . . help me."

Paul stepped back, his mouth dropping open in revulsion and surprise, his hip crashing into a table behind him, knocking whatever was on it to the ground.

Hopkins put his hands up defensively. "I can explain everything.

She's been bitten. I just wanted to see how the virus infiltrates the body, its progression. She's going to die anyway."

"You sick fuck," Paul said through gritted teeth.

Rage flooded Paul's mind as he stared at the man in front of him. Before he realized it, he'd squeezed the trigger twice, sending two rounds into the man's chest. The first round shattered the man's spine, while the second struck him in the neck and continued out his back, disintegrating the man's heart with its passage.

Hopkins fell back onto a gurney and tried to take a last breath with lungs that wouldn't work. He slipped off the table, face-down into the mud.

Paul shuffled over to the prone, mutilated woman and looked down on her. Her mouth was opening and closing slowly. Her eyes stared up at him and tears rolled down her cheeks to be lost in her hair.

Paul looked down at her, afraid to touch her or anything connected to her. Her organs glistened in the weak light and her heart beat an erratic rhythm.

Paul couldn't believe she was still alive and conscious. He glanced to the words on one of the IV's and he turned it so he could read it. Morphine.

A soft wheeze issued from her mouth then, the words: "Kill me . . . please," clearly audible.

Paul let go of the IV and nodded. "I'm sorry," he whispered to her while a single tear rolled down his cheek. Stepping back, he raised the rifle again. Making the sign of the cross and praying to God or whoever to give this soul peace, he squeezed the trigger, the rifle jumping in his hands.

The bullet went into her ear and blew out the side of her head, her heart skipping a beat in her chest, then stopping. The small battery-operated heart monitor filled the tent with a steady tone. Paul yanked the electrodes out and threw them to the ground.

He pulled the sheet over the corpse and stepped away. His friends were waiting for him.

Without a backward glance, he shouldered the rifle and walked back out into the sun. The others were waiting for him, looking to him for answers. He stared at their faces but said nothing.

Adam gestured into the tent. "What took so long? I thought you would have been back five minutes ago. I was about to come get you.

What were the extra shots?" Adam had expected the one shot for the little girl, but the others hadn't been explained.

With a grim look on his face, Paul fixed his glasses and looked up into the cloudy sky.

"Let's just get the hell away. There's nothing but death here." He started walking away from the tents, across the field toward one of the main streets that led into the city. He flexed his bandaged hands, the pain not as bad while he dealt internally with his grief and rage.

Adam looked back at the tent, thinking he might investigate further. As the others moved further away, he decided, "screw it," and high-tailed to catch up.

* * *

A few minutes later, with Paul and Timmy walking a few feet ahead of them, Josey tapped Adam's shoulder. When he glanced at her, she asked, "Adam, what was inside that tent? What did you two see? Why was he in there that long?"

Adam looked forward, his eyes glazing over just a little as he thought of the child on the steel table. When he was sure his voice would remain level, he turned his head to her.

His mouth opened, but then shut. Shaking his head back and forth, he picked up his pace and left Josey a few footsteps behind. He couldn't talk about it, not yet. Timmy dropped back and took Josey's hand in his, the two walking silently.

Some things were better left unsaid; better to keep them buried in the closet, out of sight from prying eyes and ears. Some things Josey didn't need to be burdened with.

But Adam knew what he would have said if he had told her. To him, what he saw was the end of life the way he and everyone else had known it. To him, life had hit a dead end and now they were stuck at the end of the road with nowhere to go.

They were trapped and would remain that way until the last human being was dead or turned into one of . . . them.

He knew whatever happened, he would fight to his last breath. After all, what else could he do? The only other option was death, and frankly, Adam was too scared to die.

Not yet, for Christ sakes, he thought, *I'm only eighteen years old!*

He caught up to Paul and the man looked at him, giving him a half-smile. Paul slapped him on the back and nodded. The gesture saying, "We're okay. Everything's going to be fine."

They slowed down, letting Josey and Timmy catch up. With the buildings blocking the sun and casting shadows across the deserted street, the four survivors moved on. They needed shelter and food in that order.

Overhead, a black crow floated on a tail wind, eyeing the group and watching everything.

CHAPTER 30

The four survivors were now deep into the city, the sun sitting high overhead in the clear blue sky. The clouds from earlier in the day had burned off, leaving the sky a pure blue that filled each of them with hope.

Adam and Josey were walking side by side again, while Timmy was with Paul in the front.

Adam was watching Josey as she picked her way around some debris and she turned and looked at him.

"What? Why do you keep looking at me?" she asked

Adam shrugged. "No reason. I was just thinking about back at the gym. When you shot that guy and Ellie, I mean, those were some pretty damn good shots. If it wasn't for you . . . well, let's just say I don't think I would have made a good appetizer." He held out his arm for her to see. "All skin and bones."

Josey chuckled. "Thanks, Adam. I appreciate that you noticed. You know, Paul still hasn't said anything about it."

"How come?"

She watched Paul's back while he walked in front of her. Lowering her voice a bit to make sure only Adam could hear her, she whispered, "It's probably because I'm a better shot than he is, though he'd be damned if he'd ever admit it."

Adam's eyes lit up with mild surprise. "No shit?"

Josey nodded. "Yup. Every time we go the shooting range, I always get the better score. Drove him crazy that a woman could shoot better than him. He's a good man, Adam, but he's still a little old fashioned in a few departments."

Adam listened and continued walking. A severed hand lay in the road, covered in flies. Adam stepped over it and moved on.

It was funny, he thought. Funny what you could get used to if you had no choice.

Up ahead, Paul had stopped walking and raised his hand for the others to stop, as well.

For a tense minute, no one moved. Paul was focusing his attention on a side alley between two buildings. He leveled his rifle, his finger hovering over the trigger.

A trash can crashed in the alley and a mangy dog bolted from cover, running down the street. Paul had been just a hairsbreadth away from shooting the animal.

Everyone let out the breaths they were holding and Paul turned to the others.

"A dog. Haven't seen much animal life since we entered the city," Paul stated.

Josey nodded. "Except rats, that is. Think the zombies eat them too?"

Paul shrugged. "Maybe, if they can catch them. Maybe all the dogs and stray cats just got the hell out of Dodge." He looked up at the sun. It had reached its zenith and would soon start its downward journey. They needed to find shelter for the night.

So far none of the buildings had seemed safe. Either the glass doors were shattered or doors had been ripped from hinges. They would have no choice but to pick a spot, but Paul was hoping the next street would produce a safe haven for himself and his friends.

Timmy looked up at Paul. "Uncle Paul, are we gonna stop soon? I'm hungry and my feet hurt."

"You know, the kid's got a point. We've been walking for hours. I could use a break, too," Adam added.

Josey moved next to Paul. "Why don't we take a few minutes to rest, Paul? There's still a few hours of daylight left."

Paul considered their requests, but already knew the answer. While he was their defacto leader, he was still ruled by democracy. Better to give in gracefully than to be vetoed.

"Fine, let's take a break." He looked around the street, searching for a decent place to rest, when he spotted a small delicatessen a few doors down.

"Over there. Maybe there's some food and water inside." He moved out, the others following behind him in single file.

Reaching the shattered glass doors, he stepped inside the shadowy storefront. Banners hung on the walls, displaying the specials of the day. Tables were overturned and debris littered the floor.

Paul took a few hesitant steps further in. His boot crushed a Styrofoam cup, the noise as loud as a shotgun blast in the empty room.

The place appeared empty. No smell of decay came to him. Paul kicked in the double swinging doors that led to the back of the building and a moment later returned with the same grim look on his face.

"I guess there's good news and bad news," he told to the others.

"What's the good news?" Adam asked.

"The good news is there aren't any dead guys, the place is clean."

"So what's the bad news?" Josey asked.

"Well, the place is clean. I mean, not even a box of crackers. Whoever did it took everything that wasn't nailed down."

"Scavengers?" Adam suggested.

Paul shrugged. "Could be. Guess it really doesn't matter." He picked up an overturned chair and sat on it. Rubbing his beard, he lay the M-16 across his lap.

"Okay, let's rest here for half an hour or so, then move out. We need to find shelter and our food is really getting thin. If we don't find something soon, well . . ." He left it hanging, the others knowing full well what he meant.

Josey unpacked from their meager supplies, noticing they had more ammunition than food. Everyone ate a little less than normal, giving their extra rations to Timmy.

Sipping tepid water from battered water bottles, the three adults sat quietly. Paul had a good view of the street and he kept watch while munching on one of their last packages of jerky, followed by a candy bar from the gas station.

Adam and Josey shared a can of peaches, leaving just under half for Timmy. The boy ate greedily, tipping the can to his face to drink the syrup left in the can. When he was finished, he wiped his mouth on his shirtsleeve.

Josey was about to discipline him and teach the boy about etiquette, but decided it really just didn't matter anymore.

Taking the can from him, she held it, not knowing what to do with it. She searched the room for a barrel. Paul noticed this and frowned. Leaning forward, he held out his hand for her to give him the can.

"Here, honey, let me take care of that for you," he said.

She smiled and gave him the can. "Thanks, Paul, that's nice of you."

Paul stared straight into her eyes as he threw the can over his shoulder. The can bounced off the counter and fell to the floor to be lost in the rest of the debris.

Josey frowned. "Now I could have done that."

"Then why didn't you?" he asked.

Her sharp answer was interrupted by the sound of an engine coming from outside. Paul jumped to his feet and moved to the open door, his rifle up and ready.

"Who is it? Do you see them?" Josey asked.

Paul shook his head. "No, they're not close enough. Plus, the damn echo out there is terrible. I can't get a fix on what direction they're coming from."

Adam moved next to Paul, his M-16 ready. "Think it's the National Guard, or maybe the Army?"

"Don't know. Until we know de, I say we stay out of sight," Paul answered.

The rumbling grew louder until it sounded like the noise was right on top of them. Before either Paul or Adam saw it coming, a large SUV with an open rear bed came charging around the corner and down the street. They couldn't see the passengers in the front cab, but there were two men on the back bed plainly visible.

They were whooping it up like teenagers on a Saturday night binge. Each had weapons, but from where Paul sat, he couldn't tell what they were. Handguns, that's all he knew for sure, and there was at least one rifle of some kind.

Paul and Adam ducked down, hidden from view. "Well if we're gonna say hi, we better do it quick. They're gonna be on us in a second," Adam said, kneeling low at the door.

The SUV was coming straight down the street, the engine roaring, the driver revving the engine like a race car driver on drugs. The front bumper was knocking aside anything that got in its way, the vehicle a metal bull.

Paul was still deciding if he should let it pass, not wanting to give away their hiding place if the vehicle was hostile, when Timmy jumped from his chair and ran to the door.

"I want to see the car!" he yelled, curious.

Before Paul could pull him away from the door, the SUV had passed. Paul thought the vehicle would continue on, but, no. The driver hit the brakes, the tires locking up and the smell of burning rubber filled the immediate area.

The driver side door opened and a man stepped out. Paul had pulled Timmy undercover, but he knew the damage had been done.

The driver was yelling to the other men, giving directions and pointing at the deli. With weapons drawn, the three men climbed from the SUV and formed up on the sidewalk.

Adam leaned in to Paul. "Shit, man. They saw Timmy. Maybe they think he was a zombie. We need to tell them we're people before someone gets shot . . . like me." Adam whispered.

Paul was thinking, weighing their options. Finally, he nodded and turned to Adam. "You're right. I just hope they're open to parley." He looked down at Timmy, lying on his side on the floor. "Son, you might have just gotten us all killed. Now you listen to me. No matter what happens, you stay quiet. Hear me?"

Timmy nodded, on the verge of crying. He'd just wanted to see the car, not get them into trouble.

Paul looked at Adam. He handed him the rifle and the other weapons on his back. "You stay down. If it looks bad, then you start shooting. No mercy, Adam. Okay?"

Adam nodded. "No mercy. Cobra Kai!"

Paul shook his head. Josey had crawled next to his side, and with a gentle squeeze of her arm and a parting smile, he stood up and called to the men out front.

"Hey there, wait! I'm unarmed!" he called. A shot rang out near his head and he ducked back down, cursing himself for a fool. Of course they'd be trigger happy. He should have called out first instead of making himself a target.

With the gun blast echoing off the walls, he heard a gruff voice yelling to cease fire. Then, after hearing a few choice profanities about the stupidity of the gunner, he heard the same voice calling out.

"Hello in there! Sorry 'bout that, my man thought you was a zombie. It's safe now," the voice said.

With a deep breath, Paul stood up and made himself a perfect target. If one of the gunners wanted to, they could easily put a bullet in his brain or chest before he knew what had happened.

Paul scanned the street in front of the deli. The driver was standing in front of the SUV, a weapon in his hand, but the muzzle was lowered to the cement.

"Come on out of there with your hands up and we won't shoot!" the man called to him.

Paul did as requested and stumbled over the door frame and into the light of the day. His hands were in the air as requested, the dirty bandages looking like gloves.

Four men gathered around him. All wore clothes that appeared to be worn, but clean. All were clean shaven and their skin was free of dirt and filth. These men had bathed recently.

The man who appeared to be the leader walked up to stand no more than a foot from Paul. He had a hard face, the eyes holding no warmth or compassion. Paul swallowed a little harder then he would have liked. The man saw this and grinned, the gesture not carrying to his eyes.

He looked Paul square on and said: "Hi there. My name's Roy, and I'd like to know what the fuck you think you're doing in my city."

CHAPTER 31

Paul blinked at the question. "*Your* city? What the hell are you talking about?"

Roy turned and looked at his men and smiled, like he was putting on a show. "The man doesn't know what I'm talking about," he said for their benefit. Roy called Tom over to him. "Tom, why don't you fill him in."

Tom nodded and stepped up, hitching up his pants.

"Roy is the new mayor of this here city," Tom said with a grin.

"What? That's crazy. Why the hell do you think that?" Paul asked.

Roy stepped so close to Paul, he almost knocked the man over. "Why? Because there's no one left to say I'm not! That's why. Now answer me, what are you doing in my city? And how many do you got back there in that deli?"

Paul decided he should have just let the whole mayor thing go. He decided to try the truth.

"To answer your first question, my friends and I came to the city for the rescue station. We've been holding up in my cellar since the outbreak first started, but we ran out of food and water so we had to hit the road. From the look of the rescue station, or what's left of it, I'm glad I stayed put when the order to evacuate was given. And to answer the second question, there's just my wife and friend and the little boy you saw. All armed and aiming their guns at your heads," Paul smiled slyly, "just in case we don't get along."

At that answer all the men looked harder at the deli, fingers hovering dangerously close to triggers.

"Now, now, there's no reason why we can't all be friends," Roy said smiling. "Why don't you have them come out? We're holed up in a church about a mile or so away. There's a little over a hundred of us now. Mostly women, children and old men. We could use a guy like you. We've also got plenty of food and water."

Roy looked up at the sun, just starting to touch the horizon.

"Besides, you don't want to be out here when it gets dark," Roy finished.

At that statement the other men started to laugh. Paul joined in, trying to put them at ease. When the joviality was done, Paul looked at Roy and grinned.

"I would be happy to accept your invitation. Can I put my hands down now?"

Roy nodded curtly. "Sure, we're good, just had to make sure you weren't one of them cannibals or somethin'. Crazy bastards are eatin' people if you can believe it. You seen any of 'em?"

Paul decided discretion would be wise and shook his head no. "No, only people we've seen are you fellas." Paul turned to the deli and waved, calling out for Adam to hear.

"Looks okay, Adam. Come on out!"

Hesitantly, Adam stood up. His .38 was in his hand, with his rifle on his back, but seeing that the men around Paul all had weapons pointed towards the ground, he did likewise.

"Come on, Josey, it looks safe. They seem to just be talking now," Adam said, stepping through the shattered glass door and onto the sidewalk.

Josey followed with Timmy holding her hand.

Once everyone was on the sidewalk and introductions were finished, Roy clapped his hands for attention.

"All right then," he said as his eyes wandered up and down Josey's figure, "why don't you guys climb up into the back. And make sure to hold on tight, it gets bumpy back there. The city hasn't had any street sweepers in a while; the streets are a little dirtier than you might remember." The henchmen chuckled at that, thinking of all the corpses lying in the streets and on the sidewalks.

While everyone started to climb into the truck, Roy called to Paul.

"Hey, Paul, wait a sec', will ya. I want to ask you something."

Paul gave Josey's hand a squeeze and turned around, walking over to the front of the SUV.

"What's up?" he asked.

Roy shrugged casually, and pulled his hand from behind him, holding a 9mm Glock. Before Paul could do or say anything, Roy shot him.

Paul went flying back like a giant hand had swatted him. He landed in a heap of limbs, face-down in the gutter.

Anthony Giangregorio

Adam or Josey each had the barrel of a gun shoved into the back of their heads before they could ask what the gunshot was. The two of them were quickly disarmed and tied to the metal supports of the truck bed. Adam had been gagged with a dirty rag from the floor of the SUV bed. Timmy cowered next to Josey, not understanding what had just happened, scared out of his mind.

Josey had tears in her eyes, her face twisted in pain and rage. Only her husband's arm was visible from where she was tied up in the truck.

"Why, why did you do that? He meant you no harm! We mean you no harm." she said. "Why?"

Roy stepped over Paul's body and leaned into the rear, his eyes hot. "Why? I'll tell you why. From the second I saw that guy, I knew he'd be trouble. I just figured I'd get rid of him now instead of later. But don't worry, honey," he said, gently caressing her arm with the barrel of his Glock, "I'll keep you company at night from here on out."

Adam tried to jump at the man, his bonds stopping him. His eyes flared hatred, the vein in his temple throbbing with his rage.

Roy chuckled at the burst of emotion. "How touching. It's nice to see loyalty isn't dead."

He climbed off the bed and moved to the driver's side, but paused for just a moment. Turning around he looked at Adam.

"Believe me, buddy, I'm not doing you any favors. Once you see what I've got planned for you, you'll wish I'd just shot you in the face." Then he walked to the door, climbed into the driver's seat and started the engine.

One of the men had just retrieved the group's remaining supplies and weapons bags from the deli and he climbed up into the back of the SUV, slapping the roof with the palm of his hand.

With a buck and a jerk, the SUV started forward. Roy turned up the tape player, an Aerosmith song about 'sweet emotion' pouring out the front of the cab.

As the vehicle rolled away, Josey, Adam and Timmy looked behind them at the prone figure of Paul. The SUV sped up and soon Paul's body was out of sight.

Josey hung her head down and cried, her sobs racking her shoulders.

Timmy hugged her and stared at the men with frightful eyes.

One of the men growled at him and he ducked his head into Josey's chest, closing his eyes and trying to pretend it was all just a bad dream.

The SUV gone for only seconds, the body of Paul lie still in the gutter. The sound of the gun shot that had laid him low had alerted every one of the undead around.

Through openings in broken doors and darkened alleyways, the walking corpses shambled out into the light, looking for the noise that had disturbed them.

While Paul lay motionless, the undead slowly started to surround him.

In the sky overhead, a single crow circled for a moment and then flew off after the SUV. Perhaps there would be something more interesting there than watching a single man devoured by an army of the dead.

CHAPTER 32

Roy was true to his word. The SUV jumped and bumped over the bloated remains of corpses. They were everywhere, in the street, on the sidewalks, sprawled across parked cars and in doorways. Rats ran screeching into the darkness, the growl of the engine frightening them away until the SUV had passed. They came back out to feed on the corpses en masse and with renewed fervor.

Adam and Josey watched the urban landscape drift by, still in shock from losing Paul. The sun was starting to set, the sky turning orange with a hint of crimson.

The SUV swerved in and out of the wreckage in the streets with wild abandon, but yet never connected solidly with any of the dead vehicles, as if Roy knew what to do by heart.

Adam assumed the man had driven this route many times before and had probably memorized it. He looked over at Josey, and she returned his gaze. Their eyes locked for a moment and he nodded to her. Hopefully, that would be enough comfort, because bound and gagged, that's all he could offer.

The cloth in his mouth tasted like burnt oil and he struggled not to gag as the material inched down his throat. His anger still seethed inside of him and he wanted nothing more than to shove a gun in Roy's mouth and pull the trigger, however unlikely that particular event seemed.

The SUV came to a jarring halt in front of a modest stone church with a tall steeple. Adam looked up at the structure, taking it all in. For just the briefest of moments, he could have sworn he saw someone in the tower, but he blinked and the figure was gone. There was a large fence built around the stone steps of the church and Adam quickly saw why.

At a bleating of the horn, the church's wooden doors were thrown open and men and women walked out into the waning daylight at a brisk pace. A woman opened the gate that led to a smaller opening and the people started offloading the boxes of food and other items of value that had been found by the foraging team.

The whole setup reminded Adam of how prison gates would be set up. This way even if a zombie managed to get through the first gate, the second gate would be closed. He couldn't help but be impressed by the ingenuity of the people.

Adam and Josey were untied from the metal bar on the SUV, their hands still secured). They, along with Timmy, were taken off the rear bed of the vehicle. Adam jumped when rifle cracks sounded behind him.

Twisting his head, he saw a few of the men and women shooting at some undead who were approaching, attracted by all the noise. Adam noticed the pile of burned bodies off to the right of the gate and figured that this sort of thing was routine here.

Roy herded the friends into the church.

With Josey and Timmy next to him, Adam stepped into the church's wide grand portal. The first things he noticed were the odor of unwashed bodies and the smell of cooking food. Despite the danger he knew he was in, he felt his mouth watering from hunger.

He was ushered down the middle aisles, trying to take in everything at once. People stood or sat on almost every pew. They'd spread out blankets and odd bits of clothing, claiming that this was their spot. Some of the eyes watching belonged to children. That gave Adam hope. Whatever might happen to him and Josey, at least Timmy should be all right.

A gun barrel pressed into his back to move faster, and Adam walked up to the front of the church. He was made to stand near a podium on a small stage that overlooked the grand theatre and the parishioners below. Josey and Timmy stayed at floor level, separated from him.

Roy walked up to the podium and banged a gavel on the wooden top.

"Attention! Listen up everybody! I found these people out in the city. When we found them, they tried to shoot us and take our transportation." He paused for effect. The faces below remained mostly blank. "Now, the world may not be what it was, but we still need laws. We still need rules. With the Reverend sick, I've taken up his responsibilities. I've managed to keep you safe and fed. I know I've had to make some hard choices, but what you all need to know is that I do it for all of you. In all our foraging, we've only found a handful of other survivors. I think we're it. The rest of the city is nothing but . . . them.

"We are an island of the living in a sea of the dead, and we have to stay strong and work together." He turned to Adam and pointed at him accusingly. "Tomorrow morning, this man will feed the zombies. Satan's minions, as the good Reverend calls them. For trying to kill one of us, he will receive the ultimate punishment. Are you with me?" he yelled to the crowd.

Whether they truly agreed with him or were just too beaten to argue, the crowd clapped their hands and threw epitaphs at Adam. Roy smiled. A good sacrifice will keep the rabble in line and take their minds off their troubles for a while. Finding these people was the best thing that could have happened to Roy all week.

Stepping down from the podium, Roy called Tom to him.

"Have the woman sent to my quarters," Roy said, looking at Josey with a leer.

"What about the boy and the meat?" Tom asked, gesturing to Adam.

Roy had to give that some thought. He wasn't used to keeping prisoners. Usually he would just throw their asses off the balcony and be done with it. But this was a special case. He wanted the crowd to get riled up a little in anticipation of what would be coming the next day.

When he couldn't think of a proper place he just shrugged. "Shit, I don't know. Just put him with the Reverend. The door's got a lock and that crazy bastard probably won't even know anyone's in there with him. Keep him tied up though. I don't wanna take any chances."

Tom nodded brusquely and waved for Steve to come to him. Tom saw Roy talking to Kate and a wave of jealousy flooded through him. That bitch was taking his job. He knew she needed to have an accident or he was going to be pushed out of the inner circle. He liked what power he had, and he'd be damned if he was going to give it up now.

Steve trotted over to him and waited for instructions. Tom turned to him and said, "Here. Take this guy and lock him up with the Reverend. Keep his hands tied, though. Roy doesn't want to take any chances."

"What about the gag?" Steve asked.

Tom shrugged, indifferent. "I don't care, do what you want," he snapped. Then he took Josey by the arm and started to take her to Roy's quarters. Tom looked around for the kid, but he was nowhere to be found. He decided it was irrelevant. What could a nine-year-old do?

He pushed Josey forward. "Come on, bitch. You've got a date with the Boss."

"Fuck you, you piece of shit. When I get free—" Josey said.

Tom squeezed her arm hard enough to make her wince.

"Shut the hell up, bitch. Roy didn't say what condition you had to be in when I brought you to his room."

Josey stopped talking, but eyed daggers at him. Tom chuckled.

As the crowd talked amongst themselves, Adam and Josey were dragged from the theatre to their different destinations.

━━━━●◆●━━━━

From the third pew down from the front, Timmy hunkered down low and watched as his Auntie Josey and Adam were made to leave the big room.

People were everywhere, the noise deafening because of the acoustics in the church. He'd never been in a church before and the building had an oppressive feel to it. He had never been as scared in his young life as he was right then. He had no idea what to do.

Timmy sat on the floor and started to cry. The tears flowed freely down his cheeks cutting streaks through the dust on his skin as he thought of his Uncle Paul. He missed his parents and he missed Josey.

As he sat there crying, a pair of shoes stopped in front of him. His crying slowed and he looked up at the face of a pretty blonde girl. She smiled and knelt down so they were face to face.

"Hi, my name's Eve. What's yours?" She asked.

Through sniffing and small bouts of crying, Timmy managed to tell her his name. She nodded at that and held out her hand.

"Those were your friends that just came in, right?"

He nodded. "Uh-huh, their names are Adam and Josey."

"Okay, that's good. Listen, Timmy, I don't like it here either. If I help you get them free, will you take me with you when you leave?"

Timmy had to think about that one. "Well, I guess, but we'll have to ask them."

She chuckled at that. "Okay, that's a good answer. But I'm pretty sure if I save their lives, they'll let me come, too."

She held out her hand for Timmy to take.

"Come on, let's get out of here. We can go to the basement. From there I can tell you how you can help Adam."

Taking his hand, she led him through the throng of people until they reached a set of side stairs that led down into the dark. Lighting a candle that was sitting on the top stair, she headed down under the

187

church, Timmy next to her.

An idea was already forming in her head, and if it was going to work, she had to act fast. If all went well, then by the next morning Timmy's friends would be free and she would be with them.

CHAPTER 33

Adam was pushed roughly through the back hallways of the church until he came to a large wooden door. He scanned everything, looking for a way to escape, but nothing presented itself. Looking at the door, he saw damage where the latch met the frame, but on a closer inspection he realized it was from long ago and now appeared to be stronger than ever.

Steve leaned past him and opened the door, pushing him in with the heel of his hand. Adam stumbled inside, hoping he was at least done playing prisoner for the day.

Steve picked up a chair lying on its side in the corner of the dark room. What he could see made it look to Adam like an office. The room was shrouded in shadows, the sun finishing its descent outside the church's windows. Adam could barely see in the dull gloom.

Steve forced Adam into the seat. The henchmen quickly and skillfully retied his bonds to the chair and when he was finished he stood up with a cracking of knee joints.

He pulled the gag from Adam's mouth and tossed it into the corner of the room.

Adam's mouth was so dry he couldn't talk, the taste of motor oil covering every corner of his mouth. He started to suck on his tongue to try and salivate.

With relief, he slowly regained some moisture. Adam looked up at Steve.

"Hey, pal, how 'bout a sip of water to wash the taste of that rag out of my mouth?"

Steve chuckled. "Shit. Do you think I give a flying fuck about what you feel? Screw you." Steve turned around and exited the room.

"Asshole," Adam called to his back.

Steve raised his hand as he closed the door, giving Adam the one-finger salute. Then the door clicked shut and Adam was alone.

Or he wasn't.

From behind him came a rustling sound of cloth against cloth. Adam couldn't turn his head far enough to see what was behind him. Struggling with his bonds did nothing but dig them deeper into his skin. He tried rocking back and forth in the chair, but it was too heavy, too sturdily-built for that. As thirsty as he was, a new sweat sprang out on his forehead.

The rustling grew louder behind him and he struggled fruitlessly in his chair. Ways to get loose drifted into the back of his mind, slowly being replaced by a numb terror. His heart was pounding in his chest and he figured for one lucid second that if he had to deal with any more bad shit this day his heart would just explode out of his chest, leaving a gory mess for the guards to find the next morning.

He caught a black shape on his right, just at the edge of his peripheral vision. The figure shambled forward, hands in front of it to grab Adam and tear his throat out.

Adam couldn't take his eyes off the figure, and while his heart pounded a drum solo, he managed to build up enough saliva to take one good gulp. Then it was too late, the figure jumped out of the shadows directly at Adam.

Adam could only shut his eyes and pray it was quick.

———— ••••• ————

Josey was dragged up a flight of stairs and down a small hallway. There she was thrown through a door and unceremoniously dumped onto a twin-size bed that was covered in rumpled, filthy sheets.

The bed was just a mattress on the floor, no frame, and she landed with a soft bounce, her head striking the wall, stopping her.

She saw small spots in her vision for a few moments and shook her head to clear it.

Tom smiled down at her. "Now, you just relax here, my lady. When Roy's done with his business, he'll be coming to visit you."

With a chuckle, Tom slammed the door. A soft click told Josey it was unlikely she'd be just walking out the door.

She thought of Paul and a pang of grief hit her hard. She forced it down. There would be time to mourn her husband if she managed to get out of this alive.

Sitting up, she took a look at her prison. It looked like an old stockroom or storage room, now made into a bedroom. The place was a mess, Hustlers and other nude magazines covered a far corner and a small footlocker sat half-open across from her, with a portable DVD player and a stack of movies inside it.

The other side of the room was piled high with books and boxes full of clothes. They were labeled as part of a Goodwill drive the church had been funding before the city had fallen into chaos.

Sliding her butt down the bed, she placed her feet on the floor, then after rolling off her side, she managed to stand upright. Walking around her prison, her eyes darted back and forth, trying to find something sharp to cut her bonds with. The ropes cut into her wrists, making her wince each time she moved.

She walked over to the footlocker and kicked it open all the way. Immersed under the DVDs was a jumble of sour smelling clothes and an extra pair of boots, nothing she could use to free herself. With a sigh she was about to turn away when she noticed the outside corner of the locker. From years of use, the decorative metal corner had worn and separated from the wood. Now it was a sharp piece of metal on the edge waiting to slice the flesh of the first careless soul to wander too close.

Dropping down into a crouch, she brought her hands up against the sharp corner and started rubbing frantically. The nylon rope that bound her was strong and wouldn't break easily.

She couldn't keep track of time, but she kept working at cutting the tough nylon rope for just about forever.

She heard footsteps on the other side of the door. With her heart in her throat, Josey started to rub harder, heedless of the cuts and scrapes on her wrists and palms.

She could hear voices now, deep guttural voices coming from just outside the door. With sweat dripping into her eyes, she kept at the ropes, knowing it was her only hope.

Her eyes never left the doorknob. Her heart lightened when she felt the rope loosening just the smallest bit. Was that her blood just making it slicker? She didn't care.

The voices had stopped and her breath stuck in her chest when the doorknob began to turn.

All she could do was keep scraping at her bonds and hope for the best.

Eve moved through the basement, Timmy in tow. The candle flickered as they walked across the wide open room. The last of the light from outside was barely penetrating the dirty windows. Shadows moved across the glass, dozens of legs surrounding the church. The windows were covered with ornate metal work; the welds more than strong enough to resist any undead tampering.

They were relatively safe, Eve thought. It wasn't the monsters outside the church she had to worry about. It was the ones on the inside.

She sat Timmy down on a box of canned beans and handed him a small bottle of water. He drank it down greedily, some spilling out of the side of his mouth, wetting his shirt.

"Whoa, there. Slow down. There's more if you want it."

Timmy nodded and handed her the empty bottle. "Yes, please."

She handed him another one and sat down next to him. "Look, Timmy, we don't have a lot of time. We need to get started before everything quiets down for the night. Are you with me?"

Timmy looked up at her, his big blue eyes boring into hers. "You really think I can help Aunt Josey and Adam?" he asked between gulps of water. He was drinking slower now, his thirst partially slaked by the first bottle.

Eve nodded and smiled. "I sure do. In fact, I can't do it without you. I know where they took Adam, and only you can get to him. I'm too big to fit."

Timmy's eyebrows lifted in curiosity. "Really, you need me?"

"Uh-huh, the other kids here all have someone to watch them, they have no reason to want to leave here, they think they're safe. But you know what's really happening. You've been outside the church and seen things. Your friends didn't really try to kill Roy and the others, did they?"

"No way!" he said standing up, his hands curled into fists as he remembered what had happened.

"They shot my Uncle Paul and left him in the street, then they tied up Adam and Josey and took all our stuff. We just wanted to be friends."

Eve rubbed his shoulder. "I know, honey. I'm so sorry about your friend. See, that's why we need to leave. I know where the keys to the Suburban are. Once your friends are free, we can take it and leave here forever."

Timmy smiled at that. "I'd like that, Eve."

"Good," she nodded, "then this is what I need you to do."

She filled Timmy in on her plan. Timmy was a bright kid and he understood easily, only asking questions to clarify.

With darkness covering the windows of the basement, Eve continued telling Timmy what he needed to do, making sure the boy knew the plan inside and out.

Time was quickly running out for Adam and Josey, and Eve knew she needed to act fast or it wouldn't matter. If her plan didn't work, then Timmy's friends would soon be dead and she would spend the rest of her life in this church.

However short that might be.

CHAPTER 34

Adam's eyes were closed as he waited to become dinner. But after a few tense seconds of nothing happening, he opened his left eye just a little and snuck a peek.

In front of Adam stood a man, not a monster. He was wearing a black gown and had what looked like a rosary around his neck. Deciding he wasn't about to get killed, Adam opened his eyes fully and looked at the man in front of him, who appeared to be praying, making the sign of the cross and then bending over and mumbling some more.

Without seeming to notice Adam, the man moved away and lay down on a cot in the corner of the room, all the while mumbling and praying.

Adam tried to crane his neck around so he could see him, but he couldn't do it.

"Hey, Father or Reverend or whatever you are. How about untying my hands?"

The man's devotions didn't even slow.

Adam frowned. If the man wasn't crazy, he thought, he was most definitely almost there.

Adam had no way of knowing that Reverend Bernie had succumbed to his illness and slipped into a perpetual state of madness. Visions of God and Satan constantly flooded his consciousness, never giving the man respite.

He was utterly insane.

Adam struggled with his bonds, but only managed to become more uncomfortable. His shoulder was killing him and he badly needed to stretch, the cramp only getting worse each time he tried to shift position.

He was exhausted. He'd walked all morning, and now that he was alone and immediate danger gone, the adrenaline rush was wearing off, making his extremities tingle. With the come-down he was starting to feel sleepy, as well. He couldn't believe that he was going to fall asleep at a time like this, but there it was.

With the man behind him mumbling about devils and gods, Adam slowly drifted off into a light sleep. When the Reverend would move, Adam would open his eyes, but soon he succumbed fully, drifting away into a dreamless and deep slumber.

Adam awoke an hour later, wondering what had brought him out of his doze. Behind him, Rev. Bernie still ranted and the door was still closed.

Then he heard a scraping noise coming from behind the wall. He watched the wall intently, jumping when he heard it again, which caused the pain in his shoulder to flare up.

Rats maybe? In the walls? With all the dead just lying in the streets, it had only been a matter of time before the rat population had become immense. Just thinking about it sent a shiver down his spine. To be buried under a sea of rats, their small mouths and teeth digging into his flesh, burrowing deep into his stomach.

The noise in the wall continued, pulling him out of his morbid thoughts, and he followed the sound with his ears until it finally stopped. Adam was looking at a heating vent about a foot off the floor. It was covered by a metal cover, nothing fancy, just simple strips of metal that could be angled to direct the flow of warm air.

Adam's eyes went wide when he saw small fingers sticking through the vent, then the sound of scraping began again. This time the sound was more like a prying, like with a tool. Minutes passed and Adam sat there watching, not sure what would come next.

Finally the vent popped off and fell to the floor with a rattling of loose metal. Timmy stuck his head out of the vent and climbed into the room, covered from head to toe with dust bunnies and black soot. His little body was probably the first thing to move through the ductwork since it had been built decades ago.

His face was black and his teeth gleamed white in his mouth. "Hi, Adam, miss me?"

Adam was shocked. "Holy shit, Timmy, what the hell are you doing here? How did you manage to find me?"

Timmy skipped over to him and used the Swiss Army knife Paul had given him to cut Adam's ropes. It was the same tool he had used to pry the vent from its moorings.

"There's a nice lady named Eve. She said she'd help us if we take her with us when we leave. She showed me how to sneak through the vents in the wall. I had to crawl around for a while until I found this room," Timmy said, working at the ropes. The nylon was proving harder to cut with the small knife. He concentrated on cutting, the tip of his tongue between his lips.

"Can she come with us?" Timmy breathed while working on the ropes with hope in his voice. "She's really nice. And I kind of promised."

"Sounds fine with me, if we *can* get out of here. Oww, easy kid, that's my arm you're cutting!"

"Sorry," Timmy said.

Minutes passed and Adam felt his ropes loosening. He was now able to pull his hands apart a little, allowing Timmy more room to slice at the ropes. As soon as he didn't have to worry about Adam's wrists, Timmy was able to redouble his efforts and soon later Adam pulled his hands free.

"Yes!" he yelled as he jumped out of the chair. Despite aching and cramped limbs—and a small amount of blood on his wrists from Timmy's knife slips—he turned and picked Timmy up, hugging him.

"You are the man, kid. You know that?"

Timmy smiled bashfully, then jumped when the Reverend stood up suddenly.

"Relax, Timmy. That guy's crazy, but he seems harmless."

Adam steered the Reverend back to his cot and set him down, then moved back to the door, listening for sounds in the hall.

After a full minute passed with no noise, he relaxed. There was nothing at all, just the distant sound of people in the main theatre of the church. He tried the door and it was locked. *Well, what did I expect?*

"What do we do now?" Timmy asked.

Adam frowned. "That is a *good* question. My hands are free, but we're still stuck in here."

Adam was racking his brain, trying to figure out what to do when the sound of a key being slipped into the lock of the door filled the room. Adam looked left and right, not knowing what to do. He looked down at Timmy.

"Quick, find a place to hide," Adam whispered to the boy.

Timmy dove under the cot. Above him, the crazy man continued mumbling to himself.

Adam sat down quickly and placed his hands behind his back the way he'd been left earlier and waited for the door to open. Adam's pulse was going a mile a minute as he braced himself for what he would have to do next.

Less than two seconds had ticked away after he had returned to his sitting position in the chair before the door swung open and Steve walked in.

The man had a slight grin on his face as he stopped in front of Adam.

"Roy wants me to get some information from you. Like where you got all the weapons and ammo from. He said there was some good shit in that bag, primo stuff. I volunteered since you and me got along so well before."

Adam looked up at Steve, his face void of emotion.

Steve grinned wider at his helpless captive, savoring the feeling of power. I lasted until Adam rocketed out of the chair and wrapped his arms around Steve, taking him down in a tangle of arms and legs.

Steve was a scrapper and recovered quickly.

Before Adam could get off a punch, Steve hit him in the kidneys, causing Adam to loose his breath and curl up. Adam's knee shot up between Steve's legs quite on its own, slamming into Steve's testicles.

The larger man let out a high squeak and his face turned white. He was unable to take in another breath, his eyes wide in agony.

Adam started swinging, not caring where his punches were connecting. He could only hit hard and hope for the best.

Steve recovered quickly and took Adam's blows on his arms, then threw a right hook that sent Adam flailing in a daze. As he fell, Steve climbed to his feet and kicked Adam hard in the stomach. Adam curled into a fetal position, hoping to lessen the blows, but Steve was on a roll.

Steve knelt down and punched Adam in the face, slicing the meat inside his mouth. Through blurry eyes, Adam looked up and waited for the next blow, which Steve was already getting ready to deliver.

Instead, Steve screamed and his hands went to his back. Adam didn't know what was happening, but he figured that it would be a good time to fight back.

Swinging his legs around, he brought up his knees and kicked with everything he had. Steve flew across the room and struck the far wall, back-first. His animated face went slack. Then, like a puppet with its strings cut, he fell forward and landed on the floor, bouncing once, then lying still.

He didn't move after that.

Adam made it as far as his knees before nausea got the better of him. His head was dizzy and his sides ached, and puking did *not* help.

Well, maybe it did. He felt a little better. Maybe. Timmy was next to him, trying to help him up, but he was way too small to do more than give moral support.

After a minute, Adam managed to stand up and stumbled over to the open door. Making sure it was unlocked, he closed it softly, then looked down at the man who had wanted to beat him to death.

Steve lay on his stomach, stone dead. In his back, just below his shoulder blades was a small knife handle.

Adam nudged Steve with his boot. The prone figure remained immobile; he was stone dead.

Adam leaned down and hugged Timmy. "Thanks, kid. That was quick thinking."

Timmy had tears on his cheeks. "I didn't want to hurt him, but he was going to hurt you. I'm sorry."

Adam chuckled. "Don't be, Timmy. He was a bad man and he got what he deserved, and that's all there is to it. Listen, just give me a second to catch my breath and then we'll go get Josey, okay?"

Timmy nodded happily and hugged Adam again, a few more tears sliding down his soot-stained cheeks. Adam winced from the pressure of the hug, but accepted it.

Adam noticed a small pistol sticking out of Steve's waistband and bent over the body, pulling the handgun free. It was a small .22 and Adam popped the clip. He grinned when he saw it was full.

He nodded; at least now he was armed.

Adam looked back to the Reverend and he began to feel dizzy so he sat down on the chair and placed his head between his legs. While the adrenaline continued pumping, he thought about what was coming next. After a couple minutes, he started to feel better.

The Reverend, still in his own world, hadn't noticed the scuffle.

After a full five minutes, Adam decided he was feeling as good as he was going to. Standing up, he prepared to open the door.

"You ready for this, Timmy?"

"I guess so," the boy answered quietly.

"Okay. Just stay behind me, and if you hear gunshots, then find someplace to hide until I come get you."

Timmy nodded, fearful eyes wide.

Taking a few quick breaths, Adam opened the door and stepped into the hallway, pistol leading the way.

"Find Josey and Eve," he whispered to himself. "Then fight through Roy's men and escape into a nightmare city filled with blood-thirsty, walking corpses. No problem," he said. "Just another night in zombie world."

He crept slowly down the hallway, expecting to be discovered at any moment. With a firm resolve, he moved deeper into the church.

After Adam moved away from the room, leaving the door open, the Reverend sat up on his cot. His eyes lit up when he saw the door. Standing up, he too left the room. But he had a very different agenda then Adam's.

Deep in his madness, he remembered the zombies in the court-yard; Satan's soldiers waiting to do battle on their Lord's behalf. He knew he needed to set them free so they could return to their master and tell him their cause was lost.

He remembered there was a pair of doors that led directly out to the courtyard on the first floor. There was a curtain over them now, and the newer parishioners had no idea it was there.

Reverend Bernie moved down the stairs to his destination, and God was on his side.

CHAPTER 35

The door swung open slowly, and Josey threw herself back onto the mattress.

Roy stood in the doorway talking to Tom.

"Fine, just take care of it. Now leave me the fuck alone for a while. I want to break in our new guest," Roy said as he leered at Josey over his shoulder.

"Sure, Roy, no problem. I'll see that everything you want gets—" Tom's voice was cut off as Roy slammed the door. Josey could hear Tom's footsteps as the man left to do Roy's bidding.

Roy stood over her, looking down like an animal eyeing its prey.

"That Tom. He's a good guy, I guess, loyal to the last, but he's kind of a dumbshit." Roy chatted with her while he unbuttoned his shirt, like they were lovers.

Josey stared at him with hate in her eyes. "You disgusting prick. First you kill my husband in cold blood and now you think you're going to rape me? Well, bring it over here buster, and I'll bite it off," she snapped.

Roy pulled two Glocks from behind him and set them on a stack of books in the corner and turned back to her.

Leering, he started to unbuckle his pants.

"Well, thanks for the warning, sweetcheeks. Until you're broken in, I'll just stay away from your mouth. 'Sides, there's plenty of other holes to keep me occupied."

His pants and underwear dropped to the floor. He was already growing stiff, the anticipation making him harder by the second.

Josey chuckled as Roy stood in front of her. "Shit. If I knew you were that small, I wouldn't fought so much," she said.

Roy's hand met her face with a loud smack.

"That's enough, bitch! Say something else and I'll cut your tongue out and feed it to you!"

Her head spinning from the slap, she kept quiet. Josey could tell, this man meant what he said. Roy knelt down and caressed her breasts through her shirt, his member bobbing with excitement.

Josey looked away and continued struggling with her bindings. Roy pushed her shirt up and squeezed one of her nipples hard, getting her attention.

"Don't look away from me. I want to look you in the eyes when I take you," he breathed.

Roy leaned down and pushed her onto the bed, bouncing her head off the wall. Roy started to kiss her and reached to unbutton her pants. Josey continued to work at her bonds. Roy took that as her squirming while she tried to shy away from him.

She could smell him, a mix of sweat and something else. If she had to try to name it, she would have called it pure evil. She remembered Roy's face when he'd gunned down her husband and her pulse quickened. He had enjoyed it. He'd enjoyed snuffing out the life of the man she had loved for almost twenty years.

And all she wanted was to see this man dead.

Roy climbed on top of her; the only thing preventing him from pushing inside her was his own patience. He liked to make them wait for as long as possible. Their fear and terror was what actually got him off; the sex was just a bonus.

Both his arms were now straddling her head as he prepared to slam inside of her and violate her the way no form of beating ever could.

The last few strands of nylon separated and she found her hands were free. She brought them around hard and slapped both of his ears like she was clapping a pair of cymbals.

Roy shouted and fell back, sex pushed out of his head.

Josey kicked her right leg straight up, crushing Roy's testicles into his stomach. He let out his breath in a whoosh and fell down as Josey rolled off the bed.

Jumping to her feet, she pulled down her shirt and grabbed her pants for later.

She reached for the doorknob, mind racing on where exactly she was supposed to go once she got out of the room. She saw the two guns sitting only a few feet away from her and reached for them, but there was no time. Roy rolled to his feet, and with a savage growl jumped to attack her. Her hand on the knob, she pulled the door open and dashed into the hall.

"You'll pay for that, bitch," he wheezed from behind her. "In blood."

Before she'd gone more than six feet, she was stopped in the hall-way by a pair of strong hands that grabbed her and pulled her to the side, and she screamed.

"No, I was so damn close!" she cried to the world as she felt all her energy slip away.

She could see Roy stood up straight and prepare to retrieve his property.

Her shoulders slumped; it was hopeless. She was caught only sec-onds after escaping. After everything she and her friends had suffered through, it was all for nothing.

She had tried and she had lost.

It was over.

CHAPTER 36

Josey sagged in the strong arms holding her tight, all hope flowing out of her like water from a broken cup.

Then she turned her face up to look into her captor's eyes and her mouth fell open and her eyes went wide with shock.

"Adam! Oh my God! But how—"

Adam cut her off. "No time. We need to get the hell out," he said.

His eyes caught movement in the room Josey just left, and he swung her to the side, bringing up the .22 and snapping off two rounds. The first went high, striking the lintel of the doorframe, but the second flew through the open doorway. Roy jumped back, kicking the door shut, his curses loud enough to be heard in the hallway.

"Shit, people are gonna hear that. We need to go now!" Adam said, moving back down the hall.

Josey picked Timmy up and hugged him tight. "I'm so glad I found you," she said, moving behind Adam.

Timmy hugged her tight. "Me too, Auntie. I was scared."

She rubbed his shoulder and picked up the pace. "Where are we gonna go?" she asked Adam.

Adam had stopped at the top of the stairs. Below him he could hear men yelling to each other. It would probably be only seconds before they had company. "Who I look like, James Bond? I have no damn idea. I've just been making it up as I go," Adam said.

Timmy jumped down and pulled Josey into a side door. "Come here, you guys, follow me."

With no other options, Adam and Josey followed the boy. He brought them into a room that was empty except for an opening at the far wall. Timmy went to the door and opened it.

Adam and Josey looked down an open shaft that led straight into darkness.

"We have to go down there," Timmy said.

"What, are you crazy? We have no idea what's down there. We could end up with broken legs or trapped in a boiler," Adam said.

Timmy shook his head. "No, listen to me. Eve told me about this. She says it goes right to the basement. She said she put stuff there to break our fall."

"Who's Eve?" Josey asked.

Adam waved the question away. "No time. A friend, she's helping us."

Footsteps were clomping down the hallway outside as guards started checking the adjacent rooms, searching for them. Doors were being opened and slammed closed, shaking the walls around them.

The doorknob started turning on the door to their room, only the cheap lock keeping the searchers out.

Adam looked at Josey and shrugged. "Looks like we're out of options," he said. Before he could stop the boy, Timmy jumped into the hole and disappeared into the dark, his feet the last to go.

The door rattled in its frame as men tried to break it in. With one last glance, Josey climbed into the opening, and uttering a small squeak as she started downward, slid into the shaft.

The door crashed in and Adam turned and fired two quick shots at the intruders.

They fell away from the doorway, one of them bleeding. There would be others soon.

A round flew by his head, lodging in the wall behind him. Adam jumped head first into the shaft.

Roy was so pissed off, he couldn't put it into words. The anger was something he could taste, a bile in his throat that would not go away. He'd just finished getting dressed, his balls aching like they'd been put in a vise and squeezed as hard as possible. He'd retrieved his guns, and they felt good in his hands.

That little bastard had almost shot him. The damn bullet had come so close, Roy had felt its passage.

He heard more gunshots . . . his men must have found the boy and the woman. And the woman, oh man would she pay when he got hold of her. She'd be lucky if he just decided to give her to the zombies. He smiled grimly. She wasn't going to be that lucky.

Opening the door warily, he saw Tom, Kate and four more of his men at the end of the hallway.

They must have them cornered in that room, he thought, striding forward and pushing through the crowd.

"Wait, Roy, it's not—" Tom said.

Roy pushed the man out of the way and stepped into the room where his prisoners should be, either dead or cowering on the floor.

"What the fuck? Where are they?" he demanded.

"That's what I was trying to tell ya. They jumped through some kind of laundry chute. They're gone."

"Bullshit, they're not gone. Get down to the basement. Where the Christ else could they go? This goddamn church isn't that big." He looked at the faces staring back at him. "Well, what the hell are you idiots waiting for? Find them!"

As one, the group headed for the stairs. Their heavy footsteps flooded up the hallway as they charged down the stairs toward the basement.

Roy smiled again. It wouldn't be long now.

Roy stopped short from following his crew down. A staccato of gunfire sounded from below. Men and women started to scream, their shrill cries sounding like they were being ripped apart.

After that second of hesitation, Roy set his jaw and started down the stairs, both Glocks in hand, wondering what the hell he was about to wade into.

He was halfway down when he stopped cold. A zombie was in the stairwell, looking up at him with dead eyes. Behind that one was another, and another. Each walking corpse was struggling to get up the stairs, only their lack of co-ordination slowing them down.

Roy's mind raced. How the hell had they gotten inside the church?

He cursed. The church was the only safe place he'd found in the city. If he didn't take it back, all of them were doomed.

He fired at the first walking corpse, striking it in the shoulder. The bullet went through harmlessly, but it hit the next zombie directly in the nose. It slumped down, clogging the stairwell and slowing the others behind it.

Roy retreated up the stairs. There was another set of stairs on the other side of the building. He could use it to return to the first level and take command before everything fell the fuck apart.

He shot one more time down the stairwell, not hitting anything.

Cursing his marksmanship, he turned and ran back the way he'd come. He passed his room and continued onward, cutting through a storeroom and popping out on the other side of the hallway.

The stairs were only a few feet away. He could hear screaming and the weapons discharge, but he kept running. He picked up the smell of smoke, but he dismissed it.

He hadn't worked this hard taking what he wanted to give it all up now.

Reaching the stairs, he brought up his weapons and charged down them. Whatever he'd find, he knew he was ready for it.

He hit the ground floor running. There was a smoking curtain in front of him. He pushed it aside and charged into the theatre.

He stopped running and stared at the chaos that greeted him there. As he watched the fire and destruction in front of him, he quickly retracted his last statement in his head.

He was definitely *not* ready.

CHAPTER 37

Adam was scared out of his mind.

He shot down the vent in total darkness, the wind whipping by his face. He had no way of knowing what was at the bottom. Visceral scenes of him crashing head-first into a stone floor flashed into his mind, making him even more terrified.

Without warning, a dim light hit his eyes and he fell into something soft. His arms and legs went bouncing and he was seriously worried about breaking something.

He lay perfectly still, eyes screwed shut and surprised he was still alive.

Opening his eyes, he saw three faces looking down on him. Two he recognized; the third belonged to an attractive young woman in her early twenties.

"Hi," Eve said, "nice trip?"

He blinked up at her, Josey and Timmy. Josey helped him to his feet and he stood on wobbly legs. After a minute or so he was doing better and was able to stand without assistance.

"I want to ride it again," he whispered.

"Yeah, I know. I found it one day when I was cleaning. I think they used to use it for laundry or something. The church used to let people stay here, you know, homeless guys and stuff."

Adam was barely listening, still not at peak performance.

He just nodded. "Uh-huh, yeah that's great," he said.

His eyes lit up with recognition of where he was. Looking at Eve, he grabbed her arm and dragged her to the middle of the room.

"We're in the cellar? Where's the door out of here?" Adam asked her.

She shook her head no. "There isn't. It was boarded up and barricaded so the zombies couldn't get in. It would take us forever to get it open."

Adam saw the windows were all high up on the wall with metal gratings on them. Plus, he could see the shadows of legs from the moonlight. There would be no escape from the church through those windows.

"Look, we've got to go. I'm sure Roy and his goons will be down here any second and I don't want to be trapped down here. Can you get us back upstairs? From there we can get out the front doors and get lost in the city."

She nodded quickly. "Sure, I can do that, but are you sure it's safe?"

Josey answered. "Honey, there isn't anything safe anymore. We need to get out of this church, that's all I know."

"Okay, then follow me. There's a small service stairway that will bring us upstairs to the middle of the main floor near the north wall," Eve told them.

"Sounds good," Adam said. "Let's go."

They followed Eve across the cement floor to a small wooden door that opened out. One by one, they filed into the gloom-filled stairwell and Josey closed up behind them. Eve produced a candle to light their way.

Timmy held Josey's hand tight as the four of them moved up the thin stairway. Shoulders rubbed the sides of the wall while they crept upward as quickly and quietly as they could.

Adam shortly found out their worries about making too much noise was completely unfounded. Gunfire and screams were clear through the walls.

Adam turned to Josey with puzzlement in his eyes. If they were on the stairs, then who was fighting with whom up in the theatre?

Josey shrugged slightly at his unspoken question.

Reaching the top, Eve slowly opened a skinny door barely large enough to fit an adult. It was carved into the wood of the wall, so from inside the church, no one would know it existed. As Adam slipped by her, he felt breasts rubbing lightly against him. Despite everything, he still felt a tingle in his stomach. Then he passed her and the tingle was forgotten.

He poked his head out halfway around the door. To his right was the podium and to his left were the large wooden front doors.

They were still closed tight. The front of the church was pandemonium as men and women fought zombies off in the midst of a fiery blaze. The church was filled with smoke, blurring his eyes and snatching at his breath.

No one had been prepared for this and they were slowly being slaughtered. The guards, in their haste to destroy the ghouls, wasted bullet after bullet firing into torsos instead of heads. Charred and burning bodies were everywhere, some not moving, others still writhing in pain.

Adam ducked back into the stairwell and closed the door.

"You are not going to believe this. The church is overrun by zombies *and* it's on fire." He spread his hands. "Seems like a good time to go. The fire is near the podium, but it's spreading fast. There are a few . . . *things* in our path, so keep calm and let me take care of anything that gets too close."

"If we can get out of here, I know where they keep the keys to the SUV," Eve said.

"Good, then that's where we'll go first. Once we're outside, you lead us," Adam said, and Eve nodded understanding. "Okay, then. Everyone ready?"

Everyone nodded. "Well, let's go," Adam said and turned to push open the door as wide as it would open.

Adam stepped out first, right into dead arms.

Ten minutes earlier

Reverend Bernie stumbled out of his chambers, his destination clear. While Adam went straight, the Reverend headed down the stairs to the first floor.

A few people saw him but paid him no mind, simply saying hello and continueing on with their chores. The Reverend reached the bottom of the stairs and then slipped into the large area behind the podium.

In a few quick steps he was at the curtain. He pulled it aside, the large door exactly where he remembered it to be.

He pushed on the handle, disengaging the lock and opening the door wide. The smell of death and decay flooded into the church.

In the courtyard, the zombies turned as one, then charged the door.

Reverend Bernie stood perfectly still; the door now wide open to the courtyard.

Just as the first undead hand reached for him, his mind cleared and his eyes focused, and a single second of clarity struck him.

In that fleeting second, everything that had happened in the past month flooded into him and the revelation of what he'd just done by opening the doors and letting the zombies into the church hit him like a freight train.

"Oh my Lord, please forgive me," he whispered.

He was knocked over and crushed as ghouls fell on of him. His body was torn limb from limb as claw-like nails tore and scraped for a piece of flesh.

In less than a minute, he was nothing but gobbets of flesh and scattered bone as the horde of undead poured into the church.

The parishioners had no time to react. They heard the Reverend screaming and then ghouls were flooding into the church, devouring everyone they came close to.

Torches and oil lamps were knocked over, flowing curtains catching on fire and consumed in seconds. Blossoming fireballs shot up over the front of the church, the material igniting like dried newspaper. The now oil-soaked carpeting flared to life, orange and red flames licking at everyone's feet. Within minutes, the front of the church was a blazing inferno, the living and dead alike, stumbling around on fire.

Some people were too petrified to move and just sat in the pews, praying for their God to save them until they were pulled to the floor and devoured.

Children screaming as their parents desperately tried to protect them and failing, the sudden orphans quickly joining their parents in death.

What was once a church was quickly a charnel house of fire and blood, and no Lord or Savior was there to prevent it from happening.

This church had no God . . . and never would again.

CHAPTER 38

Adam screamed as the waiting arms of a male zombie grabbed him. The face of the dead man was sloughed to the left and there were holes in his face where worms poked their heads out, wiggling back and forth. The dead man opened his mouth and growled at Adam, and it was apparent the ghoul had no tongue.

Trapped in the ghoul's embrace, Adam had his gun pointing towards the ground. No Tongue tried to bite Adam's nose off, the zombie's head snapping like a chicken pecking seed in the barnyard. Adam tossed his head back and teeth snapped on empty air.

Adam head-butted No Tongue on the nose. Cartilage crunched under his forehead and the ghoul paused for a fraction of a second.

Josey stepped out and picked up a statue from the side wall of the theatre, and brought it down on No Tongue's head.

Skull gave to stone and the skull cracked like a melon. The odor of rotten brains flew up Adam's nose and it took all he had to keep from vomiting onto his sneakers.

Eve came out next and squealed when she saw the corpse at Adam's feet. Behind her, Timmy gave her a shove so he could get out. He stepped over the body and waited for the rest of them to move.

Adam took a step back and flashed Josey a smile of thanks. She nodded and pointed to the doors. Behind them, more of the undead were crawling over pews and gutted bodies to get to them.

Adam shot at the closest one. The ghoul lost his balance and fell head first into a pew. Adam turned and ran for the doors, the others close behind him.

A dead woman got in his way in a blood-stained gray power suit, and he shoulder-checked her into one of the pews. She went flying ass over teakettle and her dress fell down around her torso. Adam got a quick flash of her naked pubic region, maggots and worms squirming around her dry orifice.

He turned away and wondered if he'd ever want to have sex again.

Adam stopped at the doors and looked at Eve. "You said you knew where the keys for the truck were, right?"

She nodded. "They should be in the visor. Tom told me that one night when he was finished with me."

"*Should* be? Fucking should be? You mean you don't know for sure?"

"Look, that's what I was told," she said. A stray bullet whined off the door and everyone ducked behind the pew. Adam peeked over the pew-back and saw Roy standing on the other side of the theatre, staring at the carnage, mouth hanging open.

Adam decided this was his chance. Lining Roy up in his sights, he slowed his breathing and squeezed the trigger. The shot went a few inches wide and Roy ducked, looking for the shooter, his own pistols coming up.

Roy's eyes lit up when he spotted Adam and he sent two shots of his own. Both went wide. Roy called some of his men to him and Adam realized that he wasn't shooting to hit them, but to keep them pinned down.

Roy rallied his men and they formed a firing line on the podium. They started moving forward slowly, mowing down every zombie that strayed into their line of fire, staying out of reach of the flickering flames and decayed, grasping hands of the ghouls.

In less than a minute, every rotting body was laying still, the horde destroyed. Most of the parishioners were either dead or dying from bites of flames.

Roy ignored them and set his sights on Adam.

Adam ducked down and looked to the others. "They're coming. It's now or never."

Josey and Eve nodded. Timmy smiled grimly, too old for his years.

"Let's get the hell out of here," the boy said. His eyes were starting to water from the spreading smoke and his breath was coming in heavy gasps.

Adam stood up, firing his pistol as fast as he could. Across the church, Roy and his men ducked for cover behind the closest pew, some of them caught between Adam's gunshots and the licking flames.

Eve pushed on the waist-high horizontal bars on the large front doors, unlatching the locks. The doors began to open wide, the fresh breeze sucking out the smell of blood, death and smoke from the burning church.

The fresh air fanned the fires, feeding them anew. The flames doubled in size and reached for the roof of the church, the white ceiling blackening. There was a scream as one of Roy's men was caught in the growing blaze, his hair already singed off.

Roy cursed at the man and shot him in the chest, silencing his screams.

Eve, Josey and Timmy, ran out of the church and onto the stone steps. Adam fired until the slide locked back on empty, running backward through the doors, then pushed them shut on a hail of bullets. Looking around, he spotted a two-by-four and told Eve to grab it.

Picking up the wood, she ran up the stairs and handed it to him. Adam shoved the piece of pine wood between the curved door handles of the two doors. His breathing was coming easier now, the air outside free of smoke.

Adam turned away from the doors and his mouth fell open. All around the fence were hundreds of the living dead. Whatever passed as reasoning in their dead brains said the only food left was in the church.

The alleys on both sides of the building were wall to wall bodies; walking corpses pushing against one another, waiting to feast. The heads and shoulders of the dead seemed to ebb and flow like the tide as they jostled for position.

At first glance, Adam thought the dead were burning, as clouds of smoke hovered over their heads. But then the sound of high pitched buzzing filled his ears and he realized that there was no smoke. There were thousands of flies surrounding the rotting bodies.

The smell was beyond overwhelming. The odor of decay was so strong Adam thought he could have cupped it in his hand like soup.

Rats darted and climbed between the ghouls as they feasted on dead flesh. The rats and insects the only living things in the city that were still flourishing.

Adam and the others stood stock still, shoulders sagging in defeat. The church doors shook in their frames. The double doors were strong, but the two-by-four was not. One piece of wood would not stop Roy for long.

The doors shook again as men threw their shoulders against the other side.

Adam heard Roy yelling through the doors. He screamed and the door would vibrate from more impacts of bodies.

Adam sat on the stone stairs and set the empty pistol next to him, so much useless iron.

Josey and Eve came up and sat down, as well. Josey was hugging Timmy and Eve was holding the boy's hand. Timmy and Eve had grown close very quickly, Adam thought.

He stared out at the undead faces pushing on the fence. The fence sagged in the middle, but it held. The moans of the dead were like a song of sorrow, pulling at his heartstrings and making him want to just give up, just lie down and die. He thought of Paul then, and wondered what he would have. Adam wished he was here. He felt as though he'd lost two fathers to this nightmare. He looked up again at the fence, watching it bend and flow with each surge of the bodies pressed against it.

Now that the little group was out on the stairs, the undead were more agitated. Adam could see more and more of them were pushing on the fence, and if he was right, in less than an hour, it would give, and they would be swallowed in a wave of teeth and claws.

Looking down at his pistol, he wished he had saved four bullets.

The door shook again and the two-by-four started to crack, small stress lines appearing where the wood was jammed into the door handles.

It wouldn't be long now.

Josey and Eve curled up next to him and tried to block out the moans of the ghouls. Adam, too, closed his eyes, and tried to spend his last few minutes on earth thinking of something better, a happier time, when the world was full of promise.

CHAPTER 39

The doors shook in their frame again. The two-by-four was only seconds from breaking in two, the soft wood not nearly up to the task of what was being asked of it.

The four of them stood and waited for the inevitable. Adam was hugging everyone, scared out of his mind. The worst thing was thinking what would happen to Timmy.

He tried to block out the images of the boy being either ripped to pieces by the undead or killed by Roy, but it didn't work. Every time the doors took a hit, all four of them would jump just a little.

They were moments away from death. Adam fingered the empty pistol and thought that he could charge the men and get them to shoot all four of them.

It'll suck, but it'll be quick, he thought.

The doors shook again, probably the last impact the fractured two-by-four would take.

Then the sound of a horn filled the street, the loud blast getting all of their attention.

As one, the four of them turned around and saw in the middle of the undead sea a green National Guard truck with a cloth-covered bed working its way through the crowd.

The truck was high enough that the zombies couldn't get on it, their muscles and tendons unable to support them. As some fell, others would step on top of the bodies, the corpses becoming steps that would bring others closer to the edge of the truck.

These undead were rewarded with a firing M-16 in the face. The rifle would buck and the corpses would fall away into the crowd. The truck slowly made its way until it was less than a hundred feet away. The truck pulled over with its driver's side facing the church. The driver climbed out the window and over the roof into the rear compartment.

For a few heartbeats nothing happened, then the side cloth of the truck was rolled up and metal glistened in the moonlight.

Then came the unmistakable thunder of an M-60 machine gun. White hot tracers flew over the zombie's heads until the gunner got his range. He swept the gun back and forth, spitting steel-jacketed death and mowing bodies down, spent casings falling to the ground in a brass rain.

Heads were separated from shoulders and bodies were ripped in half as if a scythe had swiped from above. The almost 360 degree field of fire took down hundreds in seconds, the fusillade enough to rattle the few intact windows in nearby buildings.

The machine gunner slowly worked his line of fire up to the fence, and as the four survivors leaped for cover, he cleared all the ghouls out. Bullets ricocheted off the fence, the sparks lighting up the night.

Behind the four escapees, the doors shook one last time and the two-by-four shattered, falling to the stone and being swept aside as the doors opened. Smoke billowed out of the open door and Roy looked like the Devil walking out of his flaming kingdom.

Caught in the middle, Adam and the others backed down the stairs. Roy stepped out onto the stone landing and looked down at the four terrified people.

"Got you, you bastards, I win," he said.

Adam and the others hit the sidewalk and covered their heads, waiting for the next shoe to drop.

Roy looked at them, then he looked out into the street. He saw the truck and the man standing in the back holding something.

A stream of smoke shot out the back end of it and something shot out the front on a trail of flame. Roy turned and jumped back into the church. An instant later, the LAW rocket struck just above the doors, and rock and smoke exploded out.

On the sidewalk below, Adam and the others covered their heads with shaking arms. None of them had ever seen this kind of thing before.

When the dust settled, Adam rolled over and stood up. Josey and Timmy were fine. Eve was dazed, but unhurt.

Adam looked up. The church doors hung askew in their frame, burning slightly, the tops black and charred. Stone rubble and debris littered the steps. The arch over the opening nothing but blackened stone and mortar, the bricks still falling while Adam watched.

The National Guard truck had started again and was moving closer through the wide path made by the M-60. Shattered bodies of the undead were everywhere, but the front of the fence was clear. The truck revved its engine and surged forward, swaying up and down as it drove over corpses, crushing skulls and torsos, flesh caked in the tire treads.

Near the fence gate, more ghouls came out of the alley and were only seconds from filling in the gaps from their fallen brethren as the National Guard truck hit the front of the fence. The grille and left fender crumpled under the impact.

Adam and the others turned away from flying debris as the fence and its moorings were pulled from the ground.

Paul stuck his head out of the driver's side window and flashed them a smile. "You guys need a lift?"

A bullet bounced off the hood of the truck and Adam turned to see Roy at the doorway to the church. He had a bleeding forehead, but otherwise seemed fine.

As he shot another round at Paul, other shapes came out of the dust, more of Roy's men.

Paul raised the M-16 and fired at the doorway, forcing Roy and the others under cover.

"Come on, guys, we don't have any time!" Paul yelled over the roar of the M-16. He turned his gun on two zombies who were nearing Adam and the others.

Paul pulled the truck forward and brought the bed even with the opening in the fence. The undead swarmed in. Paul shot at them and Adam fought with nothing but his hands and feet. In the chaos, Eve and Timmy became separated, already more than six feet away and getting further with every passing second.

Paul shot a ghoul directly in front of Adam. The younger man waved a quick thanks, then called out to Eve.

"Eve, you take Timmy to the Suburban and we'll take the truck!" He hoped she could hear him.

She slipped out the side of the fence with Timmy to where the SUV sat in the side alley.

Paul covered her, taking out a few ghouls that were getting close until Eve and Timmy were safe inside the vehicle.

Adam and Josey climbed into the rear of the truck and Paul waited for the SUV's headlights to come on.

Adam was inside the rear bed of the truck and he had his hand out for Josey. As she started to climb up, snapping jaws popped out from under the truck and bit into her pants. She screamed and kicked the zombie away before it could chew through. Bits of her pant leg went with the ghoul. Adam pulled as hard as he could and they both fell into the back of truck.

Paul got what he was waiting for. The SUV's headlights flared on, brightening the area in front of the vehicle into day. The vehicle bucked a few times while Eve got the hang of the clutch and then surged forward. It flew out in front of the National Guard truck, rolling over everything in its path.

A bullet whined in the inside cab of the National Guard truck, ricocheting off the roof and hitting the passenger door. Paul sent suppressing fire at the church doors and then put the truck into gear.

Roy and his men dove for cover, their arms no match for the military rifle fire.

With a grinding of gears, Paul pulled away from the shattered fence and headed off into the night.

Roy popped his head up at the sound of the truck's engine. As it pulled away he ran out onto the stone stairs and sent round after round at the receding taillights. Cursing at the top of his voice, his anger a tangible thing, Then the truck's headlights were gone, the street thrown back into darkness.

He looked to his right and stopped. Behind him, the rest of his men had come to help, Tom and Kate at the head of the pack.

Tom took a look at the approaching wall of walking corpses and ran back inside. Roy rallied his people, trying a firing line like he had in the church. But there were far more living dead than before.

The line sent round after round into the undead army, each corpse that fell away replaced by two and three more. Bodies piled up, the ghouls crawling over their fallen brethren to reach Roy and his men.

The dead were unstoppable. The dead were invincible.

The side fence collapsed, weakened from the rest of the barrier being torn apart, and Roy and his people were cut off from the church.

Roy fired again and again until his Glocks ran dry. He threw them at the closest undead and then tried to retreat. The undead had surrounded them and Roy screamed for God to help him.

With his loyal people around him, Roy was torn apart on the steps of the church. Roy's last sight was the cross that had sat above the wooden doors on the front of the church, now hanging upside down from the explosion.

As his insides were ripped from his twitching body, he looked up at the inverted cross and wondered if he'd been wrong about the whole Heaven and Hell thing.

His last thought was that he'd be finding out soon enough.

Tom ran through the church, tossing away his empty handgun. A few of the surviving parishioners that were trying to fight the fires stared at him, wondering what the hell.

He covered his face with his arms and jumped through the flames. When he landed on the other side, he found himself on fire. He quickly patted the flames with his hands, the fire burning his palms.

Reaching the back exit, he threw the doors open. He ran out into the alley and looked where the Suburban was supposed to be. Blinking his eyes clear of smoke and breathing the clean night air, he froze in place. The car was gone, like it had never existed.

He spun in a circle, not believing the vehicle was gone. There was a silver ring laying there in the dirt. He picked it up and turned it over in his hand. It was the ring he had made Eve wear.

A scuffing noise made him turn. He was surrounded by ghouls.

He fell to his knees with tears on his face.

"Eve, you fucking bitch!" he screamed to the night sky. Then he was swallowed by bodies. His screams lasted for quite a while as he was slowly ripped apart, piece by bloody piece.

CHAPTER 40

The small convoy of two pulled over to the side of the road about a half mile from the city limits. The road was pitch dark, only the beams of the halogen headlights illuminating the area.

When the National Guard truck stopped, Josey jumped off the back and ran to the front of the vehicle as fast as she could.

Paul was just climbing down from the cab and she flew into his arms, hugging and kissing him.

"Oh my God, I can't believe you're alive," she said, smothering him with kisses. He reciprocated for a minute and then tried to disengage himself from the ecstatic woman.

"All right, all right, give me some air. I missed you, too."

Adam strolled up and held out his hand to Paul. He took it and shook it with a big smile on his face. Adam pulled him close and hugged him, Paul slapping Adam on the back a few times before the two men disengaged.

"What's wrong with you people? You'd think I was the second coming of Christ?" Paul said.

Adam grinned at that. "Yeah, pretty much. We thought you were dead."

"Dead? Nah, that guy only winged me," he said, pulling back his green camo shirt to show them his bandaged shoulder. "It was a through and through. Still, even only getting clipped it nearly knocked me out. I tell you, getting shot, *is not* like they show it in the movies. It friggin' hurts like a motherfu—" he saw Timmy heading towards him and paused. "I figured if I moved, I was dead, so I just played possum until you left. Good thing that Roy fella didn't decide to shoot me again for kicks."

"Possum? You were playing possum?" Josey said, hitting his good shoulder. "I thought I'd lost you for good." She hugged him again a little softer than before, but still with passion.

With Josey around his neck, he looked down at Timmy. "Hey squirt, did you take good care of my wife for me?"

Timmy nodded. "You bet! And we killed a whole bunch of monsters!" He started to tell more, but Paul put his hand up to stop him.

"Whoa, hold on there, there's no time for that now. Right now, I think we should keep moving." He scanned the edge of the light from the headlights and the darkness beyond. "Who knows what the hell's out there? We'd be overwhelmed before we even had a chance to say 'whoops.' Best to move on and we can talk more when the sun comes up."

Paul looked at Eve, standing quietly behind Adam.

"And who's this young lady?" Paul inquired.

Adam gently took Eve by the arm and pulled her closer.

"This is Eve, and from what Timmy told me, she's a big reason why we're free. Who knows what might have happened if not for her," Adam said.

Paul held out his hand for Eve. "Pleased to meet you, and thanks for saving my friends and my wife."

She shook his hand. "No problem. I needed to get out of there and you folks seemed to be the best route available."

Paul nodded at that. "Fair enough. Welcome to the team." Paul clapped his hands together, softly thanks to his bandages. The once white bandages on his hands were a charcoal black and needed desperately to be changed. "All right everybody, let's load up and get moving."

With a flutter of activity, everyone returned to their vehicles. Timmy stayed with Eve, enjoying the feeling of sitting in the big SUV, while Josey climbed into the front of the truck to be with Paul.

Adam was about to return to the back of the truck, where he planned on stretching out and relaxing when Paul called to him.

"Hey, Adam, wait a second. I need to talk to you."

Adam stopped and turned to Paul, not liking the look on his face. Paul seemed to be wrestling with something. His taciturn eyes looked back at Adam and he stumbled over his next words.

"Look, Adam, after you guys left, I had to deal with a bunch of zombies. I was wounded and dazed and I had to make it all the way back to the rescue station. Night was falling, the fuckers were everywhere, and I was severely limited on what I could do."

He sighed for a moment, choosin his next words carefully.

"What I'm trying to say, is that while I made it to the trucks *alive*, I didn't make it there *unscathed*." He rolled up his left sleeve to show Adam a red bandage. In the light of the Suburban's headlights, he pulled off the bandage to show Adam a set of teeth marks, the skin around the bite already turning gangrenous.

Adam leaned against the truck, shocked. "Oh, Christ, Paul. No," he whispered.

Paul replaced the bandage and slid his shirtsleeve back down. "Look, Adam, it's okay. I should have died when Roy shot me. Everything after is gravy. Besides, it's worth it if my Josey is okay."

Adam didn't know what to say, so he just stood there, quiet.

Paul smiled at him, then turned to climb up to the cab. "I'll tell Josey while we're driving. Don't worry, she's a strong woman. She can handle it. Shit, she had to handle it once already, right?" He didn't wait for an answer.

Paul climbed into the cab and shut the door. With a roar, the engine surged to life. Adam shook his head and ran around to the rear and jumped up. Eve and Timmy waved to him from the SUV and he waved back, lying back in the truck bed.

The truck rumbled forward and Adam tried to get comfortable. As the truck rumbled over the road, he closed his eyes, not relishing what would happen when they stopped again.

Inside the truck, Josey rubbed her leg. It was hurting something awful. She figured she must have whacked it somewhere during their escape, but she couldn't remember where.

Paul was silent next to her, his attention on the road.

For a while she just sat next to him, laying back, breathing in his smell. But then her bruised leg started to itch and she sat up.

Paul gave her a quick glance, not wanting to take his eyes off the road for long. Behind him, the Suburban followed at a respectable distance, two lone vehicles following the thin yellow double line.

"What's wrong, you okay?" he asked her.

She made a face. "Yeah, I guess so. My leg is killing me, though. I must have whacked it somewhere," she said, rubbing it.

"Well, put on the dome light and see what it is. If it's something serious, we need to take care of it. Last I checked, the emergency rooms were closed," he laughed.

She made a face at his joke but did what he said. In the dim glow of the dome lamp, she pulled up her pant leg. On her calf muscle was a deep scratch. Paul slowed down a little to take a closer look. As he stared at the wound, he saw the clear indentation of what looked like a tooth mark. That alone would have been only ominous, but in the wan light he saw prominent veins shooting off the wound and up her leg. The wound was a bright red and seemed to almost pulse in the gloom of the cab. He had seen something similar recently, on his own arm.

His face went grim.

Josey pulled her pant leg down and sat up. She looked at him and realized he saw something he didn't like.

"What's wrong, what did you see? It looks like a bruise, that's all," she said with worry in her voice.

Paul had been putting off telling her he'd been infected, but now he realized he had no choice. He turned to her, one eye on the road and one on her.

"Honey, I have something to tell you that you won't like." He said this just loud enough for her to hear him over the engine. Then he hesitated, his statement hanging in the air between them.

"Well, tell me for Christ's sake!" she demanded.

Paul sucked in a deep breath, held it, then let it out, his stomach feeling like there were a hundred rats fighting to eat their way out. Then he sighed and told her what had happened to him in the city, and what her "bruise" was.

In the back of the truck, Adam perked his head up. He thought he'd heard a yell but the engine was too loud for him to be sure. After a moment, when the sound didn't occur again, he lay back down on the bed of boxes and relaxed.

He absently rubbed his arm where he had picked up a circular scratch fighting off the zombies at the back of the truck with Josey. The scratch oozed a few small droplets of blood, but otherwise seemed fine.

It would heal in time.

Not giving it much thought, he closed his eyes and let the rocking of the truck soothe him back to sleep.

CHAPTER 41

Adam snapped awake, realizing the truck had stopped. Rubbing his eyes to wake up, he stretched and climbed down out of the bed. The sun was coming up. He realized they must have driven all night.

Eve and Timmy were just hopping down from the Suburban.

Adam waited while Josey walked around the front of the cab and wrapped herself around Paul. The two of them walked arm and arm to the rear of the National Guard truck. As they grew nearer, it looked to Adam like Josey had been crying.

As Paul moved closer, it looked like he might have done some crying, too.

Adam waited for them. While he waited, he absently scratched his arm and leaned against the side of the truck.

Paul noticed this and pointed, most casually.

"What's wrong with your arm? You hurt it?"

"Yeah, I guess so, but for the life of me I can't remember where."

Josey seemed to chuckle at that, but it was a sad chuckle, not jovial. "Yeah, there seems to be a lot of that going around," she mumbled.

Paul moved closer and held out his hand. "Adam can I take a look at it?"

Adam shrugged and held out his arm.

Paul turned Adam's arm over so he could see the bruise. It resembled Josey's in almost every aspect . . . except for the absence of veins and the redness. Paul figured everyone's metabolism was different and the infection worked faster or slower in different people.

Paul frowned. "Jesus, Adam. I think you were bit. One of the fuckers must have got you before you made it into the truck."

Adam's world fell out from under him. He was infected?

He was going to die. And then, he was going to turn into one of those monsters. He slumped against the truck and slid down to the road. He ran his hands through his hair, head sagging down.

He would have cried, but it was too early for that. He had yet to wrap his head around it.

Josey leaned down next to him. "Oh, Adam, I'm so sorry. I know it's no consolation, but I got bit, too."

Adam looked up at her, surprised. "Oh, God, not you, too," he whispered.

She smiled wanly. "Yeah, I'm afraid so. Paul told me what happened to him. At first I couldn't believe I got him back only to have him taken away from me again, but now, well . . . at least we'll die together. As corny as that sounds."

Adam looked at her and shook his head. "No, that's not corny."

Paul held out his hand for Adam. "Think you can stand now?"

"Yeah, I guess so," Adam said and took the offered hand.

Eve and Timmy stood there, not quite understanding what was happening. Then Paul asked Eve to come over to him while Josey went to Timmy.

Eve's eyes were wide as she waited for Paul to speak. "Look, Eve, Josey and I talked about a few things while we were driving, and I know this is the best thing for Timmy."

She was puzzled. "What about Timmy? What do you mean by that?"

Paul sighed and rolled up his sleeve. "I got bit before I got to you guys and so was Josey. Adam, too. Look at his arm if you don't believe me. You know what's going to happen to us in a few days. Timmy can't stay with us. Once we turn, he'd either be alone or we'd kill him. That can't happen."

Eve was looking at Adam and then her eyes turned to Timmy. Josey was kneeling down talking to the boy. Timmy didn't seem to like what she was saying; his cheeks were covered with tears as he tried not to cry and his head was moving back and forth in slow motion.

Paul took Eve's hands and made her look at him again.

"Listen, Eve, Timmy needs to go with you. We'll give you as much gas as we can take out of the truck, and you can have the M-16. I found a good amount of ammo for it, and we'll load the Suburban up with as much supplies as will fit. The only thing I don't have is food and water, just a few K-rations I found. But they're yours."

Eve stood quietly. She was so frustrated. She finally made it away from the church and now all the people she escaped with are going to die.

"Jesus," she said, scratching her head. "It's not like you're leaving me with a lot of choices here."

Paul chuckled at that. "You're telling me? I'm not exactly pleased with the hand I've been dealt either, lady."

"Oh, Jesus! I'm sorry about that. I don't mean to—"

"I know, but I need an answer. Like now. The longer we stay together, the more dangerous it could get."

Eve sighed. "Shit, Paul, you already know my answer. Of course I'll take him."

He nodded. "Good. Let's get to work. There's a lot of crap to transfer out of the truck bed and I want to be finished as soon as possible."

Josey and Timmy walked over to them and Josey nodded to Paul. "He understands, but he doesn't like it one bit," she said.

"This sucks," Timmy said.

Paul leaned down and rubbed his hair. "I know it does, buddy. But we have to adapt and do the best we can. This is one of those times."

Timmy sniffed, not wanting to hear it. "I don't care, this sucks!" He ran into Josey's arms and started to cry. Full blown tears were now pouring down his cheeks as his sobs filled the morning.

Josey smiled softly at Paul. "He'll be all right. He just needs to let it out."

Paul nodded and turned to Adam, who was in his own world, facing his mortality.

"Come on, Adam, there'll be plenty of time to mourn ourselves once Timmy and Eve are on their way."

Adam looked at him and sighed. Paul was right, he had the rest of his life to worry, however short that might be. Right now he needed to make sure Timmy and Eve would be safe.

For the next hour, the survivors transferred all the remaining supplies to the back of the Suburban. Timmy seemed to be doing better, working and running distracting him from the goodbyes that would be on them all shortly.

Adam siphoned the gas from the National Guard truck with some tubing he found in the rear bed. Using an empty water bottle, it took almost an hour to siphon the tank empty. When the SUV's gas tank was full, the surplus was put into some spare gas cans the Suburban carried in case Roy's foraging crew found fuel.

Paul kept watch. A few lone zombies had come close, not too intimidated by the sunlight. Paul stitched them from stomach to head, putting them down for good.

The road was quiet, and there were only a few houses set back from the road. A crow flew by overhead, curious as to what the survivors were doing, but when it realized there was no food, it flew off in a northerly direction.

The sun was high overhead when they were finally finished with their work and ready to say their goodbyes.

Paul took Eve aside and showed her how to work the M-16. She practiced with the magazine and slide for a few minutes until she had it, then Paul had her take a few practice shots into the foliage lining the road.

Once she became used to the kick and the muzzle climb, she became a pretty good short-range shot.

Paul slapped her back gently and laughed. "Good enough for government work."

She smiled, proud of herself, then she lowered the weapon and turned to him. Before Paul realized it, she hugged him, surprising him. After a second, he returned the hug. She let go and stepped back, tears in her eyes.

"Thank you for saving me, even if I was just along for the ride. Don't worry about Timmy. I'll take care of him as if he was my own."

He smiled back, his eyes filling with emotion. "Even if I didn't have a choice, I'd still do it. I know you'll protect him."

The two walked back to the rest of the group. Timmy was crying hard, his tears like a river. He kept hugging everyone, not wanting to let go. Finally, when they had put it off for long enough, Paul picked Timmy up and carried him to the Suburban. Eve was saying her goodbyes to the people she had just met that already felt like family to her.

Paul sat Timmy in the passenger seat and buckled his seatbelt. Timmy's tears were still flowing strong, but he had managed to get the crying under control.

"Now I need you to take care of Eve, like we took care of you when your parents left you with us, okay?" Paul asked him quietly.

Timmy blew out his breath in a raspberry. "Please, Paul. I know my parents are dead. The monsters got them. But then you guys took me and now I have to go with Eve, and I don't want to. I want to stay with you guys."

"I know, pal, but you just can't. Me and Josey and Adam are going someplace you can't go yet. That's why you need to go with Eve."

Timmy folded his arms across his chest and turned his face away. He was done listening. Paul knew that look. After giving Timmy a kiss on the forehead, he stepped away and closed the door.

Walking back to the others he pointed to the SUV.

"Better get moving, Eve. He's calm for the moment, but I don't know for how long."

"He'll be okay. If there's one thing a kid at that age can do, it's bounce back," Adam said.

Eve gave everyone one last hug. When she got to Adam, she kissed him softly on the lips.

"Thank you," she whispered, "and good luck."

"You too," Adam breathed, the kiss giving him pause.

Eve walked to the Suburban and climbed into the cab. The engine started and she put it in gear, the vehicle rolling forward.

She beeped once as she drove by the others, Timmy's sad face plastered to the passenger window.

"Bye, Timmy! I love you, and don't you ever forget it!" Josey called to the retreating vehicle.

The three of them stood there well after the Suburban had disappeared over the rise in the road. Not talking, just staring, each lost in his or her private thoughts.

After a sufficient time had passed, Paul broke the silence.

"Come on, guys, we still have some gas left, let's see where it takes us."

Everyone silently climbed into the truck and Paul drove away, leaving the road empty once more.

CHAPTER 42

The engine sputtered for the last time and finally died; the truck rolling to a stop in the middle of the two-way blacktop. The road went on straight for miles until it was lost on the horizon.

The rearview mirror told the same story. Paul placed the truck in park and laid his hands on his lap. Next to him in the cab was Josey, and Adam sat against the passenger door.

"Well, that's it. We're outta gas," Paul said, frustrated.

"Are you just saying that so I'll neck with you?" Adam asked. Paul shook his head. "So where do we go?"

Paul gave him his patented shrug. "I have no goddamn idea." He opened the door of the cab and climbed down to the asphalt. Scanning his surroundings, he noticed a few rooftops peeking over the tops of the trees. One rooftop in particular caught his eyes.

"Hey, guys, come here. I think I see something," Paul said.

Josey and Adam sighed and climbed down from the cab. Walking around the truck, they stood next to him on the cracked asphalt.

"What is it, honey? My damn leg is killing me," Josey said.

"I know, hon' and I'm sorry, but take a look over those trees, what do you see?"

"I don't know, a roof?" Josey answered him.

He nodded. "Exactly, a big roof. A roof implies a building, and if we have to go somewhere . . ."

Adam studied the roof. "That might be farther away than you think, Paul. Do you really want to go hiking through the woods?"

"Sure, why not? It beats sitting in that cold truck waiting to die." He turned to Josey. "What do you say, hon'? Will you take one last walk with me?"

Holding back tears, she smiled at him. "Yes, of course, you romantic asshole."

"Great, let's get what gear we have and get going. It would be great if we're there by dark," Paul said, already moving to the back of the truck.

All three went to the rear and retrieved the few things not given to Eve and Timmy. Two bedrolls, a flashlight—Eve had taken two with her—a couple of heavy pipes used for supporting the cloth covering the rear bed, now makeshift weapons, and a few other things that might come in handy. No food, no water, no guns. They'd given all that to Eve.

Paul figured they were dead anyway, so a few days without food wouldn't really matter. Adam was kind of regretting that decision now. He was starving and, whether he would die in a few days or not, he still wished he could eat.

The three of them set off across the double-yellow line and crossed over to the opposite shoulder of the road, the only moving creatures in sight.

A few birds chirped in the trees and insects buzzed around them. Other than that, the forest was quiet.

They walked in silence, Paul and Josey holding hands and Adam behind them, the third wheel.

Hours passed and they took a break, the smell of the forest intoxicatingly sweet after all the death and decay in the city.

Paul's arm was giving him some trouble and his bullet wound was infected. Josey tried to help him, but he just shrugged it off.

"Jesus, Josey," he snapped. "It doesn't fucking matter. I'm dead anyway. Who gives a shit if my shoulder gets infected?"

"Fine, then die in pain if you want," Josey answered back, then turned her back on him and began walking away. Adam noticed she was limping while she moved away.

Paul stood up and ran after her, catching her at the top of the next rise. Adam just heard the words, "I'm sorry," from Paul and then Josey began crying and they hugged. Adam waited below the ridge, giving them some much-needed space.

When they recovered, Paul waved him on. Adam reached the top and Paul held out his hand to help Adam over the slope of the ridge. Once Adam was next to him, Paul grinned and slapped him on the shoulder.

Adam understood it was Paul's way of saying everything was okay, at least for the moment.

An hour later they reached a break in the tree line, the foliage thinning until there was nothing but overgrown grass. The forest had been cut away by man, the few stumps clearly visible in the tall grass.

They exited the forest at the back of a large building. The three survivors stepped onto the hardtop of a large parking lot and headed for the two-story, sprawling structure. The closer they came to the building, the more it became clear what it was.

"A shopping mall? You want to hole up in there? I've seen that movie. It doesn't end well," Adam said.

Paul grinned at that. "So life imitates art, so what? Deal with it."

"Besides, Adam, we don't have anywhere else to go," Josey said. "This is the best place to stay. Who knows, maybe the pharmacy has antibiotics and we can fight off this damn infection," Josey added, still the optimist.

"Fine, fine, we'll go," Adam said, giving in. They were right, what other options did they have?

The bricks looked brand new, as if the mall had been built recently; no watermarks marred its pristine surface. No entrances were evident. Plenty of exits. The fire doors had no handles or locks on the outside, making entry impossible.

With Paul in the lead, they walked around the building, the names of popular stores and franchises plastered on signs that hung from the sides of the structure.

Paul walked around the side-corner of the mall and then jumped back as if he'd been shot.

"What's wrong, are you all right?" Adam asked.

"Yeah, I'm fine. I'm fucking great. But we're not the only ones to find this place."

Adam looked around the corner and saw what Paul meant. The parking lot was full of the walking dead. The undead banged on the inch thick, glass doors and wandered aimlessly around the parking lot, weaving in and around the parked cars like Christmas shoppers after a long day of spending.

"Shit, they're everywhere. Do you think there's a sale? How the hell are we supposed to get in?" Adam asked, pulling his head back.

Paul looked out into the parking lot, at the dozens of parked cars that would forever be parked in the exact same spot until time stood still.

Paul turned and looked at Adam and Josey with a big smirk on his face.

"That's simple," he said. "We go for a drive."

CHAPTER 43

The three friends ran as fast as they could towards the farthest block of parked cars. Keeping low as they ran, they made it more than halfway before the first ghouls spotted them. Like a well choreographed team, they split up, Adam moving away from the cars and Paul and Josey continuing forward.

The first zombie's head swiveled, and dead eyes opened wider, then it started forward.

Prey, at last.

Others soon followed, and when Adam looked again, there were more than fifty walking corpses shambling towards him. Despite his pulse pounding in his ears, he was glad they were following him. That meant that Paul and Josey could get to the cars unobserved.

Adam moved away from the mall, running in a wide circle. He just needed to draw the undead away long enough for Paul to hotwire a car, then Paul would swing around and pick him up.

Stage one.

Adam kept running, his breath coming in gulps. He'd eaten nothing for almost a day and had just finished a long hike through the forest. Now he was running a race where, if he lost, he was torn to pieces and eaten by the winners.

He just hoped Paul was a good car thief.

———————◆·••◆•••◆———————

Paul and Josey weaved their way through the parked cars. Every surface of every vehicle was coated with dust and dirt. Paul ran on by willpower alone. His shoulder was killing him and his arm throbbed like it had its own heartbeat. He slowed down and waited for Josey to catch up to him. She was faring no better, her limp becoming much more pronounced.

He didn't care. He refused to give up. He would keep fighting until his last breath.

Now that he was in the maze of cars and trucks, he started to examine them more closely. He passed vehicle after vehicle, not liking what he was finding.

"What are you looking for? Let's just take one," Josey whispered to him impatiently.

"Can't," he said. "We need an older model, something from the 1980's or before. The older the better."

"Why?" she asked, breathing hard. Her lungs worked overtime for each gasp of air.

"Because I don't know how to hotwire the new cars. They have too much computer shit in them."

His eyes lit up when he found what he wanted. A 1978 Buick Apollo sat near the end of the lot. It was covered in gray primer and as Paul moved closer to it, he saw someone had lovingly done all the bodywork; all the car needed was a paint job.

"Bingo," he exclaimed. "Josey, I found one."

She turned and ran to him. She got there as Paul broke the driver's window with a rock, the safety glass spreading across the driver's seat and falling onto the floorboards.

Opening the door, he slipped under the dash, pulling wires out as he tried to remember if it was blue to red or yellow to blue. He racked his brain as his shoulder screamed in protest. His shirt felt wet and he knew he was bleeding again. His newly bandaged hands made it difficult to handle the small wires. "Fuck," he croaked.

Josey took a quick look to make sure they were alone and then stuck her head into the car.

"Where the hell did you learn how to hot wire a car?" she asked.

Paul's muffled voice floated out from under the dash.

"Jesus, Josey, I had a life before I met you, you know." He grunted for a second and then continued talking. "I knew a guy in high school, good guy, but he was always getting into trouble. One night we were bored, so he showed me how to hotwire a car. We went for a joy ride and ended up getting chased by the cops. Let me tell you, that was one of the scariest nights of my young life."

"So what happened, did you get caught?" she asked, curious now.

"Nah, we ditched the car and cut through the park. I guess the cops didn't feel like chasing us." Josey heard Paul pressing the gas pedal with his hand, priming the carburetor. The sound of the starter came from under the hood and Josey crossed her fingers.

"Yes!" Paul's voice called out and the Apollo's engine surged to life. With Josey's help, Paul crawled out from under the dash. He brushed some stray glass from the seat and climbed in. Paul leaned over and unlocked the passenger door for Josey while she ran around and opened it, sliding into the car next to him. Paul had to keep his foot on the gas pedal, babying the engine to keep it from dying.

"Sounds like the choke is sticking," Paul said.

"Is that a problem?" she asked.

He shook his head. "Nah, I should be able to keep it running, it just means it won't idle. Besides, it's not my car." He slammed the automatic transmission into reverse and backed out of the car's parking space with a squeak of dry ball joints, then he revved the engine twice and hit the gas.

The Apollo surged forward, its six cylinders more than up to the task at hand.

He raced through the lanes until he was in open lot. He easily swerved around the few dead people and shot after Adam, who was still running around in circles, more than half of the undead chasing him like they were playing a game of tag.

While Adam was faster, the ghouls outnumbered him and were slowly surrounding him.

The Apollo shot through the middle of the undead crowd, knocking bodies to the side like candlepins. Adam saw Paul and his face seemed to radiate pleasure.

"About goddamn time!" he yelled, dancing out of the way of a dead meter maid.

Paul cut him off and Adam jumped over the hood of the Apollo, misjudging and almost going head-first onto the pavement. He reoriented himself and managed to land on his feet, although more sloppily than he planned.

Josey threw open the passenger door and he jumped inside the car, all but falling into the back seat.

"What the hell are you waiting for? Go!" Adam yelled as a dead security guard bounced off the passenger window, leaving a yellowish-red smudge on the glass.

Paul hit the gas and the Apollo surged forward, plowing through the shambling corpses. Bodies bounced off the hood and rolled under the car, the Apollo bouncing like it had hit a patch of large potholes.

Paul managed to right the car and point the grille towards the mall entrance.

Breathing heavily, Adam looked over to his friend. "So, where to now?"

Paul grinned like a man who knew he was going to die and didn't care. "We go shopping," he exclaimed and stomped on the gas pedal. The Apollo surged forward like it had been shot out of a cannon and Adam looked away from Paul and out the front windshield. The car was heading straight for the glass doors of the mall.

"If you break those doors the zombies will get inside! Even if there's some already in there, there's hundreds more out here! We'll be overwhelmed!"

Paul shrugged. "So what? In two days we'll all be dead. Shit, we'll be joining them. As long as we get to be comfortable until then, who cares what happens later? Brace yourselves, this is gonna hurt!" Paul yelled, the Apollo surging forward and barreling at the glass doors.

Four dead men were standing there when the car struck the doors. The zombies were cut in half, their torsos flying into the windshield and protecting the car's glass from shattering.

The Apollo shot through the glass doors, the sound of the shattering glass echoing off the walls of the shopping area.

Paul lost control of the automobile as it flew through the opening. The car slid across the smooth tile and ended up crashing into an escalator. The world went quiet. Sound came rushing back into Adam's ears and he pulled himself up from where he'd slid down on the seat.

Next to him, Josey was dazed. She had a small cut on her forehead. Paul was just shaking off the crash, his eyes already starting to focus.

"That was awesome! How come we never did this before? Never mind. Let's get going before we're surrounded," Paul said.

The three survivors half-crawled, half-stumbled out of the car, resembling their undead adversaries for a few seconds before righting themselves. Paul picked up a *"NO RUNNING"* sign and swung it into the face of the nearest zombie. It fell away as if slapped by a giant fly swatter and Paul helped Josey up. Then they all took off at a fast trot deeper into the mall.

The wide hallway had had only a few ghouls in it, all spread out like shoppers on a Sunday afternoon, but thanks to Paul's stunt more were pouring in by the dozens. The three live ones hobbled down the hallway, shoving away anything undead that came near.

Rounding a corner, Paul saw a CVS with the metal grating down. Crossing his fingers, he ran to it, leaving Josey alone for a minute. She leaned against the wall and tried to stay standing, her face covered with perspiration.

Paul's hopes were dashed when he saw the lock was still in place.

"Shit, we're not getting in there."

Adam pointed to another escalator at the junction of four bisecting hallways.

"Up there, maybe?"

Paul nodded and together the two men helped Josey up the escalator. A pretzel shop had the gate half-up, half-down and Paul pushed it until the three of them could rush inside.

Paul turned and pulled the gate closed, the lock was still hanging on its hook on the grating and Paul snapped it shut just as three ghouls appeared and snapped at his hand. He pulled his bandaged hand back like it had just been burnt; he narrowly missed losing a finger.

With the gate secured, the three of them fell to the floor and took a breather.

Through gasps of breath, Paul tried to talk. "We did it, we're safe. They can't get us."

Josey rolled over and hugged her husband. "You did it, Paul, you saved us. For however long we've got, we're alive." She kissed his cheek.

"Jesus, Paul. I can't believe you pulled that off. We should be dead," Adam said breathlessly.

Paul rolled over onto his side so he could look at Adam.

"Don't rush it, Adam. It's coming soon enough." Then he lay back down, closed his eyes, and rested.

Just a few feet away on the other side of the hardened steel grate, more and more zombies arrived, shaking it ineffectively.

The three exhausted friends ignored them and took a much needed nap.

***

An hour later, Adam snapped awake. Sitting up, he saw his undead fans were still clawing at the gate, trying to get inside.

Paul and Josey were still asleep. Adam took a good look at both of them. Their complexion was milky white, their skin was covered in sweat and their eyes had large black bags under them.

The infection was slowly killing them as they lay sleeping.

Oddly, Adam felt fine. He checked his arm and saw it was in the same condition as the day before. For the first time he wondered if perhaps he hadn't been bitten and had just cut it on some stone debris or something.

He looked down at his sleeping friends. If that was true, he was trapped inside a pretzel shop with two people who were about to become zombies. And he had nothing to protect himself with.

"Irony of ironies," he whispered.

Paul stirred on the floor and opened his eyes. He saw Adam watching him and he slowly sat up, wincing as he did. He noticed the zombies, but ignored them.

"What's up?" he asked.

"Oh, nothing. I just woke up myself. How you feeling?" Adam asked, already knowing the answer.

"Like shit, that's how." He looked down at his wife and brushed the hair from her face. "It's not fair, you know. We've come so far and survived so much to have to die now."

Adam remained quiet, letting Paul talk. "You know, I could take dying if I knew she was going to keep on living, to keep on fighting, but now . . ." He let out a deep breath. "Now it just sucks."

"I am so sorry, Paul," Adam said quietly.

"It's not your fault, Adam. It's just . . . fate. Besides, it's not where you end up that matters, it's the road you take and the people you meet along the way. That's what matters."

"That's very poetic," Adam said with a smile.

Paul gave him a shrug. "Yeah, well, I'm a sensitive motherfucker." He shook off the melancholy and the old Paul was back.

"I'm starving. Does this place have any food?" He asked this in a more cheerful tone.

Josey opened her eyes. "Did someone say food?"

Paul helped her up and they were happy to find the shop was fully stocked. The pretzels were beyond stale, but they were edible, and the survivors gorged themselves. Warm soda quenched their parched throats as they each drank what seemed like their own weight in liquid.

But Adam could tell he was eating much more than they were, their appetites only half as large as his. He pretended not to notice and focused his attention on choking down another stale pretzel.

When the meal was finished and everyone had rested and used the non-functioning bathroom (sink) in the back room, Adam found a back hallway that seemed to connect all the stores on that side of the mall. The three went exploring and wound up in a clothing store.

This is where they decided to call home for as long as it mattered. Letting Paul rest with Josey, Adam was able to scrounge a few pieces of furniture from different sections of the store and the back offices and laid them out in what resembled a rough living room, complete with a non-working television. Josey even helped some, though the work exhausted her. Adam tried to stop her, telling her he could do it, but she made him leave her alone, saying she wanted to do her share. Paul told Adam to leave her be.

They were close to the glass doors and metal grating that led to the main hallway, and were able to see into the rest of the mall, thanks to illumination from the overhead skylights that covered more than seventy percent of the mall.

Paul and Josey lay on a small loveseat and relaxed while Adam fussed around. He was exhausted, but seeing his friends like this just made him antsy. He wanted to do something for them, but there was nothing he could.

Paul saw him fidgeting and called him over.

"Adam, let me see your arm," he asked.

Adam gave it to him and Paul held the arm close to his eyes, looking at the cut. Even through the bandages on his hands, Paul's hands felt cold.

Paul nodded. "Well, I'll be dammed. Your cut is fine. Good news, buddy, you're going to live. Bad news, you're going to live, trapped in a clothing store with two potential zombies."

Adam gave Paul the shrug. "Yeah, it sucks, but the news is still better than the alternative."

Paul nodded and looked down at his wife. Her eyes were closed and Paul shook her awake. Her eyes fluttered and she looked up at Paul, though her eyes remained unfocused.

"Huh, what Paul? I'm so tired, just let me sleep," she muttered.

"You can't, Josey. If you sleep you won't wake up. Josey, come on, honey, don't do this to me." It was no use. She had drifted off to sleep again.

Paul lowered her back down and let her rest. He was feeling pretty tired himself and it was only his iron willpower that was keeping him awake.

He looked over to Adam, his jaw set, his eyes cold. Adam knew that look. Paul used it when he was deadly serious.

"Adam," Paul said. "I want you to promise me something."

"Anything. Just name it, man, you know that," Adam answered, his voice shaking.

"I want you to promise me that when we turn, you'll put us down. I don't want to be walking around out there with you looking at me."

"Oh, Jesus . . . Paul . . . I—" Adam stammered, not knowing how to reply to his request.

"Stop it, Adam. No bullshit, Promise me damn it, on your life!"

Adam nodded. "All right, I promise." A tear slid down his cheek.

"Good," Paul said harshly. "You better. And Josey, too. God rest her soul.

Adam nodded, too choked up to answer.

Paul held out his hand for Adam to take. "It's been a pleasure knowing you, Adam. I hope you make it out of this, just don't give up hope. Do that, and you're fucked."

Adam took his hand and squeezed it hard, pumping it up and down. Then Paul let go and lay back on the couch.

"I'm tired, Adam. So damn tired I can't tell you. I'm gonna take a nap now. I honestly don't think I'll wake up." Paul bent over and kissed his wife softly on the cheek. She was in a coma, one she'd never awake from as Josey.

"I love you, baby. And I'll see you in Heaven," he said softly into her ear. Then he curled up next to her, and with his hand holding her tight, he closed his eyes.

Adam sat there for hours, watching his last two friends sleep their last slumber on earth.

The tears flowed freely now and he wasn't ashamed. There was no one to see him even if he did.

He watched both Josey's and Paul's chest rising slowly for the rest of the night.

As the sun rose the next morning, first Josey's and then Paul's chest stopped moving. Adam sat perfectly still, knowing what was coming, but too scared to move.

Then, almost in perfect synchronicity, Josey's eyes snapped open, followed by Paul's. Taking a deep breath, Adam stood up and reached down for the lead pipe he'd found in the back room the night before.

He knew what he had to do.

Epilogue

The crow flew across the city, its black wings catching every updraft, keeping it airborne. It left the city and continued onward, stopping to feed on what it could find and then taking flight once again.

Looking down from high above, the crow spotted a shopping mall.

A single man was on the roof, jogging around the edge. A water bottle and a sweat shirt lay near a fire door. Below him were more than a thousand zombies, shuffling in and out of the shattered doors of the mall. The man didn't seem to mind.

The crow flew on, realizing there would be no food here. It flew on for miles, sleeping and eating and then taking to the air once more.

Soon, it was flying over mountains, miles and miles of forest with no sign that man had ever invaded this tranquil place.

Only nature existed here, now.

The bird spotted a small dirt road, from above, looking like a thin line that trailed up the nearest mountain. Curious, the crow followed this road, dipping up and down with the air currents.

Something flashed in the sun and the crow dipped closer. One of man's vehicles was stopped in the middle of the road, the doors flung wide and the tailgate open. Footsteps led away from the vehicle, the trail easy to follow on the muddy road.

The crow dipped low, only a few feet off the ground. There might be eagles in the area and the crow didn't want to be another animal's meal today.

Up ahead was a small cabin, the chimney built of solid stonework and a small wooden porch in the front. There was a small vegetable garden on the side, the crow noticed, but it wasn't a vegetarian.

Landing on the wooden railing, the crow cawed at the door. A minute passed and the door creaked open. A young boy stepped out, no more than ten. He saw the crow and smiled. He picked a small piece off the sandwich he was eating and tossed it to the crow. The bird dipped down and scooped it up, cawing for more. The boy smiled and tossed him another piece.

A woman stepped out then, and put her arm around the boy. "That's enough. That sandwich is for you," she said.

"Aww, I just wanted to feed it a little," the boy said.

The blonde woman shook her head. "I said no, now come back inside and finish your sandwich, then we'll play a game." She turned and disappeared back into the cabin.

The boy looked at the bird and then back into the cabin. Since he wasn't being watched, he ripped off another piece of his sandwich and tossed it to the bird. He put his finger to his mouth and said: "Shhh, don't tell."

The bird cawed again.

The woman's voice floated out of the cabin, a little upset now.

"Timmy, will you leave that bird alone and come in here? Please?"

Timmy waved goodbye to the bird and closed the door.

The crow cawed again, watching the door. He liked it here and decided he'd stick around for a while.

At least until the boy ran out of food.

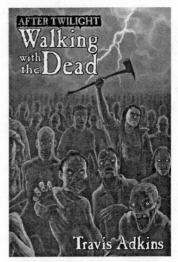

DYING TO LIVE
LIFE SENTENCE
by Kim Paffenroth

At the end of the world a handful of survivors banded together in a museum-turned-compound surrounded by the living dead. The community established rituals and rites of passage, customs to keep themselves sane, to help them integrate into their new existence. In a battle against a kingdom of savage prisoners, the survivors lost loved ones, they lost innocence, but still they coped and grew. They even found a strange peace with the undead.

Twelve years later the community has reclaimed more of the city and has settled into a fairly secure life in their compound. Zoey is a girl coming of age in this undead world, learning new roles—new sacrifices. But even bigger surprises lie in wait, for some of the walking dead are beginning to remember who they are, whom they've lost, and, even worse, what they've done.

As the dead struggle to reclaim their lives, as the survivors combat an intruding force, the two groups accelerate toward a collision that could drastically alter both of their worlds.

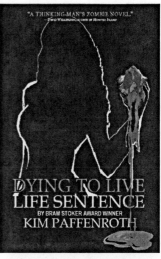

ISBN: 978-1934861110

EDEN
A ZOMBIE NOVEL BY TONY MONCHINSKI

Seemingly overnight the world transforms into a barren wasteland ravaged by plague and overrun by hordes of flesh-eating zombies. A small band of desperate men and women stand their ground in a fortified compound in what had been Queens, New York. They've named their sanctuary Eden.

Harris—the unusual honest man in this dead world—races against time to solve a murder while maintaining his own humanity. Because the danger posed by the dead and diseased mass clawing at Eden's walls pales in comparison to the deceit and treachery Harris faces within.

ISBN: 978-1934861172

Permuted Press
The formula has been changed...
Shifted... Altered... *Twisted.*™
www.permutedpress.com

Zombies, Vampires and Texans!
Oh, my!
The Novels of Rhiannon Frater

As The World Dies: The First Days
A Zombie Trilogy
Book One

Two very different women flee into the Texas
Hill Country on the first day of the zombie rising.
Together they struggle to rescue loved ones,
find other survivors, and avoid the hungry undead.

As The World Dies: Fighting to Survive
A Zombie Trilogy
Book Two

Katie and Jenni have found new lives with
the survivors of their makeshift fort, but
danger still lurks. Nothing is easy in the new
world where the dead walk and every day is
a struggle to keep safe.

Pretty When She Dies:
A Vampire Novel.

In East Texas, a young woman awakens buried
under the forest floor. After struggling out of
her grave, she not only faces her terrible new
existence but her sadistic creator, The
Summoner. Abandoning her old life, she
travels across Texas hoping to find answers to
her new nature and find a way to defeat the
most powerful Necromancer of all time.

All novels are available in both paperback and Kindle
eBook versions are available at smashwords.com.
For more information on the author, her upcoming appe
http://rhiannonfrater.blogspot.com/

THE PLACE TO GO FOR ZOMBIE AND APOCALYPTIC FICTION

  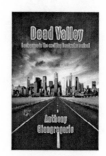

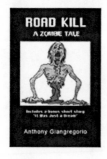  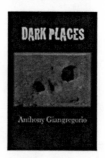

LIVING DEAD PRESS
WHERE THE DEAD WALK
www.livingdeadpress.com

LaVergne, TN USA
13 October 2009
160700LV00004B/2/P